"The stuff my rock-star dreams are made of. A thrill ride. I felt every stomach dip in the process. And I want to turn right around and ride it again. Every girl who's ever had a rock-star crush, this would be the ultimate fantasy."   —*Maryse's Book Blog*

"This book rocked my world! *Lick* is an addictive blend of heartwarming passion and lighthearted fun. It's a story you can lose yourself in. The perfect rock-star romance!"   —*Aestas Book Blog*

"An engrossing, sexy, and emotional read."   —*Dear Author*

"Scrumptious and delicious. Firmly in my top ten best books this year!"   —*The Book Pushers*

"Fun with great characters, a rocker story line, good angst, and plenty of sexy times. I would strongly recommend this book to anyone looking for something sexy and heartwarming."
        —*Fiction Vixen*

"A nice start to a rock-and-roll series. Very much looking forward to the next one."   —*Smexy Books*

ALSO BY KYLIE SCOTT

Lick
Play
Lead
Deep
Dirty

Twist

Kylie Scott

ST. MARTIN'S GRIFFIN ❦ NEW YORK

TWIST. Copyright © 2017 by Kylie Scott. All rights reserved. Printed in the United States of America. For information, address St. Martin's Press, 175 Fifth Avenue, New York, N.Y. 10010.

www.stmartins.com

The Library of Congress Cataloging-in-Publication Data is available upon request.

ISBN 978-1-250-08322-7 (trade paperback)
ISBN 978-1-250-08328-9 (e-book)

Our books may be purchased in bulk for promotional, educational, or business use. Please contact your local bookseller or the Macmillan Corporate and Premium Sales Department at 1-800-221-7945, extension 5442, or by e-mail at MacmillanSpecialMarkets@macmillan.com.

First Edition: April 2017

10 9 8 7 6 5 4 3 2 1

To my readers, thank you

ACKNOWLEDGMENTS

First, to all of the reviewers and bloggers who take the time to read my books, thank you. To Rose and the awesome team at St. Martin's Press, to Cate and Pan Macmillan Australia, and Catherine and Pan Macmillan UK. To Amy Tannenbaum, agent extraordinaire and keeper of my sanity, and everyone at the Jane Rotrosen Agency. To the Australian Romance Readers Association for their unfailing support. To the Groupies, go, you good things. To my claimed sister, Mish, who does everything all the time <3. To my babe, Sali Pow, love you. To my beloved husband and babies, my friends, family, and everyone who's had my back during this amazing, and at times tough, journey, thank you so much. To By Hang Le, you still haven't responded to my offer to run away together, it's beginning to get a bit awkward. Lastly, to Joanna Wylde, I have nothing to say to you.

If there's one thing I've learned over the last few years, it's this . . . it takes a tight posse to keep things together and a community to make you whole. I got my posse, and I got the romance community. And for both, I am extremely grateful.

Twist

CHAPTER ONE

Screw playing it safe.

I stood outside the Dive Bar, hands shaking, heart crashing around inside my chest. Goddamn nerves. Let them do their worst. No way would I scurry back to Seattle and hide. Not now. Beware, beautiful hot man from the Internet. I had arrived. Yes, fate in the form of me, and a return-trip plane ticket, had come to Coeur d'Alene, northern Idaho.

Right. This was it.

I took a deep breath and fluffed up my hair (shoulder length and brown). My bestie, Val, had applied my makeup several hours earlier and the woman knew her shit. None of it would dare move. I smoothed out the creases in my dress (little and black). Shoulders back, boobs out, as per instructions. And okay, sure, my toes were turning into frozen stumps in the stupid sky-high black suede heels, and my bare legs and arms were covered in goose bumps. But never mind. Val and the girl in the shop had sworn I looked amazing in this outfit. Definitely doable and about a billion times better than normal, care of the push-up bra above and the Spanx below.

So what if I felt a little like a high-class hooker. Never mind. First impressions were important. And if Val and the salesgirl were right, this particular first impression was the way to go—as opposed to my usual boring date attire: boots, jeans, and a blouse. But then, I wasn't usually gaga about the guy in the way I was about Eric Collins. Those dates were solely about scratching an itch.

Yes, I know. Shock horror. A single woman regularly indulging in casual sex. Absolutely not even a little attachment to the male in the equation. Burn me at the stake and drown me in a river. Valerie called me an emotional coward, but I liked my life uncomplicated and largely spent alone at home dressed in pajamas. And relationships? They were one hell of a complication. Yet, here I was in northern Idaho hoping to get all sorts of involved and complicated, against my better judgment. The outside world terrified me, but Eric Collins mattered too much to just be relegated to the role of some passing Internet fancy. I had to see him, to find out why a week ago he'd up and disappeared on me. Turning up at his birthday party just added a bit of serendipity to the event.

Maybe I'd played with Bridal Barbie once too often when I was young. I don't know.

The closed sign hung in the restaurant window, the outside lights were dimmed. Inside, however, things were happening. Muted music and the sound of low chatter carried through the cold night air. Lightning crashed in the distance, the breeze picked up. Even the weather was telling me to stop procrastinating.

Despite the sign, the door was unlocked. Carry-on suitcase bumping along behind me, I ventured inside. No one noticed me at first. A good dozen or so people were hanging out at the long wooden bar, drinking and eating. My stomach turned inside out at the scent of delicious pizza. I'd been too nervous to eat anything on the flight or beforehand.

I gasped. There he was.

Holy shit, his profile photo hadn't begun to do him justice. The man put supermodels to shame. He literally glowed, his long dark hair shining beneath the lights, and his pearlescent smile even more so. (Not that I didn't admire and respect him for his mind, because I did. After all, our relationship had so far sat entirely at the platonic level of cyber-messaging. I was overdue for seeing a little flesh. So there.)

All of the tension inside me unwound, my shoulders sagging in relief. The smile on my face, however, just grew bigger and bigger. People said nobody told the actual truth about themselves on the Internet. Lying to strangers and sharing cat pictures were basically why the World Wide Web had been invented. And yes, it'd been a huge leap of faith to get on that plane. He could have been some five-hundred-pound pervert hoping to get pictures of my tits to whack off to. He could have been married with five wives and forty-three children, hoping I'd be willing to join the family and push out some more bambinos.

But no. The man was everything he'd said he was. I just hoped I lived up to his expectations. The tension inside me wound right back up into a hard ball. I'd told no lies about my thunder thighs or my modest bra size. Either he'd like me in real life or not. There was nothing I could do about it now.

First one person turned, noticing me. Then more followed, until the whole party was hushed, waiting.

"Hi," someone said. "I'm sorry but we've already closed for the night. This is a private party."

"I know," I answered, circumnavigating the tables, walking

toward him. Not taking my eyes off the man for a second. Tears welled, the absolute thrill of the moment threatening to undo me. I'd never forget this night as long as I lived. He was so gorgeous, so wonderful. I'd crushed on him hard just through reading his emails, but it was this, us finally being in the same damn room together and feeling the connection between us, which sealed the deal.

Eric Collins was going down. The dude would be wooed so hard it hurt and I, Alexandra Parks, would be doing the wooing.

Once I got close, I couldn't hold back any longer. I burst into action, flinging myself at him. And just as I'd known he would, he caught me.

"Happy birthday, Eric," I said, my smile trembling from both nerves and joy.

"Thanks."

I laughed. It sounded only slightly hysterical. "I can't believe I'm really here."

Exquisite jade-green eyes stared down at me in shock.

"So . . . surprise," I exclaimed.

"Wow." A pause. Then, gazing down at me, he licked his perfect lips and said, "Do I know you?"

Everything stopped.

"What?" I asked.

A low, masculine, yet distinctly uncomfortable chuckle. "We've met before, huh?"

"Eric," I chided.

He said nothing. Just kept looking at me in confusion. As if I was a total stranger.

"Is this a joke?" I asked, my whole body stiffening in his hold. "Eric, it's me. Alex."

Nothing.

Absolutely positively not a fucking thing.

Everyone was watching, the same bewildered look on all of their faces. Eyebrows raised and hesitant smiles, etc. God. For months I'd played this moment over and over inside my mind. It most definitely never turned out like this. Whatever this was.

I stepped back from my supposed beloved's arms, doubt trickling through me, first a little, then a lot. Soon it was a whole damn tsunami of disbelief crushing my heart and mind. I was drowning, panic slowly but surely closing over my head. This is what came from stepping outside of your comfort zone. Bad things. Deeply shitty soul-crushing things. Why the hell had I ever left home?

"I don't understand," I said, voice rising in pitch and volume. "Of course you know me. We've been talking for months. E-mailing."

Still nothing.

"We met on Heartingdotcom. Remember?"

They were still watching me with blank stares. Eric included.

I glared back at him. "So you've just been stringing me along, haven't told anyone about me, and now you're just going to deny everything? That's how you're going to play this? Really?"

"Or maybe I haven't told anyone about you because I have no idea who you are," he countered, looking me up and down. Something close to doubt flitted across his face. "Hold up. Are you the chick I doggy-styled in the walk-in closet at that party in Spokane?" His smile somehow managed to be sympathetic, apologetic, and leering all at once. "Shit, you are, aren't you? I'm sorry, I should have known you right away. Maybe if you'd shown me the back of your head."

I had nothing.

"It's just sometimes it's hard to remember faces after a big night, you know? And I'd been mixing Flaming Blue Jesuses for them. You know, with the rum, peppermint schnapps, and peach liqueur, with the thinnest layer of tequila on top." He licked his lips. "I really do like those."

Slowly, I shook my head. "You didn't dog-style me in a closet."

"No? Are you sure?" he asked. "Can I just see the back of your head for one minute?"

"We didn't meet at a party, Eric," I said through gritted teeth. "Emailing. You and me. Constantly, for months."

"Not me."

"Yes. You."

"Come on, that's not even realistic." Eric put his hands on his slim hips. "Everyone in this room knows that's not me. My attention span just isn't that long."

"True," said someone. Lots of nods from other people. And he might be persuading them, but he wasn't fooling me.

"Right," I shot back. "So I've just been, what? Imagining all of this?"

"Depends." He smirked. "Did I start *constantly* emailing you around the time you went off your meds?"

"Eric," scolded one woman. Slim, redheaded, and pregnant.

"You're Nell." I gave her a finger wave. "He told me about you, sent me pictures of you all and the Dive Bar."

The woman's eyes widened.

"He never mentioned you were expecting, though. Congratulations."

"Thanks," she said hesitantly.

Next I turned to the other redhead in the room. A tall, nicely built guy covered in ink. "And you're Vaughan, Nell's brother. You're a musician. You recently got engaged to Lydia there, the lovely blonde at your side. Hi."

"Hi." Lydia's lips thinned in surprise. "Huh."

"If I'm a crazy person, how would I know these things?" I turned back to Eric, my own hands sitting on my own damn hips. "How would I know that you went to school with most of these guys? That you only lived a couple of streets away from each other when you were kids?"

Eric's mouth opened but nothing came out.

"Oh my God." A familiar gorgeous, dark-skinned woman with a head full of corkscrew curls stepped forward. "Are you one of those psychics? Mom's always watching that shit on TV. I never believed before, but . . ."

"Nah, she's a stalker," said Eric. "Got to be. I was bound to pick one up eventually."

"I am not a stalker." Given how tight my fingers were rolled up into fists, however, I might soon very well be accused of assault and battery.

"Do me," said the dark-skinned waitress. "Who am I?"

"You're Rosie, one of the waitresses here."

"Got it in one!" Rosie smiled. "Can you tell me anything about my future?"

"I'm sorry. I'm really not psychic."

"Oh." Her smile turned upside down. "That sucks."

"What's going on?" asked a deep, booming voice from behind us.

I spun, staring straight into the startled eyes of a man who could only be described as a blond Bigfoot, a case of beer casually hoisted on one enormous shoulder. His golden mane flowed down over his wide shoulders, a beard covering the bottom half of his face. I guess it kept him warm in the winter, but seriously. Who needed that much hair?

"Hi, bro, welcome to the crazy." Eric slapped the big man on the back. "You didn't happen to send me a psychic stripper for my birthday, did you?"

Dark shocked eyes fixed on me. Joe. It was his brother Joe, of course. The man was just a whole lot bigger in the flesh than I'd ever imagined. Not that I'd spent a lot of time imagining him or anything.

"What?" He shook his bearded head at Eric in confusion. "No. Of course not."

"A stripper?" I asked in disbelief. "Seriously?"

Eric's gaze went straight to my shoes. "You got to admit, those are some serious heels."

He had a point. Still, I highly doubted I looked like the kind of woman who wore pasties at parties on a regular basis. Let alone as if I had any dancing skills or could even attempt to climb a pole.

"All right, enough," ordered Nell. "I think this poor girl might be the victim of identity theft."

I froze.

"Look, ah . . . obviously something's up here. Why don't we take this into the back office?" said Joe. "Somewhere a little more private. We don't want to embarrass her."

"I think I've pretty much reached peak embarrassment overload," I said, giving him a forced smile. "But thanks."

Strange, the man's skin, the bits visible, at least, had turned a kind of ashen color. He honestly looked ready to hurl at any moment. That or faint.

"You okay, man?" asked Vaughan, also noticing.

"Yeah, yeah. Never better." It was a wonder the guy's pants didn't catch on fire. Even I could tell that one was a blatant lie.

"So you've never met Eric in the flesh before?" Nell asked. "Only online."

I nodded. "Yes. We only ever swapped emails."

With a pained look, Nell came closer, lowering her voice. "It couldn't have been Eric. I'm pretty sure he couldn't even find a computer's on switch, let alone write actual emails on a regular basis. It took him forever just to learn how to spell his own name."

Eric screwed up his forehead. "Hey. That's beside the point."

"Shush." Nell waved a hand at him. "I doubt it was him who set up the account on this dating site at all."

"I did set up the account," said Eric, distinctly unimpressed. "For fuck's sake, Nell. Stop acting like my half of the baby is going to be dumber than your half. It's not."

"Do not call my baby 'it,'" warned Nell, poking him in the chest with a finger.

And suddenly it was all clear to me. It was all horribly, perfectly clear.

"That's your baby?" I asked the sleazoid male standing in front of me. "It is any wonder you're pretending you don't know me? God. You asshole. All of those things you said to me and meanwhile, you're playing house with her."

"What?" Eric's "you're crazy" look tripled. "No. I . . . shit. Joe helped me set up that stupid dating account and then I pretty much forgot about it. Didn't need it. So I told Joe . . ."

Silence.

"Joe," Eric repeated. Then he blinked and turned to his brother. Nell too turned to face the big blond guy.

Joe squirmed under their gaze. He had that look about him as if he wanted an emergency trapdoor beneath him to disappear into.

"You email her, bro?" asked Eric.

"Yeah." And the blond Bigfoot did not look happy about it. "Yeah, I . . . we've been talking for a while. We know each other."

"No, we don't." I frowned at the man who was most definitely *not* my type. His brother? Yes. But him? Nuh-uh. "I know Eric, not you."

Bigfoot sighed.

I pointed an accusing finger at the beautiful dark-haired man of my dreams. "That's the guy who was in the profile photo. The one I basically bared my heart to. Not you. I don't know who you are."

"Let me explain." Joe/Bigfoot's gaze intensified, focused wholly on me. His dark brown eyes were so earnest, as if he could will me to understand this shit storm. "I read your message and . . . I don't know. You seemed like someone—"

"You could lie to?"

"No." He dragged a hand across his face. "Fuck. You were so funny and real and—"

"Real?" I could only shake my head, taking another step back.

"Yes. Real. At first I was just helping out my brother. Trying to get him interested in someone nice for a change. Someone who had more to recommend them than the size of their breasts." His gaze dipped to my uplifted, yet still extremely modest, chest and panic flashed across his face. "Not that you're not—"

"Don't even bother."

"But then I started to get to know you better and you were someone I could really talk to." The side-eyes he gave the assembled crowd were purely sheepish. "I guess I was lonely. I don't know."

Aw, was the poor asshole embarrassed? My heart bled for him.

"But it was Eric you'd reached out to, so . . ."

"So?"

The man said nothing.

"Are you actually trying to tell me that your motives were pure? Seriously?" All I could do was shake my head. In wonder or horror, I don't even know. "I believed in you and you were nothing but a lie. All along, just lies."

His lips firmed. "That's not true. I'm your friend."

"Bullshit. A friend would never do this."

Murmurs circled from the people gathered round. And seriously, whatever this was, fuck it. Fuck Eric, Joe, all of mankind, the Internet, and all of my hopes and dreams. I was running straight back to my apartment and staying put. I retreated another step, my butt bumping the back of a chair. It made the most awesome crashing noise as it toppled over, hitting the floor. "Shit. Sorry. I, um . . ."

The faces surrounding me blurred and a rushing noise filled my head. Christ. All those personal, deeply private things I'd told him. How honest I'd been. But I was just one more stupid girl dreaming of love and a life that was somehow larger. There was nothing for me here.

Time to go.

I turned and made straight for my suitcase. Grabbing the plastic handle, I ran back out the door, the cold night air like a well-earned slap in the face. Out on the sidewalk I tripped in the stupid shoes. Then I continued. I walked faster and faster, putting as much distance as possible between me and the whole debacle.

My case rattled and rolled over the asphalt. From top to toe I felt numb. Nonexistent. The first few drops of rain should have passed right through me instead of soaking into the cotton of my borrowed dress.

"Alex," a voice yelled from behind me. A male voice. Him.

It only spurred me onward. No cars or signs of life ahead. The whole world seemed to have emptied out. There was just me, that voice, and the storm.

God, I'd been so wrong to come here. So damn wrong.

What the hell had I done?

CHAPTER TWO

Heterosexual female age 29.

Graphic Artist. Works from home.

Seattle born and bred.

Enjoys reading romance, watching action, sci-fi, and horror movies, and shows about building renovations.

No pets unless the squirrel in the tree outside counts. His name is Marty.

Most prized possession is my laptop. All of my work is on there. Except the backup USB I've entrusted to Marty.

Most proud of establishing and running my own graphic design business.

In five years' time I see myself further developing my business, investing in a property, and dabbling in renovating.

Looking for someone who is employed, artistic, neat and attractive, has a sense of humor.

Looking for a fun night out with a new friend.

Sexual compatibility is important.

Most important value in a relationship is honesty.

Heterosexual male age 28.

Restaurateur.

Northern Idaho born and bred.

Enjoys movies and music.

Most prized possession is family and friends.

Most proud of establishing and running a restaurant/bar business all on my own.

In five years' time I see myself settling down with the woman of my dreams to raise a family in a home we've helped to build with our own hands.

Looking for someone who is attractive.

Looking for someone who is open to developing new friendship starting with a fun night out.

Sexual compatibility is extremely important.

Most important value in a relationship is open-mindedness.

"Alex!" called a deep male voice.

I should have known better than to take a chance. Such an idiot. I should have just stuck to crushing on various men on TV. Much safer. As for Valerie encouraging me to buy the plane ticket and instilling me with all of that false hope, the chances of her being beaten over the head with a wet fish in the near future were exceptionally high. And those bastards. Those heartless, soulless assholes playing me for a fool. Men sucked more than any known creature.

"Hey, hold up." Joe's big hand wrapped around my arm, bringing me to a halt.

I didn't even think, just bared my teeth at him.

"Whoa." He took a hasty step back, setting me free.

"Do not touch me," I said coldly—right as the heavens opened and rain poured down. Awesome. Just awesome.

"Okay, okay," he said. "I'm sorry."

"Go away." I sucked in a harsh breath. "Joe, Eric, whoever the hell you are, it doesn't matter. Just leave me alone."

Face set, I turned and continued on my way, in whichever direction would take me far from the Dive Bar and those people, as fast as fucking possible.

"Wait, please," he said from behind me. "Alex, you have to let me explain. I know I shouldn't have lied, but Eric was never going to get back to you. I was just going to send a note, telling you not to worry about it. But then I liked talking to you."

"Good for you."

Head down, shoulders drawn in, I trudged on. Strands of wet hair clung to my face, the cold seeping into my bones and making me shiver. I was top heavy on account of the padding in my push-up bra absorbing roughly twenty-one ounces of rain on either side. Dolly Parton didn't have a damn thing on me. And my end-of-season-sale, four-hundred-dollar designer suede shoes were ruined, but there wasn't much I could do about that. The money was already gone from my "hoarding for a dream home" savings account. Yet another reason to hate the guy.

Shelter was required. Shelter, dry clothes, and a large alcoholic drink, in that exact order. Heavy-assed footsteps splashed along beside me as thunder rolled across the dark and cloudy sky.

"Look, I'm sorry you feel let down. I know you're after a pretty boy with all the smooth moves and that's definitely not me," he continued. "You're not exactly my type either, for that matter. No offense."

Douchecanoe.

"But I still think you're great and us being friends, it's a good thing. We support each other, Alex."

I walked faster.

Sadly, with his long legs, the man had no trouble keeping up. "We can talk to each other about anything without any worries about being judged or gossip getting around. I swear, these last few months, you've pretty much been the only thing keeping me sane."

I trotted along as fast as possible, trying to escape him. It still didn't work.

"Fuck. I told you we should put off meeting."

I ground to a halt. "Wait, are you actually trying to turn this around on me?"

"No," he growled. "What I'm trying to do is make a point."

"And what might that be?" I made my mouth a mean line. "Hmm?"

Water dripped off his beard, soaking into the T-shirt already plastered against his body. I suspected he was carrying off the storm-drenched look better than I was. Bastard. Even by street-light it was obvious he was fit and strong. A big guy. More barrel-chested where his brother was lean. "My point is that we work as friends and that's worth saving. And also, I get that you would not have been interested in talking to me if Eric's photo hadn't been attached. Would you?"

"I guess we'll never know."

"Bullshit."

"Fuck you," I spat straight back at him, stabbing him in the chest with a finger. "You lied to me. Over and over again, you lied. You let me believe you were someone else. Does that really say 'friend' to you? Blame it on your insecurities, your loneliness, sibling rivalry, whatever. I don't care. But you made the choice to do that. Not me. You. The end."

And I meant it. I strode on, leaving him standing there, scowling up a storm. Pun intended.

Lumbersexuals were clearly the worst. Truth was, I'd never been especially into beards. At best, I'd been indifferent. Now, however, I outright despised them. Horrible hairy frames for lying lips and duplicitous tongues, that's what they were. Loathsome whiskery bastards. Burn them all in a fire.

"It's late at night in the middle of a storm," Captain Obvious bellowed out after me. "Where are you going, Alex?"

I ignored him and kept walking. Midtown, where the Dive Bar was located, didn't offer many options. A couple of shops, all currently closed. Coeur d'Alene itself, however, was a decent-size place. As soon as I escaped my stalker I'd pull out my cell and call an Uber. Find the nearest hotel or something.

"Downtown's another six blocks. You seriously going to walk all that way in the rain?"

And now I knew I was heading in the right direction.

"At least let me help you with your suitcase."

I gripped the handle of my half-rolling, half-bouncing suitcase harder, and ignored him.

A steady flow of grumbling punctuated by more than the occasional profanity followed along behind me. It was pretty much just him, me, my rattling suitcase, and the sound of the rain. He had to give up and go away eventually. Surely.

But he didn't.

When I at long last trudged up the steps to the Lake Hotel, it was with him still in tow. All the way I'd ignored him. Now he stood, waiting patiently out in the rain, as I entered the building. The place was nice. A glowing fire pit with a leather lounge, and big floor-to-ceiling windows looking out into the darkness.

"Can I help you, ma'am?" A polite young man stood behind the front desk, smile frozen in place.

"I'd like a room, please," I said with as much dignity as I could muster. Not easy with me dripping on their tiled floor. Oh, and my legs were splattered with drops of mud. The designer suede heels had turned a sad sort of brown from walking through puddles along the side of the road. Lovely. The cold rain had almost frozen me solid and blisters covered what remained of my feet. I couldn't have felt more sorry for myself. "If you have one available?"

"Of course." It took a moment longer than it should have for his gaze to move from me to the computer. Fair enough. "I have a Classic or we also have a—"

"Does it have a hot shower and a mini-bar?"

"Yes, ma'am."

"Then I'll take it."

He blinked. "Ah. Yes, ma'am. I'll arrange that for you right now."

I almost wept with gratitude. But the boy behind the desk looked weirded out enough by my sodden self already. Ever so subtly I peeked over my shoulder. The street was empty. He was gone. Phew.

I wondered how long it would take for this whole little adventure to turn into some funny story I told people. Except no part of me was amused. Not even a single cell. *My* Eric, the beautiful man from the Internet, didn't exist. Not really. Because the guy who'd charmed me with long, rambling emails about life and everything was a liar. And everyone knew, you couldn't trust a liar.

Again I gazed over my shoulder, out into the rain. He was still gone. I'd probably never see him again and that was for the best. It was. Tomorrow I'd go home. Back to the safety of my apartment and my neatly organized, uncomplicated life. Eventually I'd forget all the things we'd shared in those emails, the sense of companionship and the excitement of seeing that name in my inbox. The way I'd started to shuffle my life around reading his nightly missives. For not the first time tonight, I blinked back tears, ignoring the sting of saltwater in my eyes.

Yep, it would all fade. And I'd be fine.

CHAPTER THREE

Message received six months ago:
Alex,
Saw your profile. Looking at traveling to Seattle for business
soon. Would love to take you to dinner if you're available?—
Eric

Message sent:
Hi Eric,
Nice to meet you. What dates are you thinking you'll be in
town? I'd be interested in hearing more about your restau-
rant. Are you seriously considering working on your own
house? I've got grand schemes to update my one-bedroom
apartment sometime. But a whole house . . . wow.
Alex

"You're kidding," cried Val, her outrage coming through on my
mobile as a tinny squawk.

"Nope." The elevator doors slid back and I stepped out into the hotel lobby. The bright morning sun glaring through the hotel's windows mocked my crap mood. "Wish I was."

"Lying fucking asshole."

"You said it." I stopped to blow my nose. The sound was anything but pretty. Yes, care of the delightful walk in the rain last night, I'd woken up with a raging head cold. Sore throat, red and runny nose, and pounding head. It basically felt like someone had hung me upside down and filled my nasal passages with quick-dry cement. Just when you thought things couldn't get better.

"God, you sound horrible," she said. "To think, he friend-zoned you before you'd ever even met. I'd had such high hopes for him."

"You and me both." I sighed.

"And I encouraged you." A pause. "Shouldn't you be pointing out that deep down you were right and I was wrong? You should probably also be lecturing me about your uncomplicated-life theory."

"Meh. You've heard it all before and I don't have the energy."

"Aw, you poor thing. If you can't even manage an 'I told you so,' then you really are feeling sucky." She huffed out a breath.

Valerie and I'd had each other's back since the same group of bullies had targeted us in eighth grade. I'd always been mousy, clutzy, and generally clueless. An easy target for the cool kids wanting to establish their supremacy in the school hallways. Back then, Valerie had been Vincent, and he'd never fitted in either. We'd nursed each other through all manner of insults, broken hearts, and then a sex change. So I guess it fell under her job description to get up in arms on my behalf now. But I, on the other hand, was done. Mostly dead and emotionally spent. Every last fuck I had to give had fled during the night, never to be heard from again.

"I'm coming out there," she announced, voice firm.

I scrunched up my face. "Why on earth would you come out here? Hopefully, I'll be on a plane home this afternoon. Tonight at the latest."

"Doesn't matter. This Joe-Eric-jerkoff needs his ass kicked. I'm coming."

"You're not coming."

"I'm coming and I'm wearing my fiercest pointy-toed stilettos," she said. "You haven't seen these ones, they're new. Leopard print. That boy's ass is grass."

"Oh, that reminds me. The heels got trashed."

She gasped. "Not the half-price YSL!"

"Yep. I told you I couldn't be trusted with designer."

"But those shoes looked so good on you. That settles it. I'm definitely coming out there to hurt him."

I took a deep breath. Through my mouth, not my nose. My nose just wasn't an option.

"God, you sound like shit," said Val.

I grunted and blew my nose. A mucus factory, that was me.

"Yuck. That's disgusting. Seriously, I'm not sure you should fly in that condition," she said, voice concerned.

"I'll be fine." I shoved my wad of tissues back into my jeans pocket. "I just need coffee."

Even from behind my sunglasses the early morning light dazzled. I stepped out of the hotel and paused, giving my eyes a chance to adjust. Downtown Coeur d'Alene was quiet first thing in the morning, with the odd car cruising by, and a couple of signs advertising cafés sat out on the sidewalk farther up the street. All of the assorted fancy-clothes and gift-shop-type places were still closed. The cool air tickled dangerously at my nose and throat. Stupid cold.

A heavy sigh from Val. "Are you sure I can't come out there and commit violence in your name?"

"I appreciate the thought."

"There's lots of woods in that area. I promise they'd never find the body."

"Be rational," I said. "You know you hate nature."

"You never let me have any fun."

"I know, I'm the worst."

"Call me if you change your mind," she said. "I'll be here . . . sharpening my shoes."

"Thanks." I laughed softly. It was the only semblance of mirth I could manage. "Later."

Coffee. Right.

I could do this.

A beat-up silver Bronco sat at the curb. The thing was basically a monster truck—probably normal around these parts. Getting up hills in heavy snow would take some work. Though it wasn't the truck that caught my attention. Nope, it was the ridiculous tangled mass of blond hair and beard pressed against the side window that made me stop in my tracks.

Damn. It couldn't be. I stepped closer. "Eri . . . Joe?"

Sleeping Beauty slept on.

Don't tap the glass. Let sleeping stalkers lie. Don't tap the glass.

And yet . . . ever so politely, I tapped on the glass.

"Huh?" A groan accompanied the batting of eyelids and much squinting. "Yeah, yeah. I'm awake."

Slowly, the window rolled down.

"Hey," he said, voice still thick with sleep. "Morning."

We just kind of stared at each other, perplexed.

"You slept in your car?" I asked.

A shrug. "Didn't want you to leave before we had a chance to talk."

I turned away, crossed my arms.

"Look, Alex . . . can we talk?" The car door cracked open and I took one giant step back as he stood tall on the sidewalk. He looked beyond rumpled, fitting, given the circumstances. Before beginning his vigil, he'd obviously changed out of last night's wet clothes. Long legs were encased in another worn pair of blue jeans, and a faded gray hoodie covered his upper half. The width of his mighty shoulders was stretching the material a little. Equally large feet, or at least seriously large sneakers, completed the outfit. I wondered, did guys ever buy oversize shoes to try and benefit from the feet-to-penis-size belief? Was there a market for that? And I was standing there staring at the man's crotch in a total daze.

My gaze darted to his face, cracked wide yet again on a yawn. Thank goodness he hadn't caught me. That would have been bad. I really needed to get my sick wandering thoughts under control.

"Please?" he asked, eyes all intense.

"I'm pretty sure we covered everything last night."

For a moment he hung his head, then he looked me straight in the eye. "I'm pretty sure we didn't. Please. Let me buy you breakfast. You need food, right? Coffee?"

Sleeping in his car definitely showed commitment. Plus, I did need coffee. "Okay."

He smiled. It wasn't a full-out grin, more a cautious curving of the lips. "Great. Thanks."

I nodded.

"There's a good place just down here," he said, stuffing his hands in his jeans pocket and giving me side-eyes as we started walking.

Man, this cold sucked. I pulled out my wad of tissues and blew my nose for the umpteenth time this morning. Gah. Already, I could feel my poor nostrils chafing. Aloe vera Kleenex was urgently required, along with more aspirin. "Is there a pharmacy nearby?"

"About a five-minute drive. You sick?" He gave me a dubious once-over. "You're not looking so hot, but I didn't want to get in any more trouble by saying something."

"Wise."

The man held his silence.

"I must have caught a chill last night from walking in the rain."

He winced. "Ah, shit. I'm sorry."

I shrugged.

"Be happy to take you to the pharmacy or wherever you want to go."

"That's okay," I said, ambling alongside him. Walking any faster would have required energy. "I can go in the Uber on the way to the airport."

No reply.

Halfway up the next block he stopped outside a café, holding open the door. "Here we are."

The place seemed nice. Bright green walls covered in community notices. Only a few of the shiny old diner-style aluminum tables were taken this early in the day. He pulled out a chair for me by the window and I sat, mumbling my thanks. Breakfast was going to be awkward as all hell. Maybe I'd just caffeinate and run.

Hit the road to Spokane. Sure, I'd be loitering around the airport for hours and hours, but even that had to beat rehashing my oh-so-recent embarrassing past with this guy.

What I really wanted to do was swan-dive into a big soft bed and sleep for about a week. Too bad that wasn't an option.

Opposite me, Joe sat forward in his seat, arms braced on the table. I'd returned to my usual attire, skinny jeans and boots (there were only two pairs of socks and about a hundred Band-Aids covering my poor blistered feet) and a black bulky, comfy sweater. No makeup or hairstyling, that's for sure. If the man was surprised by the lack of last night's glamour, it didn't show.

With all the body-shaping underwear, lip gloss, heels, and tiny dress, you could almost say I'd been fibbing about who I was. His lie, however, left my Spanx and push-up bra way behind.

We both stayed silent, watching each other warily.

A cute, perky waitress appeared, smile stretched wide at the sight of Joe. A curious gaze looked me over, then dismissed me. I swear, it took the woman no more than a nanosecond to decide I wasn't any competition for my disheveled, hirsute, tattooed companion. Little did she know I'd always thought Jean Grey in *X-Men* got it right, Cyclops was a way better bet than Wolverine. All of that testosterone and bad attitude mixed with a scruffy face and general give no shits about his appearance was not so wonderful. In all honesty, I'd take cool, calm, and well kept over anger management and body hair issues any day of the week. Joe was all hers. She turned slightly and hitched her hip, subtly blocking me out of the conversation.

Oh yeah, I'd be leaving her a real big tip. Something along the lines of "fuck off."

"Hey," purred the waitress. "Good to see you, Joe."

"Hi, Jess."

"The usual?"

Joe turned to me, apparently unaware he was being oh so obviously hit on. Interesting, his eyes were hazel in the sun, chocolate brown flecked with amber. Last night they'd seemed dark and furtive, brimming over with secrets and lies, but this morning, he was just a guy. Funnily enough, one I thought I'd known, though it turned out I hadn't had a clue. Or maybe it was the other way around. I thought I hadn't known much about him, but actually in a strange sort of way I did—which only complicated things further.

"They do great coffee and fresh juices here," he said. "Excellent pancakes. Sound good?"

"Sure."

Again, a small, safe smile, then he ordered for both of us. I did my best to tune out Joe and the waitress. Proving she had all the moves, however, cute, perky waitress then placed a hand on the table and leaned forward, giving the man a clear view down her shirt. All right, so I might have had a bit of breast envy on account of my minimal mammaries. And yeah, care of recent events and my head cold, my mood registered right around crap level. But if she was the universe's way of messing with me, in an effort to pass along the message that Joe was in fact attractive, well . . . duh. I already knew that. Beards and bulk were on many a woman's wish list. They just hadn't been on mine. Could be I'd watched Keanu Reeves in *The Matrix* one too many times. That slick dark hair and cool outfits. *Rawr.*

"Are you sure I can't get you anything else, Joe?" she asked, sucking on the end of her pen in a manner that would have made a porn star feel mildly uncomfortable.

"No, I think we're good." Joe looked my way. "Alex?"

"All good over here."

"Thanks, Jess."

"Tell Eric I said hi," said the waitress.

Joe gave her a friendly smile. "Will do."

With a wiggle of the fingers, cute waitress sashayed her tiny little butt back off inside. Yes, fine. I'm a little sensitive about the size of my ass too. In all honestly, my issues are many.

"Friendly girl," I muttered, hunkering down in my black wool coat.

Joe said nothing.

"Hypothetical question," I said, my chin inching up a bit. "A waiter hits on the woman you're with, what do you do?"

He blinked. "There a reason for this question?"

"Just curious." I shook my head. "Never mind."

It's not like it mattered, because after this unfortunate breakfast we'd probably never cross paths again. So the waitress had rubbed me the wrong way. Such was life. Let it go. Move forward. Blah blah blah.

He cleared his throat. "If a waiter hits on the girl I'm with, I do nothing."

"Nothing?"

"Not unless it's upsetting her."

Hmm. "Why only then?"

"If it's not upsetting her, then the problem's mine." He settled back in his chair, stretching out his long legs and crossing them at the ankle. "Make a big deal out of it and I look like a jealous douchebag who doesn't trust his woman to ignore that sort of shit."

"What if she enjoys that sort of shit?"

"Then I'm with the wrong woman."

"Huh."

"What about you? What if a man you were on a date with started flirting with the waitress?"

"Then I'm out of there." I sighed and stared off down the street. Downtown Coeur d'Alene was a pretty place. And a somewhat strange one. "That is a very colorful moose."

Joe turned in his chair, peering through the window at the brilliantly painted statue on the corner. "Yeah. They do different art installations every summer then sell them off as a fund-raiser at the end of the season to pay the artists."

"Wow."

"Moose were the theme one year. Another time we had fountains on every corner. It was a little crazy," he said.

"Cool."

He tipped his chin, studying me.

I took the opportunity to sniffle. So feminine.

"I wanted to talk to you a bit more about what happened between us online," he said, his mouth a serious straight line. "How I came to use my brother's profile."

Ugh. "I'm pretty sure I found out everything I needed to know last night."

"I didn't mean to lie to you, Alex."

"Once is a mistake." I crossed my legs, kicking my black leather bootie back and forth. So I was a little aggravated. Sue me. "Months' worth of emails is not. You could have introduced yourself to me, Joe, told me who you really were. You chose not to. Christ, no wonder you kept putting off meeting. I should have known something was wrong."

"You're right. I shouldn't try to sell you excuses." A big sigh from my "friend." "Truth is, I'm not used to being the bad guy. Usually I'm the one cleaning up my brother's messes."

"Lucky me." Right behind my eyes, what had been a mild ache became a dull pounding. I pushed my sunglasses further back on my head, rubbing at my temples.

"Are you okay?" he asked.

"Yeah, it's just this stupid head cold. Please, continue. You're not used to being the bad guy, huh?"

His frown deepened. "I know it must feel like you don't know me, but you do. It was just a couple of details. But the person talking to you, that was me."

I shook my head. "I don't care. Look, you're forgiven. Okay? If that's what you need, you got it. All good. It's in the past."

"Thing is, Alex, I don't think I really ever saw us meeting. I don't know." He scratched his head. "It was always going to be a clusterfuck that wound up with you hating me. And I liked you too much to want to 'fess up to that."

"As a friend," I inserted. "I know."

"Yeah. But it's done. You're here now. Seems stupid if we don't take this chance to try and get to know each other face-to-face," he said. "Guess what I'm asking is if you'll stay a few days. Let me make this up to you."

"God, are you serious? No. Absolutely not," I said, resolute. "I've had liars in my life before, Joe. No. I can't. I'm going home."

He visibly sagged.

"Sucks that you're having issues being the jerk in this situation. But that's not my problem."

No response.

"Excuse me. I need to go to the bathroom." Time to go splash some water on my face. Pull myself together. Only when I pushed back in my seat and stood, the whole world whited out, spinning in dizzy circles. My muscles weakened and suddenly gravity was not my friend.

"Shit. Alex."

A strong hand gripped my arm, keeping me from keeling over. Already up and out of his chair, Joe guided me back down into my seat. Maybe going nowhere was best. Yeah, I'd just hang. No doubt this would all pass in a minute.

"You're gray," said Joe, kneeling at my feet.

"Actually, I don't feel particularly great." In fact, if there'd been anything in my stomach, I'd have probably thrown up all over him. Ha. What a statement that would have made. Only then, I'd feel bad because he was being so sweet and all.

Coffee cups clattered on the table.

"Is she okay?" the waitress asked Joe.

"You mind grabbing her some water, Jess?"

"Sure."

I heard swift footsteps. The growl of a motorcycle passing by outside.

"Maybe I caught some bug on the plane yesterday," I said, pondering my shit condition. The only swooning women I knew came out of Georgette Heyer novels. I wasn't the fainting type. "This seems a bit worse than a stuffy nose."

"You nearly passed out just now. You can't fly in this condition."

"Shit." I groaned on the inside. "I guess not. Perhaps I'll see if I can extend my stay at the hotel."

"And who's going to look after you?" he asked.

"I don't need someone looking after me."

"Hey," he said, forehead furrowed all stern-like. "You could have fallen and seriously hurt yourself just now. Hit your head or something."

"Joe . . ."

A glass of ice water was thrust in front of me.

"Thanks," I mumbled to the waitress.

"Jess, we'll take it all to go," ordered the man before turning back to me. "I better stick with you."

Oh, hell no.

"Please don't take this the wrong way, because you're being very kind. But one polite attempt at breakfast isn't about to undo months of betrayal. Anyway, I don't think I could relax with you watching me in a small hotel room, friend or not." I blew my nose and thought deep thoughts. Or as deep a thought as my muddled, hurting head would allow. "Some cold and flu drugs and I'll be fine. I'll just sleep it off. By tomorrow it'll probably be gone."

"I'll take you back to the hotel, then I'll go get whatever you want from the pharmacy," he said, as if the decision had been made. "I won't be hovering over you, promise."

I winced. "Joe . . ."

"Alex, you're sick."

"Really? I hadn't noticed. Thanks so much for pointing that out."

"And in a bad mood. But fair enough, you've got reason to be." He placed his warm hand atop mine, gently stroking with the side of his thumb. Trying to lull me into submission or something. I didn't have the energy to care.

"I pulled some crap with you that was wrong," he said. "But right now, you look terrible. You should be in bed. Why don't you crash and allow me to go get whatever you need from the drugstore then drop it back at the hotel? I can leave it at the front desk. You won't even have to see me."

"That's a really kind offer, but—"

"But nothing," he said. "C'mon, I'm here. I want to help. Give me a chance to show you I'm not a total asshole."

His offer did sound good. Extremely good. I didn't even care that he'd dissed my mood and said I looked like crap. The word *bed* floated before me like a beautiful, impossible dream.

"You've got time?" I sniffed. "You don't have to be at work or something?"

"No." He shook his head. "It's all good. And later if you decide you need anything else or want to go to the doctor I can organize that, no problem. You could just text me or something."

Heavy sigh. "Are you sure?"

His beard framed a confident smile. "I'm sure."

Even heavier sigh. "Okay."

"Good."

"I'm only staying for one more night, though," I clarified.

"Okay."

I managed a feeble smile.

Maybe he wasn't such a bad guy, despite all the lying. It didn't matter. I'd given this thing between us a chance and it had blown up in my face. Whatever kind of man Joe Collins might be, tomorrow I was going home where all was safe and sound. Home where I belonged.

CHAPTER FOUR

Message received five months ago:
Hi Alex,
Thanks for your reply and sorry about the silence. My trip to Seattle's off for now, but it'd be great to keep in touch. How's your graphic design business doing? I see you're interested in renovation. Been doing some work stripping parts of the restaurant back to original fittings and raw brick lately while also trying to maintain some of the original 70's/80's fixtures. Not much else happening right now. Seen any good bands lately? Live music scene here dies off in winter but the summer's really active. My best to your squirrel friend Marty. I'd add some joke about keeping nuts warm, but it'd probably just make things awkward. We don't know each other nearly well enough for that. ;)
Eric

Message sent:
Shit. I probably shouldn't have added that nuts bit. Hope I haven't offended you.
Eric

Message sent:
Hahaha. No worries, Eric. I'm not that delicate a petal.
Would love to keep in touch. Your renovation project sounds
awesome, can you shoot me some photos when you get a
chance? How old is the building you're working on? Business
has been crazy busy which is great. Lots of branding for new
businesses mostly, business cards etc. No plans to head out
but I just downloaded the Soviet X-Ray Record Club's latest.
Enjoying that. I'll be sure to pass on your regards to Marty
and his nuts next time I see him.
Alex

Someone had called Thor.

It was the only explanation my befuddled mind could come up with for the almighty pounding upon my door. Thor and his mighty hammer. Goddamn god of thunder. I'd been fast asleep, completely unconscious.

I struggled to sit up. And I do mean struggled.

Upon returning to the hotel, Joe had pretty much taken over. My booties and coat were removed from my body and I was put to bed. The man took my tucking-in seriously. He'd fixed the top sheet and blanket across me so tightly, I almost needed the Jaws of Life to escape. Almost.

"Coming," I attempted to bellow when the hammering continued. What came out, however, was more of a wheeze, as if I'd been involved in an amateur sword swallowing contest. My throat was annihilated and my head didn't feel much better. Oddly enough, the room was dark. Completely dark. No sunlight snuck around the curtain edges or anything. Only the dim line of light from the hallway showed beneath the door.

"Hey," I rasped upon opening it.

Sure enough, there stood Thor aka blond Bigfoot aka my supposed friend Joe. He did not look happy. "Fuck's sake, Alex. You had me worried sick."

"What? Why?" I headed back over to the bed, sitting on the end of the mattress. Oh, beloved bed. All I wanted to do was crawl back in and do some more sleeping. For forever would work.

He closed the door and flicked on the light, making me wince. One bulging pharmacy bag and one neat brown paper bag hung from his right hand. "I called the front desk six times to check and see if you'd picked up the stuff from the pharmacy. They hadn't heard a word from you."

"Huh. I must have slept all day."

"And half the night," he said, frowning heavily. "It's nine P.M. I was supposed to work until twelve, but I needed to come check on you. I've been standing out there banging on the door for ages. I was just about to get security to open it for me so I could make sure you weren't dead."

"Not dead." I feebly waved a hand his way. "Yet."

"You're still too pale. If anything you seem worse." Hands on hips, the man scowled down at me. This morning's hoodie had been replaced by a nicely fitted blue thermal. A smooth mover or not, Joe had a drool-worthy physique. Big black boots covered his feet, and he wore black jeans. He looked a little dangerous, dressed all dark and acting so moody. Even if it was just my lazy white blood cells he was mad at.

"Sorry you had to leave work," I said. "But I really am okay."

Without comment, he placed the palm of his hand against my fevered brow.

"I actually feel a little better," I lied.

"Yeah? Because you look like shit."

"Don't you flirt with me." I coughed out a laugh. "I'm not your type, remember?"

The brown paper bag, he sat on a little table against the wall. But the pharmacy bag he upended onto the bed beside me. Cold and flu tablets, aspirin, Theraflu, Advil, Kleenex, throat lozenges, cough syrup, and more. Much, much more.

"Wow," I said. "That's a lot of stuff."

"Wanted to make sure you had everything you might need."

"But I only gave you twenty dollars."

"Don't worry about it," he said.

It didn't exactly sit well with me, owing him. Maybe I'd try and slip another twenty into his coat or something. I picked up a slim purple tube. "Huckleberry lip balm?"

A shrug. He passed me a bottle of water out of the mini-bar. Then tore into the box of cold and flu tablets, popping two out of the packaging into my waiting hand.

"Thanks."

Next, he started fussing with the contents of the brown paper bag. First he removed the lid from a large take-out cup, then added one of those disposable plastic spoons.

"Nell made you chicken noodle soup," he said, handing the cup and spoon over. "Careful, it's hot. Well, I hope it still is. There's also some cookies in the bag."

"I wish my nose was working. I bet it smells great." Steam rose from the soup, warming my face. I blew on the liquid and took a small sip. Immediately my throat felt a bit better. Such was the almighty power of comfort food. "This is so nice of her. She's the chef in your bar, right?"

He flinched. "Ah, no. I mean it's not my bar. Eric owns a share of the bar along with her and Lydia. They all run different sections. I just work for them."

"Right. Sorry, I forgot to forget what I thought I knew about you."

Insert uncomfortable silence here.

The man got busy moving all of the pharmacy goods onto the table. I watched, sipping and stirring my soup. Eventually, he ran out of things to do and we were back to facing each other, a veritable life full of lies between us.

No, that was wrong. Nothing lay between us now. All of my romantic misconceptions were gone. Whatever I'd imagined could develop between me and "Eric" had died a sad and sorry death last night. In front of all of his friends, even. Little wonder Nell was making me soup. I must have looked like such a fool.

"You want me to run you a hot bath or something?" he asked.

"No. Thanks. I'm good."

Once he'd gone I'd summon up some strength to do it for myself. A nice quick hot bath. Emphasis on *quick*. Baths and I had a bad history. Long story.

He shuffled his feet, crossed his arms. I stared off at the wall, embarrassed for some reason. Being in such close quarters was weird. Would it be rude to tell him to go back to work? It felt rude. The things he'd done for me today, he'd been kind, caring. I had no idea what he thought he'd achieve here. Guess the least I could do was not be a raging bitch. Besides, who had the energy?

I swallowed hard. "Actually, could I have the Kleenex, please?"

"Sure." He tore open the box, setting it beside me.

"You'd make a great nurse." I tried to smile. It felt wrong, wonky and weak, like the rest of me. *Blergh*.

An amused glance. Then more silence.

God, the spaces between words were so awkward. All difficult and embarrassing. And I was so off balance, I couldn't help but fill them up with meaningless conversation. "Ever considered going into that field, Joe? Nursing?"

With both hands, he smoothed back his golden hair, getting it out of his face. "No. This is strictly a one-off gig."

A pause. "I do about five shifts a week behind the bar and work with my dad a few days as well. He's a carpenter, trained me too. He used to build houses until his arthritis got too bad. Now we just do renovations and maintenance mostly."

"Oh."

"Nothing as fancy as part-owning a restaurant and bar like my brother."

Wow. I so wasn't going near that comment. I drank some more of my soup, then fished out chunks of vegetables and noodles with the spoon. "That's where the interest in old buildings came from, then, working with your father?"

"Yeah." He sat down in the dumb decorative chair they always have in posh hotel rooms. Made for quite the combination, Joe and peach cushions.

Man, everything hurt. I sagged further, wilting before his very eyes. Having something hot in my stomach helped, but I seriously couldn't wait for the drugs to kick in. Every inch of me ached, but my head was a total mess. Maybe I should get it removed. At least then my nose would stop running.

Steam might help me breathe. I gave the bathroom door a longing look. A bath was starting to sound nice, it just seemed so far away. Miles. States. And I smelled funky, sweaty. Must have had a fever while I slept. Just as well Joe was sticking to the other side of the room.

"You really do want that bath, don't you?"

I just looked at him, waiting for my brain to cough up something to say.

"Look, Alex, it's okay to let me help you. I'm not going to use it against you or something."

"Ha." I smiled for real. "That doesn't make me sound paranoid or anything at all."

"I've given you enough reason not to trust me. I get it." With wrinkles all around his eyes, the guy gave me a truly pained look. The whole being-the-bad-guy thing really wasn't sitting well with him.

Good. I would not feel pity for him. The man had burned me bad. Desperately, I tried to shove any empathy, sympathy, or any of the above back from whence they came. It didn't quite work. I was such a sucker. "If you wouldn't mind running me a bath that would be great. But you don't have to, you've done more than enough already."

Without another word he got up and went into the bathroom. The sound of water rushing in to fill the fancy jetted tub was music to my ears. This had been the only room they had available when I booked back into the hotel after our conversation attempt at breakfast this morning. My original basic room had been gone. Luckily, the lady on the front desk took pity on me and dropped the price some. She probably didn't want me hanging around the lobby, infecting people with my germs. Whatever the reason, she deserved sainthood and I'd be emailing the pope ASAP. The room was damn nice.

"Done." Joe rubbed his hands together. "Shit, I didn't think to buy any bubble bath. Sorry."

I smiled. "I think just this once I can live without bubbles."

His answering smile didn't fit quite right. Guess his need to please wasn't appeased. Awkward looks started up again as neither of us knew where to go from here, what happened next. I broke the standoff by blowing my nose. Such a delicate, lady-like sound. Not the least bit like a trombone on acid with added gargling noises. Seriously, the human body could be spectacularly gross.

"Speaking of renovations," he started, sitting back down. "You ever get a chance to look at those pictures I sent you?"

"Pictures?" I played dumb, picking at the stitching on the hem of my top.

"Of the upper floor of the Bird Building where Dive Bar is."

"Oh, right."

A pause.

He shrugged. "No problem if you didn't. Just thought you might have been interested."

"I was." Internally, I gave myself a good hard slap. Then another. Might as well just paint a target on my back and be done with it, rather than admitting to being interested in his life or work any further; disappointment and disaster were sure to follow. You only had to look at our recent awesome history to see that. I should just ask him to leave. Or fake my own death and then lock the door when he ran to get help.

Gaze glued to me, the man waited.

"Hand me the laptop on the table," I grumbled.

Curiosity lit his dark eyes and he did as requested, sitting beside me on the end of the bed. Big fingers brushed mine as he handed over the computer. His skin was cooler than mine. Though not unpleasantly so. Surreptitiously, I wiggled an inch or two away from him as we waited for the machine to power up.

"You have Marty the squirrel as your screensaver?" The corner of his lips curled into a smile and he nodded at my screen.

"I don't have to explain myself to you," I said, frowning. Nervous, shaking fingers stumbled across the keyboard, entering the password then bringing up the relevant file. "Sure, Marty doesn't always remember where he's left his nuts. But he's never once misled me or done me wrong."

"Hey, calm down. I was just going to say, great shot of him." He turned back to the computer. Then he stopped and gaped at the screen. "Wow, what's all this?"

"It's nothing, really," I babbled. "Actually, let's not do this."

"Wait." He leaned in closer, tilting his head, checking things out. "No. These are really something."

"It was just . . . I was just messing around." I tucked my hair behind my ears, rubbed at the old scar high on my forehead. "Seriously, it's nothing. Not like I'm an architect or anything."

"Bullshit." The dude leveled me with a look. One that I neither liked nor took comfort in. "Alex, we need to show these to Andre."

"Who? The owner of the building?"

A nod.

"No, no. That would just be silly. Also, it would make me wildly uncomfortable."

He gave me another look. One I couldn't begin to read. Such a pain in the ass the way his beard covered half his face. The sharp cheekbones above provided me with no clues at all.

"I'm not being disingenuous, Joe," I said, trying to explain, searching for the right words. "I'm good at my work and I take pride in it. But that stuff was just play time. I had no real idea what I was doing, okay? It was something I thought we—well, me and Eric or whatever—could have a laugh over. Can we please leave it for now?"

For a long moment we stared at one another. Then he gave me a nod. It wasn't a happy one.

"Guess I should probably head off now," he said, brows drawn tight. Clearly reluctant to leave. "Let you grab a bath and then get back to sleep."

"Yeah . . ."

"Hmm."

Neither of us moved.

"Though I really should stay at least until you're out of the bath. You're on enough pain meds to put an elephant to sleep."

Oh God. I shouldn't do it. For both of our sakes, I should let him go. Except something sick and stupid stuck up its head and begged. Perhaps it was some misbegotten curiosity about the man or maybe the drugs. God, I hoped it was the drugs. At any rate, some overly vocal part of me wanted to keep him around a bit longer.

"Well, I'm kind of awake now," I blurted out before I could slap a hand over my mouth. Talk about being out of control. Shit.

He just looked at me.

"You know . . . um." Shakespeare I was not. Fuck it, I'd said it, I'd put it out there. Now I'd just have to suck it up. "We could watch a movie after I've had a bath. If you want. But if you need to be somewhere, I under—"

"No. They're not really expecting me back at work. That'd be cool." He perked right up, pulling his cell out of his back jeans pocket and firing off a text. Then he paused, gazing at me from beneath a heavy brow. "You're sure?"

"Sure." I did not sound sure. Nor did I feel it.

The man froze.

"I mean . . . so long as it's understood I'd rather never again discuss the whole, 'switched identities, you fooling me, and me feeling like a chump' thing," I said. "Okay?"

Slowly, he nodded. "Okay. We can just relax together."

"Great." We could try, at least.

Kill me now.

Everything was horrible. Truly deeply God-fucking awful. Lethargy dragged at my limbs, making me feel like I was sinking through the bed, down through the floor straight into hell. Yet my mind was drifting, lighter than air and completely confused. All of this with the added benefit of being covered in sweat. I felt like I'd been thrown into Mount Doom.

"Yeah. She took some about six hours ago," a deep male voice said. "Nothing before that for a good ten or twelve hours, I think."

Faintly, I could hear another voice responding.

Wearily, I blinked open my eyes. The damp cloth covering my forehead obscured my vision. A table lamp was on, showing Joe standing by my bedside.

"Okay, I'll get some more into her." He looked my way, face lined with concern. "She's awake now."

Another pause as the person on the other end of the line talked.

"Keep the liquids up. Got it. Thanks, Mom. I'll call you if she gets any worse."

"Mom?" I queried in a wavery voice.

"Dr. Google and Mom have got you covered. She's a nurse." He put down the mobile and picked up the bottle of aspirin, shaking two tablets out into his hand. "Can you sit up a little?"

I nodded, dislodging the cloth and rising up on one elbow, shaking all the while. "Yeah."

"We need to bring your temperature down." He sat beside me on the bed, lifting the glass of water. "Open your mouth."

In went the pills, followed by the water. Man, nothing had ever tasted so good. Nothing. I downed the whole glassful in a nanosecond.

He refilled the glass from a bottle of water. "Just sip it this time. We don't want you getting queasy."

I did as told. "Feel hot. Can we get this blanket off?"

"Sure."

Together, though mostly it was Joe, we pushed the blanket off onto the other side of the bed. My clothes literally stuck to me. Gross didn't cover it. And I was still burning up, hot as Hades. It felt like a small sun had taken up residence inside of me. While my feet pushed at my socks, I wrestled with removing the baggy thermal from my upper body. To get comfortable was the only thing that mattered. This man had already stated that he didn't see me that way, plus he and I had no future, so who cared what he thought of me in my underwear. Also, fuck modesty when I was feeling this sick.

"Want that off too?" Joe carefully freed me from the thermal top while I huffed and puffed. The white tank top underneath was plastered to me with sweat. Never mind. At least I could start to feel cool air on my skin.

"Socks, please," I whispered.

He got busy liberating my feet from the fluffy menaces. But it was still too much, and only achieving a modicum of comfort mattered. I stuck my thumbs into the top of my leggings and started wriggling about, trying to get them down. Someone had sucked the strength straight out of me. My arms just kind of flopped around. Noodle woman, that was me.

"Those too?" The big guy peeled my leggings off and *yes*. Oh, fuck yes.

"That's better." With a sigh of relief, I flopped back down. Tank top and knickers were plenty of clothing. Every part of me ached. My toes, my teeth, my freaking hair follicles. Everything.

The TV was off, along with every light in the room apart from the table lamp. It made the world look so weird, shadowy. Joe's cheekbones in particular appeared to have been carved from stone, his dark eyes glowing in the low light. It all felt like a fever dream. Reality was far, far away and sleep had started sneaking up on me once more.

"The movie finished?" I asked.

He smiled. "A while ago. You fell asleep."

"Oh."

A nod toward the couch. "Don't freak out. But I camped out over there. Just in case."

"Okay." My eyelids drifted shut. I lacked the energy to keep them open. Or to care. "Thanks."

The mattress shifted. Soft footsteps and then distantly I heard running water. He returned and placed a new damp cloth on my forehead.

"That's nice." I mumbled.

"I'm here if you need me," he said.

And that was nice too.

CHAPTER FIVE

Message sent five months ago:

Hey Eric,

So it's my turn to write and I really don't know what to say. Look, in all honesty, my life is incredibly boring. Since I'm based at home and I'm my own boss, I can work pretty much whenever it suits. Depends on how many jobs I've got going on. I can easily go up to a week only talking to the people who deliver my takeout. I've got my friends and family too, of course. But you know how busy modern life is etc. Oh, and there's Marty. He's always good company. Besides work, it's usually just me, online property sites (a girl needs her dreams), and TV together forever. Don't be mad, you had to have seen this coming. TV and the internet are just too good. There was no way you could ever compete.

Regretfully,

Alex

P.S. Hope your restaurant and life in general are doing well.

Message received:

Alex,

Damn. We haven't even actually met yet and you've chosen TV over me. That's harsh. Things are going okay here. Starting to warm up a little which is great. The Dive Bar's been busy. Can't imagine going days not having anyone around. Your bubble must be peaceful. Seems all I do is talk to people all day long. Not sure I need TV since the business isn't short on drama. One of the bartenders thinks he's Romeo. Unfortunately he has the attention span of a gnat. Makes keeping good wait staff around hard. Also our cook, Nell, is going through a divorce. She and her ex are both long-time friends of mine so it sucks to see them hurting. On particularly bad days you can hear Nell using her cleaver throughout the whole restaurant. I don't even want to think about what she's imagining chopping.

Eric

Insistent knocking on the door. Again.

"For fuck's sake."

My sentiments exactly. Only, strangely enough, I hadn't spoken. Instead, a familiar, if somewhat unexpected, masculine voice had provided the profanity. I rubbed the sleep from my eyes and checked out the other side of the mattress. Large-male alert. Oh God, what if I'd had some strange reaction to the cold and flu tablets and sexually assaulted the poor innocent man last night? It had been a while since I'd seen any action.

"Hey," said Joe, stretched out on top of the bed. He'd shucked his boots, but otherwise, all clothing remained intact.

Thank God.

"Hi" is what I attempted to say. What came out was a cross between a whisper and a wheeze. God, my throat was on fire. Raw agony. I could have cried in pain and frustration, only it would have made my headache worse. Besides appearing pitiful, of course.

The knocking continued.

"How are you feeling,?" he asked around a yawn.

"Crappy," I whisper-wheezed, beyond caring. Fucking plague.

"Shit," he mumbled. "You lost your voice?"

I nodded.

"Damn. Least you're not burning up anymore." Slowly, he sat up, stretching his neck and rolling his shoulders. Then he pushed up off the bed and went to answer the door.

The actual Eric Collins barging in made for the second surprise of the morning. Unlike his brother, he wore black slacks and a pale blue button-down, topped off with a black leather jacket. His long dark hair was tied back in a man-bun, his face freshly shaven. Besides him, Joe appeared distinctly rumpled. Resemblance-wise, you could see the shared gene pool in their high foreheads and generous lips. The slight thickness of their noses. Otherwise you'd hardly credit them with being brothers. As different as day and night.

"Morning," said Eric, dumping his load of brown paper bags on top of the chest of drawers. "Told Nell you didn't make it home last night and she made me bring over more food and stuff. Coffee's in that one."

"Thanks." Joe dove into the designated bag, pulling out two extra-large coffee cups.

"Dad phoned, wanted to know when you'd be on the job," he said. "Better check your cell and give him a call."

"Will do."

Eric turned, giving me a flirty little grin. It didn't last long, however. "Damn. You're really sick, aren't you?"

Joe's brows drew in. "I said she was."

"Yeah, just figured it was an excuse she'd made up to stay in town and make you run around jumping through hoops, doing stuff for her. Grovel. You know, make you pay penance?" He shrugged. "Bet Boyd fifty bucks too."

Without a word, Joe set down one of the cups and smacked his brother upside the head.

"Christ, man!" Eric patted his hair back into place. "Take it easy."

"Apologize to Alex before I break your fucking neck."

"Sorry, Alex," said Eric, becoming less attractive to me by the minute.

"Idiot." Dark eyes distinctly pissy, Joe turned my way. "You want coffee?"

To think I'd actually imagined Eric might be the man of my dreams. The real Eric had maturity issues, that much was certain. I shook my head and fought my way out from underneath the mountain of blankets he must have piled on me while I slept. Distantly, I could remember waking up at some stage shivering, ice cold, and demanding blankets. Otherwise, I still just had on the thin tank top and my favorite underwear. Bright yellow boy-legs with Little Miss Fucking Sunshine on the front. I only owned about five pairs of them. She was kind of my spirit animal. And to think, Joe had seen me in this glorious getup, sticky with sweat and sick as could be, and he'd still stayed and played nurse. Impressive.

I hadn't lasted through all of the movie last night, what with being on death's doorstep. Joe and I hadn't talked much. But what we did do was laugh at the same lines, exclaim over the same fight scene, and *ooh* at exactly the same time during the car chase. So our tastes in films were eerily similar, as if that meant anything. I just hadn't expected to feel quite so comfortable having him around. Early on, all I had noticed was how different he was from the guy I thought I knew. It was disconcerting to start grafting all the things we actually had in common onto this new hunk of manhood.

Anger, hate, and betrayal were harder to hold against Joe Collins than I would have liked. Let's blame it on the drugs.

No doubt on top of my questionable underwear I also had crazy bed hair, morning breath, and every other unattractive thing you could think of. But the glory of feeling like something a cat barfed up was the complete lack of caring. And let's face facts, in a day or two's time, the plague would have either turned me into a zombie or subsided.

Either way, these two men could take me as I came or get the hell out of my hotel room.

Still pouting, Eric threw himself into a chair. "There's fresh juice in there too. Apple, orange, and whatever else Nell could think of to boost the immune system. Ever since she got pregnant she's been on this insane mothering bend. Can you believe last night she tried to tell me I drink too much?"

Joe just grunted and dug through the bags in search of the juice. He brought it over to me, taking a seat on the side of the bed with a coffee in hand. "Hate to be the bearer of bad news, but I don't think you're going anywhere today."

I nodded glumly, downing two more of the cold and flu tablets before taking a cautious sip. Wow, what eye-watering goodness.

Zesty with explosions of ginger and garlic in my mouth. At least I could vaguely taste something. Everything else was *blergh*. If Nell's germ-attack juice didn't kill the evil bugs living in me, nothing would. I plucked some more Kleenex out of the box and blew my nose.

"Actually, Nell's been riding my ass about a lot of stuff lately." Eric stared up at the ceiling, all contemplative. "You think she wants me to propose again?"

Joe turned to look at his brother. "E, she tried to punch you in the balls last time you offered her a ring. So, I'm thinking no."

"Could have just been the baby hormones making her crazy."

"No, man," said Joe. "Pretty sure it was you making her crazy."

With nothing to contribute to the conversation, I kept on sucking down the juice.

The big blond guy turned back to me, taking a sip of his coffee. "Eric accidentally knocked up Nell. She was drunk."

"Doesn't mean she didn't jump me."

Joe caught my eye and gave a small shake of the head.

"I saw that," his brother bitched.

Joe winked at me. I couldn't help but smile back. It was a small, feeble thing, to be sure, but it was there. He obviously hadn't gone into detail about Eric and this issue in his emails. Guess it got too complicated.

"Started reading one of those baby books you got me. Already proving useful." Eric grabbed the closest brown paper bag, checking out the contents. "Give me a break, she packed you the triple-choc brownies. Like they have any health benefits."

"I'll take one of those." Joe half rose from the bed, stretching out a hand. His brother handed one over to him. "What about the book?"

"Well?"

"Yeah. All right." Eric slumped down in his chair, mouth lined with worry. "And don't call it *it*. That's really uncool."

No response to his brother's mini-rant. Joe just drank more of his coffee.

Suddenly, Eric was up and out of here. "I got to go. Later."

"Later."

I waved as he closed the door.

"He's actually doing better than he was," mumbled Joe, turning to look at me. "Spent the first few days after she told him about the baby pretty much hiding under a shrub out in the yard with a bottle of single malt. Wouldn't even speak. Didn't think he'd manage to open one of the books, let alone read some of it. For a guy who never planned on getting married and having kids, it's a start."

I nodded.

"Nell was going through a messy divorce from another friend of ours, Pat. Her and my brother were a drunken accident." He sighed, staring off at nothing. "It's been like getting caught in the middle of a fucking war, having this going on. We've all been friends since school, but now everything's a mess. It drove me nuts I couldn't email you about all of it. I needed some sanity."

Silence.

"Anyway." He cleared his throat. "Don't you think maybe you should go to the doctor?"

Good question. Thing is, unless modern medicine had made some miraculous discoveries overnight, they still didn't have a cure for the flu. "No," I mouthed.

"Okay. If you change your mind or need anything, I'm writing my cell number on this notebook over here. Text me." He got busy doing as much, bending over the little table half-covered in brown Dive Bar goodie bags. Whoa. Hold up. Nice ass. Seriously, the man had a good one. Something about a masculine, jeans-clad ass just beckoned to be noticed and appreciated. I still preferred my men in suits and ties, but it couldn't be denied. Joe's rear had it going on.

The man himself turned and my eyes shot up to his face. I pasted on a pleasant smile to hide the shameful guilt inside of me over perving on the poor defenseless guy. Not that I actually felt any guilt. I just probably should have.

He cocked his head, forehead lined. "What?"

I raised my brows. "Huh?"

"Is there something on my ass?" He attempted to look at said fine behind, brushing away at it with both hands.

Busted. I was so very busted. And to have this happen after he'd stated I didn't do it for him. Oh, the shame. I should ship my libido to Alaska for a season or two, cool the stupid thing off.

The brushing of said bottom continued for a moment then he fortunately moved on, picking up the spare room key. "I'm going to take this so when I come back to check on you tonight, if you're sleeping, I won't wake you with any knocking. Okay?"

Normally, no, it wouldn't be okay. But I was reasonably certain he was not a murderer. If he'd intended to do anything bad then he'd have already done it. Also, his brother, mother, friends, and the people on the front desk all knew he'd been coming and going, so I nodded. Given how woozy I'd been yesterday and my fever during the night, having someone check on me seemed wise.

"All right." A big hand brushed over his butt one more time and he frowned. "I'll see you later, Alex."

Phew.

CHAPTER SIX

Message received three months ago:

Hey Alex,

Had an interesting conversation today you might like to hear about. Andre, the guy that owns the building, got approached by some real estate people about developing the second floor into condos. They used to be offices but have just been left empty or used for storage for the last thirty or so years. No way Andre will deal with the real estate goons, but he asked if I'd be interested in developing the spaces. Doing something similar to what we did with the Dive Bar renovation. Making use of the raw brick walls and polishing up the wooden floors and that. Modernizing where necessary. I don't know. It'd be a huge commitment when I've already got a lot going on. It'd take a lot of cash to see it through, too. Cool idea, though. My brother Joe and my dad are carpenters. They could handle most of it. I guess I'll see how things go over the next while.

E

Message sent:
Eric, great to hear from you. And what a great project! Thanks
for those pics you sent. Wow—your brother looks like a
lumberjack—where's the family resemblance there? The reno
on the Dive Bar worked out so beautifully. Just imagine what
you could do changing the space upstairs into studio apart-
ments or something. It would be amazing. Please give this
more thought. You sound so passionate when you talk about
the carpentry projects you do with your dad. If there's no set
d-day on it, this could work out perfectly. Would love to hear
more about the spaces when you get a chance.
Cheers,
Alex

As promised, it wasn't knocking that woke me. It was the buzzing of my cell phone over on the table.

I'd had a quiet day, sleeping, mostly. The codeine Joe's mom
had sent over had knocked me out nicely. My head still felt light,
a bit woozy. More rest was needed. Maybe I'd take a home-cation
for the remainder of the week back in Seattle. Disconnect, and
take it easy. Give myself a break and take the time to properly re-
cover from this illness. I couldn't even remember the last time I
had a vacation. But, no biggie. I loved my work. Graphic design-
ing was not a chore, it was a delight.

A break would be good, though.

Weirdly enough, suddenly the bathroom door opened and out
strolled Joe on a cloud of steam and masculinity wearing an extremely small white towel as a skirt. There was a lot of bronzed
skin on show. A truly unnecessarily large amount. The buzzing

cell phone immediately caught his attention and he rushed on over, picking it up.

"Shit," he mumbled, putting it to his ear. "Hello?"

Standing with his back to me forced me to reassess the skirt. Actually, I'm not even sure it would qualify as a towel. It couldn't. The thing barely covered his ass cheeks. Not that I was staring. Been there, nearly gotten busted at that.

Yeah.

Well, I was kind of not staring. It's harder to ignore a mostly naked man than you'd think. Perhaps this was a real fever dream. I didn't feel particularly hot, but why else would the man be wandering around mostly naked in my hotel room? Oh my God. Unless he was thinking of putting the moves on me.

Whoa. I seriously hadn't seen that coming. What to do? Usually sex with no consequences was an easy call; I either wanted to or I didn't. Despite my best intentions to ignore Joe, he was hot. On the other hand, however, lying was not. I'd let him get close (well, virtually close, if that makes sense) and he'd hurt me. If any lingering feelings for him were still floating around inside of me, it could very well happen again.

"Yeah, I'm Joe Collins. Alex is sleeping, she's been sick. She caught the flu." He waited. "Ah, well . . ." Again, he listened. In fact, he listened for quite a while. "You're . . . I : . . . Okay, yes, I'm a raging asshole. I should never have done that to her, you're right. But . . ." He paused. Then he took an almighty big breath, letting it out real slow. "Yes. You're right, there's no excuse for such a willful act of bastardry and I definitely deserve to be castrated and burn in hell for all eternity. Um. Who did you say you were again?" The man massaged his temple, making the muscles in his upper back move. Nice. "Valerie, Alex's best friend. Right. Nice to meet you. Alex spoke about you a lot, when we were emailing." Joe winced, removing the phone from his ear for a moment as a particularly loud noise issued through the cell. "Yes, I can see how that would just remind you what a jerk I am, of course." He nodded. "No. Okay. I will never win you over with charm because I'm slime. Got it." The man hung his head. "Yes, I'm listening. She is a goddess despite her cold, hard heart and I'm a lowly animal. Totally agree." He started rubbing the back of his neck. "Okay. I'll get her to call you when she's up. Great to talk to you, Valerie. Yep . . . okay, got to go. There's a whole line of people here who also need to abuse me. Bye."

Visibly sagging, the man commenced muttering obscenities.

Over on the bed, I could hold it in no longer and proceeded to almost piss myself laughing. Valerie was the best. The absolute best.

"Oh, you're awake," he said, pushing the long wet strands of his golden hair back from his face. "I just had a little chat with your friend Valerie. Your phone kept ringing so I thought I better answer or it would wake you up."

I giggled on.

"Enjoy that, did you?"

I nodded.

"Great. I'm glad. Anyway, hope you don't mind. The heating at Nell's place is acting up and they can't fix it until tomorrow. I told her she could have my room for the night and I'd crash here again," he said. "If that's okay with you?"

I shrugged, kind of caught out.

"You're looking a little better, got some color back in your cheeks."

Given how little the man was wearing, that did not surprise me at all.

His shoulders were broad, as befitting a man of his stature. His arms were muscular and his nipples were brown. Both of them. I didn't want to take in all of these details, but what with him standing nearly naked right there, I was forced to. Wise or not, my ovaries had seized control and they wanted to make big strong babies with the man, pronto. Common sense never stood a chance.

"You don't mind that I helped myself to a shower, do you?" he asked. "Eric wanted to go for a run after work. I was already covered in sawdust so the sweat just made it even worse. We had a hell of a busy day. Dad's hands were playing up on him so he couldn't work, but he'd booked in all these jobs."

"You couldn't use your own shower?" I asked, voice sounding only a little rusty. And oh, good God. Now that he was full-on facing me, it was the bulge below his waist that was really the issue.

Not my type. The man was not my type, no matter how fascinating I apparently found his body. Once I got back to Seattle, I really needed to get laid.

"Hey, great. You got your voice back." He smiled. "Eric was in the shower and I didn't want to wait around any longer. I was worried about how you were doing. Plus, the water heater isn't that big and I wanted to leave some hot water for Nell."

"Right." I took a soothing deep breath, pretending to swallow his obvious lies. As pickup lines went, Joe's needed work. I blew my nose. "Um, no problem. But would you mind putting a towel on? Or pants, maybe? Pants would be good."

He laughed, making bits of me quiver. Bits that frankly should have known better.

"Alex, this is a towel."

"Ah. No, it's not."

"It is. See?" The man held out his arms, modeling the freakishly small piece of white cloth.

"No, no." I pressed my lips together tight, anger and aggravation growing in me by the second. "That's like a hand towel. Christ, I'm not even sure it's that. It's probably more of a glorified face cloth you've stretched somehow."

Chuckling, he shook his head. "Alex—"

"Hell, I can almost see some of the essentials. That's ridiculous."

"Yeah, but you're half hanging off the bed to take in the show."

"Oh, I am not. I just had to cough." I forced out a fake cough or two, holding my fist up to my mouth. We were in the friend zone, goddamnit. No perving allowed. Still, I could feel my face flushing, my nipples getting perky.

"Alex, relax. I saw you in your underwear. Now you've seen me in a towel. Why are you getting so worked up about this?" Hands on slim hips, his tongue played behind his cheek. Like stringing me out like this was all highly fucking amusing. Asshole. Hell, he even had a little golden treasure trail. A scattering of hair starting at the belly button and leading downward. My fingers wanted to follow the trail so badly. They basically itched, the little bastards.

"Look, it's okay. I know what you're doing," I said, my croaky voice thick with recrimination. "But I just don't think it's a good idea between us."

"What am I doing?"

"We should only be just friends," I stated. "And this goes a bit beyond that."

"Friends don't let each other use their showers occasionally?"

"Friends don't strut around showing off their assets." I did not giggle nervously. That was someone else. God, what an awkward situation. "I could see less skin at a strip joint!"

"Fuck me," he muttered, smiling.

"Normally I might be open to the idea of doing that," I said. "Just the once, mind you—for fun or to get it out of our system or whatever. But this situation is a freaking mess. I've already been hurt by you. Emotions were involved despite my better judgment. Having sex with you now, even as friends, would just be stupid."

He looked at me all wide of eye and said very slowly, "You want to have sex with me?"

Everything stopped. Every little last fucking thing.

"Alex?"

"I, um . . ." Over and over my jaw worked, yet nothing came out. Total panic stations. My brain had blanked, most likely fleeing the room. "I think maybe I'm a little high on the cold and flu meds. Yeah, that sounds about right?"

He just gave me another serving of that questioning look.

"No. No, I definitely don't want to do anything naked with you."

He blinked.

"You thought about having sex with me, though?"

"What?" I faux cringed.

"But you said—"

"Forget about what I said. And stop saying *sex*."

Joe just stared at me.

"I thought you were trying to start something. I mean, you can't blame me for thinking this is a setup." Curling my feet up beneath me I leaned forward, ready to attack. Or defend. Or something. "Somethings wrong with Nell's heat, seriously?"

He grabbed the back of his neck. "Shit. Alex, it's okay. No need to be embarrassed."

"And Eric was in the shower? That story is so lame, it's like something out of a bad porn film. You might as well tell me you're the pool boy," I said, packing in all the scorn I could manage. "I'm not your type, remember? Then you come over here, parading yourself in front of me like some lumbersexual gigolo. So that yet again I get led on and wind up looking like a complete idiot! What kind of sadistic near-naked asshole are you?"

"I'm not playing games or something, okay?" The man hung his head, slowly shaking it. "Let me clear this up right now."

Without another word, Joe picked up his cell phone off the table.

"Hey Nell," he said into the phone. "Alex just wanted to ask you something."

Circumventing the bed, he pressed the cell directly into my reluctant hand.

"Hello," I said cautiously.

"Alex! Great to talk to you," said a friendly feminine voice. "How are you doing? You're still sounding a bit off."

"Ah, yeah. Getting better, though."

"Good. Glad to hear it. Listen, if it's not okay for Joe to hang with you tonight just say so. I can always go to my brother's place. It's just that they were planning some fancy date-night thing, you know?"

"No. That's fine."

"Excellent. Let me know if you need more soup or anything."

"Thanks. Yeah. Thank you for all the care packages. That's really sweet of you. Thanks."

"No problems. What was the question?" she asked.

"Ahh . . . can I pay you for the food and drinks? I'd really like to pay you. You've been so kind."

"Absolutely not! I've got to go, but I hope we'll see you in at the bar again real soon. Everyone would love to meet you properly. And don't worry, we don't bite. Or remind people of embarrassing scenes caused by idiot males."

"Right. Thanks."

"And can I just say, I get that he behaved like a complete dick. But Joe really is a great guy."

"Ah . . ."

"It's such a shame he's been on his own for so long when he has so much to offer a woman. And I realize you don't know me from a lump of moldy cheese," she said. "But honestly, you could do a lot worse than giving him a second chance. You two looked really great together the other night."

I frowned, perplexed. "How could you tell? Mostly we were just yelling at each other."

"But there was passion there, you know? Real passion." She sighed wistfully. "That's so precious, Alex. It doesn't always come along more than once in a lifetime."

"Right. Okay." Deep breaths. "Thanks for that, Nell."

And she was gone.

Joe squatted down beside the bed, staring up at me. Good God, if anything could have made his flasher skirt even worse. I averted my eyes, despite my brain wanting another moment to imprint the memory. Idiot brain.

"Do you believe me now?" he asked softly. "I can call Eric too if you want."

"No, that's fine."

"Okay. I'm going to put some pants on so you'll be more comfortable."

"Thanks." Subdued, I set his cell on the bedside table. "Nell's a big fan of yours. You know, I think I'd like a drink. Vodka and orange, maybe."

"No problem." The man sounded way too fucking happy.

"I think we should both stop talking for a while. Watch a movie or something. Wouldn't that be nice?"

"Sure. I won't even ask you for an apology for all those nasty things you said." Highly magnanimous of him.

"This never happened," I stated most adamantly. "None of it."

Grabbing a pair of jeans out of a bag on the floor, he couldn't have smiled any more if he tried. The dude's face had to be hurting from the overload of glee. "Alex. Little Miss Fucking Sunshine."

"Shut up. You're responsible for enough horrifically embarrassing moments this week, thank you very much," I said. "Worst Internet friend ever. I think I need more meds."

"Hey. Just remember, I didn't say no."

"Well, I said no before you could say no so I win."

"Okay." The bastard gave me such a sweet, gentle smile.

I couldn't take it, not from him. "You're too hairy for starters."

"What?"

"Who needs that much hair? On your head, your face, the bits on your chest . . . it's all too much."

His brows drew tight. "That so?"

"Why, I bet there's a jungle down there. Tell me, Joe, have you had any complaints? Is the tiger getting lost?"

Tongue in cheek, he stared back at me.

"I'm just worried about you." I shrugged, all innocence. "Friend."

"Kind of you to be so concerned about my dick. Friend."

I smiled benevolently.

"See, this is why I prefer blondes. Brunettes are just so high-strung. You can never tell when they're going to turn nasty." He wrinkled his nose. "And not in the good way either."

I put my hand to my head. "You're hating on my hair color?"

"Just calling it like I see it." Stupidly muscular thick arms crossed over his broad chest. "Also, I like women with a little color. Ones who occasionally go out in the sun. You're so pale you make Casper look alive. I'd be too fucking scared to touch you. Anything I do would leave a bruise."

"Do you think maybe that's because you're so freakishly large it's hard to relate to normal-size people?"

Teeth gritted, he gazed down at me. "Now that I come to think about it. I'm not real keen on your eye color, either. What do you call that shade of green? Fungus?"

I gasped in outrage. "Yeah, well, yours reminds me of dirt after the rain. You know, when there's mud everywhere. Or maybe wet manure."

"Has your chin always been that pointy, or is that because of some childhood accident?"

A beat of laughter burst out of me. Actually, that was a good one. But I wasn't done yet. "Your toes are so furry," I said. "Is it a hassle having to shave them all the time?"

He grinned.

"And I think it's wonderful some women have a Hobbit foot fetish," I continued. "Works out damn well for you."

"That one wasn't very good."

"It was too."

"No. You just keep coming back to body hair and my size. You're being lazy," he chided. "Come on. You can do better."

"Man." I rubbed at my forehead. "Well, I'd insult other bits of you if I could see them! The body hair is a real problem. Are you related to Yeti on your mom's side or your dad's?"

"Lay-zee."

I huffed out a laugh. "I think I'm done for now."

"Okay." He perched on the edge of the bed, TV remote in hand. "I'm going to let you off. Clearly your sweet little head's been taxed enough for one day."

"Bite me."

"My point exactly."

In lieu of a response, I smacked him in the back of the head with a pillow. The idiot just laughed.

"I win," I said. "Again. And I am in no way ever interested in having sex with you. That was just all a sad misunderstanding. I mean, look at you . . ." I made a fake moue of distaste.

"Sure. Whatever makes you happy, Little Miss." He held his peace for all of about three seconds. "I don't want to have sex with you even more."

God, he was so petty. Juvenile, even. Just the same I ignored him. An act of charity he probably didn't deserve. But it's important in relationships, even just friend ones, to show that you're the better person.

CHAPTER SEVEN

Message received four months ago:

Hey Alex,

I was glad to get your email. It's been a shit of a day. My brother went after the new waitress at the Dive Bar and caused a crapload of trouble and drama I could do without. Then dad got upset with some long time carpentry customers and family friends changing over to another builder. But with his health the way it is, he's not willing to take on anything but small jobs anyway. It's damn frustrating. Enough bitching. Hope you and Marty are doing well and enjoying the sunshine for a change. Make sure you take a break now and then and get outdoors.

All right, you wanted to talk best and worst childhood memories. Let me think. Worst would be a toss-up between the time my brother accidentally dropped my favorite Transformer toy into the fireplace. I could have killed him. Optimus Prime and me were tight. Best buddies. And then there was the first time I ever brought a girl home for dinner and it turned out she just wanted an intro to my brother. Embarrassing as all hell. Are you getting the feeling he's been ruining my life since day one? Ha. He's not so bad most of the time. At any rate, he's family. What can you do?

Best memory would be when Laura from down the road decided she wanted to get friendly with me at fifteen.

xx

Message sent four months ago:
ERIC!
I can't believe you sent me a porny childhood memory about you losing it. That's disgusting. What happened next with Laura? Tell!

Sorry to hear your brother is causing you stress. Some people just seem to take up more space, time, and energy than others. I have an older brother who's in the military. I'm very proud of him but it's not like we see each other much or have a huge amount in common. He's a good guy though. I think you'd like him.

On the childhood memory front, I feel your pain over losing Optimus Prime. I myself lost Bridal Barbie in a terrible act of mutilation perpetrated by my brother's dog. Her head never was found. As for this Laura getting friendly, my worst memory is my first kiss. I thought you did it with your lips closed but the guy went in with mouth wide open, lots of tongue action. I came away confused, my face covered in spit. It took me a while before I was willing to kiss again. My best memory would have to be making chocolate chip cookies with my mom. It didn't happen often because she was so busy. But when we did, she always pretended not to notice the fact that I ate half the dough and never lectured me when I got a stomach ache. As a kid, that was always pretty awesome.

Not much else going on here right now. Work is steady. I got offered a big contract by one of the more prestigious marketing firms in town. It would be great money and experience, but I'm not sure I'm that good or that I'm ready to operate at that level so I said no. Growing the business more slowly is safer.

I've been looking online at some properties, apartments with more space, but even the ones in need of work are still way out of my price range once you factor in how much the renovations will cost. I'd do as much as I can myself but apart from scrubbing walls and repainting them, my skills are minimal.

Hope things at work have calmed down. Ever considered a chastity belt for your brother? Just a thought.

Alex x

The walls were closing in on me. Just like in the scene from *Star Wars* where they're stuck in the trash compactor, slowly but surely I could wind up squished. Reduced to nothing more than a weird stain on the carpet. Housekeeping would not be happy.

Overly dramatic, but true.

I slumped back on the bed, staring at the ceiling. Yep, still white, flat, and boring.

Normally me and my space were best buddies. Especially when I was alone. Alone meant absolutely no one giving me shit, involving me in shit, or generally being a shit. Alone was safe and oh so comfortable. Alone didn't care what you wore or how many days it'd been since you washed your hair or shaved your pits. Alone accepted you exactly as you were. It never lied to me or let me down.

For all of these reasons and more, I loved alone. One day we'd probably wed. Marty could be best man.

Valerie often complained that it took a grappling hook to get me out the front door. That or the promise of cheesecake. Being trapped in this hotel room for the last forty-eight hours, however, had somehow started driving me insane. Perhaps it was all the bland, tastefully appointed furniture and fittings. Maybe if I had my own stuff I'd be fine.

I don't know. Everything seemed so *meh*. I sat up, crossed my legs, and looked around.

My nose had mostly stopped running and there'd been no more fever, only a mild headache. Aspirin had dealt with it just fine. I'd showered and gotten dressed in my favorite blue boyfriend jeans and a simple black T-shirt. Washed my shoulder length brown hair.

Truth was, I was well enough to travel. I should have been on a plane already. Except, Joe and I had a movie marathon the night before with a room service carpet picnic and I honestly couldn't remember the last time I'd enjoyed myself so much. Not to mention the curious little side glances he kept giving me. All of the spending time together had changed things. Again. God, it was confusing.

I'd crushed on him hard.

Then I'd hated him with the fire of a thousand suns.

Now I liked him and his body far more than I should.

Outside, a magnificent sunset covered almost half of the sky. Violet and blue, gold and orange. There was also the lake and the mountains. Lots of trees. Coeur d'Alene was beautiful. It was a pity I hadn't gotten to see much of it, really. Also, I had already paid for another night just in case because, you know, it was probably good to give my body a bit longer to get over the plague.

Fuck's sake. Such confusion.

I couldn't even commit to packing. My carry-on lay on the floor, clothes, shoes, and toiletries spilling out of it every which way. A girl explosion. Panties, bras, everything was hanging out there. Even the stupidly small and expensive black hooker dress and the ruined heels. (Last time I ever let Val talk me into going shopping. Until next time.)

At any rate, it all lay there waiting . . . staring at me accusingly.

The lock clicked, the door swung open.

"Hey," said Joe, stepping into the room.

"Hi." I half raised a hand. Then stuck it back in my lap. "How'd your day go?"

"Good, good. Yours?"

"Great. Fine."

He nodded. "You're looking a lot better."

"Yeah. I'm feeling better."

"Nice."

"Hmm."

An-n-n-d we were both apparently out of small talk. Neither of us rushed to fill the silence, either. Joe's hair was damp and slicked back, his jeans and sweater were clean, nice-looking. Obviously, the man had stopped off at home, showered and changed before coming here. He'd gone for comfort, same as me. Nice that we'd both made an effort.

He cleared his throat. "In all honesty, I half expected to find you gone."

"In all honesty, I half expected to be gone." I huffed out a laugh.

Yeah. Not awkward at all.

We both just kind of looked at each other. Looked away. More silence. I opened my mouth then shut it, my mind a vast empty wasteland.

"Right," he said, like something had been decided. The mattress moved as he sat down beside me at the end of the bed. One big brown boot drummed restlessly against the carpet. "What now? Have you gone back to wanting nothing to do with me? Should I leave the key and get out? Do you hate me again? Have you already booked a flight home? Lay it on me. What happens next?"

"What? Right now?"

"No, a week from now," he deadpanned, boot still going like a freaking automaton. *Thump, thump, thump.* "Yes, now, Alex. Talk to me. Please."

"Okay, okay." Only partly ignoring the sarcasm, I sucked in a deep breath. God, the pressure. So many words. It was completely unexpected. The last few days he hadn't been nearly as chatty. Or pushy. "Umm. No, I don't hate you and I don't mind you being here. You probably don't need the key anymore, though. Just leave it on the table or whatever. Ah, yes, I booked a flight home for late tomorrow. And I don't know about right now."

"You booked your flight?"

"Yes."

The man nodded then scratched at his beardy chin.

"Did I cover everything?" My heart was racing, my head spinning in circles. "I'm not sure there's a set etiquette for this situation. You lied to me about who you were on the Internet, but you also nursed me through a gross dose of the flu. To a certain extent they balance each other out. But not completely."

"Hmm."

"Not that I don't appreciate everything you've done for me over the past few days. You've been amazing, being there for me and everything," I said. "I get that it could be confusing because there's been this certain intimacy established. I mean, hell, you've even seen me in my underwear."

"Not sure that counts since you were sick at the time." He frowned. "And you saw me in a towel."

"Yes, I did." And oh God, the memory. Such clarity and detail. I could almost give you a map regarding the muscles of his thighs, the strength in his calves, and the impressive bulge under that fucking towel. The number of little golden hairs on his bare, naked toes even. You'd think I had a photographic memory. My mind hadn't forgotten a thing when it came to Joe Collins hot, wet, and mostly naked.

What a stupid subject to have raised. Intimacy. Underwear. All of these words were bad. This was what happened when my mouth started moving. The most unwise shit came out. Thank God I had on a T-shirt bra with a little padding. Any hardening of nipples remained mostly unnoticeable. However, the warmth in my face might be an issue. Wonder if I could pass it off as another fever?

Sitting preternaturally still, Joe was watching me like his life depended on it. God. The scrutiny made me sweat.

"Anyhoo, moving on." I scrambled across the bed for a Kleenex, taking my time blowing my nose. "This is who I normally am. Jeans and a T-shirt. Valerie did the hair and makeup the other night. That's her job, she's a makeup artist. And my sexy dress and heels were a total ruse."

He said nothing. At least the Thumper foot had stopped beating.

"Disappointing, huh?"

"No."

I waited. He said no more. Awesome. He was back to using words sparingly. I was doomed.

The sunset had wound down to indigo and gray. A little lavender, maybe. High up above it all, a star twinkled.

Out of nowhere, he said, "I'm really glad you're still here. Even if it is for only one more night."

It took a moment for me to manage a smile. "Thanks. I mean, in all honesty, this situation, us emailing all the time, it was never going anywhere. We both have family and friends, established lives in different states. Long-distance relationships don't work even if we were into each other in that way. Which we're not. But . . . why would you even bother?"

"That part of the reason you were interested in Eric in the first place?" he asked.

A question far too canny for my comfort. I was Bambi frozen in headlights. Just waiting for the semi-trailer to mow my fluffy ass on down.

"Alex?" he asked. "Is it? He was a safe person to be interested in, right? He might come to town but he'd leave again too. Didn't require you moving far out of your comfort zone."

"True." Wow, the man really had me figured. Though I guess I had given him all of the ammunition.

A nod from him.

Christ, I should never have gotten caught up in Val's excitement and come to Coeur d'Alene. It would have been kinder to both Joe and me. Then I would have had his emails for a little longer. The thrill of receiving them. The sense of hope at finding a kindred spirit, of not being quite so alone.

Hold up. I liked alone. Alone was easy and exactly what I

wanted, wasn't it? Shit. There were no easy answers in my head anymore. No certainty at all.

Soon as I got back to Seattle I was resetting my dating profile to local matches only. Who knows, maybe I'd stop messing around and actually attempt a real relationship instead of just bumping hips with someone now and then. Stranger things had happened. Perhaps I could change after all.

"You hungry?" he asked.

"Yes," I said. "I went for a walk earlier. There were a few places down the road that looked nice."

"I've got somewhere in mind. Put your shoes and coat on, please, Little Miss Fucking Sunshine." He clapped his hands together, rubbing them. "We're getting out of here."

"On it." I fell upon my boots, shoving in my feet at lightning speed. What Valerie would have paid to see me actually rushing to get outside. My mild agoraphobia thingy was on hold. And to think it had only taken a small dose of the black plague and a couple of days trapped in a soulless hotel room.

CHAPTER EIGHT

Message sent three months ago:

Hi Eric,

You'll be pleased to know I left my apartment today. It was my dad's birthday. Ever since I was little, mom, dad, and I always go down to Pike Place to see the guys at the fish market do their thing throwing the fish around. It's pretty cool to see. We go buy salmon to cook for dad. It's the family tradition. My friend Valerie and her partner also came. It was busy as always at the market, but a lot of fun. My folks even managed to play nice with each other.

Valerie is a stylist and make-up artist. We pretty much grew up together so she's basically family too. Neither of us were exactly part of the cool kid crowd at school. She's a trans woman and had it rough for a long time, way worse than me getting my ponytail pulled and crap like that. Kids can be incredibly horrible to each other. But then I guess grown-ups can be too. All of the shit going on in politics at the moment makes me despair.

Ugh. Excuse my bad mood. I think I need to eat some ice

cream or something. Anyway, work is busy. Lots of interesting projects. How are things going with you? What have you been up to this week?
A x

Message received three months ago:
What's your poison? I'm a mint choc-chip man, myself.

Message sent three months ago:
Mint? No. NO. Mint is the devil's work. I'm a chocolate chip cookie dough woman to the end.

Message received three months ago:
Haha. Of course you are. And I'm going to ignore you misunderstanding mint. It just means we'll never have to share the ice cream. Probably for the best. Good to hear you had a nice time with your family and Valerie. Pike Place Markets are cool. I haven't been there in ages.

Spent a few days with an old school friend named Pat. I might have mentioned some good friends have been going through a divorce. Pat's been having a rough time with it so we went camping. Built fires. Drank bourbon. Hugged trees and beat our manly chests. That sort of thing. It was good to get away for a bit.

I'm sorry to hear you and Valerie had a tough time in school. Kids can be cruel. I was never exactly one of the cool kids either. Of course my brother was. He loved showing off about all his girlfriends and generally being a little shit. But I had my growth spurt early so no one else tended to mess with me.

If anyone pulls on your ponytail who shouldn't be, you let me
know. I'll come teach them some manners.
Eric

"Maybe I should head back to the hotel," I said.

Joe looked at me across the table, his face visibly pained. Poor
guy. His agony was so acute the facial hair couldn't even hide his
expression, for once. I was hoping his eyes were glossy from wincing, not actual tears. Given the situation, however, it was kind of
hard to tell. Nell had really gone all out in her championing of Joe
and the belief that I should give him a second chance in the something more than friends stakes. In fact, she'd gone so far out, you
could safely say she'd fallen off the edge.

"I don't blame you." He sighed, leaning forward. Shadows
danced across his face, as the candle between us flickered. "I'm
really sorry about this, Alex."

"Not your fault. I know."

"I can't believe this romantic bullshit. They're out of fucking
control."

"Nell and your friends are certainly something."

Determined or insane, it was kind of hard to tell which cate-
gory his friends and fellow staff-members fell under. Sure as hell
they were certainly convinced that Joe and I were in the throes
of some sort of epic love affair. And, bless them, they were doing
everything within their power to enhance that for us by going to
town on the Dive Bar's atmosphere. Though some of them seemed
more on the side of Satan than love.

I'm not going to lie. It was a painful experience.

Joe slumped back in his chair, delivering dirty looks to the rest
of the room's occupants. Well, all except for a couple seated at the

bar and a family of three across the way. If anything, the couple seemed mildly amused. Nice for them. The teenager, though, appeared to be acting out a series of slow deaths over at his table. At least, I hoped he was. It would be sad if the kid were actually trying to stab himself in the head with a fork.

Suddenly, the lighting dimmed yet again. If it weren't for the red candles scattered about the room, we'd be sitting completely in the dark.

"For fuck's sake," Joe muttered. Not meeting my eyes.

All of this supposed ardor, care of his friends, had squashed the easy-going flirting from last night, murdering it with hyper-awareness and embarrassment. Ironic, really; in attempting to help they'd killed our innocent little fledgling attraction. Knocked it right out of the nest.

Over on the small stage in the corner, Vaughan, the dude singing and playing guitar wound up his delightful rendition of Celine Dion's "My Heart Will Go On" to rousing applause. Eric, standing behind the bar, our friendly blond waitress, Lydia, and the kitchen staff seemed most ecstatic. Meanwhile, the teenager started making choking noises as he apparently tried to strangle himself over at his table. His parents should probably look at putting him into drama. The kid had talent.

"Now I'd like to play an old favorite of mine for you," announced Vaughan. Just like Joe, his skin was covered in ink. Not that I could make out what the tattoos were. "A little something by that great Canadian artist, Bryan Adams. '(Everything I Do) I Do It for You.'"

More applause from the kitchen staff. A wolf whistle from Lydia. Vaughan just smiled and started playing again. He too had talent. If only he'd use his powers for good instead of evil.

in my throat. I coughed and coughed then downed about half of my beer in one go. "Crap."

"You okay?"

"Yeah." I took deep breaths, tried to pull myself together. "I, ah . . . wrong pipe. All good."

"Well?" he said eventually.

Shit. "I don't know."

He held his silence.

"In all honesty, I'm not the bravest. I'm not great at putting myself out there. Guess you could say I have my . . . issues." I studied the dusty, dirty floor as if it were about to cough up the secrets of the universe to me at any moment. And while I did that, I fiddled with the zipper on his coat. "I might have been open for a hook-up at one time, but once we starting emailing regularly, really talking, things changed for me. You became important. It was scary."

Silence across from me.

"It's what I do," I said, an uncomfortable smile on my face. "Guess that makes me sound pretty stupid. Cowardly. But I don't really feel comfortable talking with many people. Not in the way I did with you. I loved getting your emails too, Joe. I would get so excited when one arrived. So, yeah . . . I think I would have found reasons to not be able to meet face-to-face in case it all went wrong."

He sat so still. "Like it did."

"Yes."

We stared at each other. Everything seemed to have been forgotten, to fade away. The room, the food, the whole wide world. I have no idea how he did it.

"Who lied to you?" he asked, taking a sip from his beer. "You said you couldn't have another liar in your life. Who was it?"

I didn't hesitate. "A boyfriend. He cheated on me. It was a very painful experience."

Joe tucked his hair behind an ear, nodding. "Okay."

It was on the tip of my tongue to say sorry. To apologize for being messed up long before he'd ever met me. I'd already revealed enough, however. Given him a close-up of my insides, the likes of which few had ever had. Time to stop and say no more. Time to run for cover.

CHAPTER NINE

Message sent two months ago:
Eric, that's ridiculous. There's no way they needed to kill off Han Solo. In fact, I hereby deny the very possibility. In my mind, Han will forever be flitting around the stars with Chevy, ripping off awful aliens and evading the authorities. I refuse to countenance any other possibility.

Message received two months ago:
Alex, be reasonable. Han had to go. He was always a man of action, so no way would he have been sitting around waiting while Leia went and tried to cuddle up to their psychopath of a son. I'm cool with Ren killing the misgonyist idiots along with Han, though.

Message sent two months ago:
You're wrong about Han. And you spelled misogynist wrong.

Message received two months ago:
You're wronger.

Message sent two months ago:
That's not even a word. This conversation is over now. So
there.
P.S. How's things going at work? Is everything okay?

"Hey," a new voice entered the room. Multiple pairs of heavy footsteps.

Joe recovered first, climbing to his feet. "Andre. Pat. Come meet Alex."

The males did some handshaking, backslapping. First came a man who had to be about mid-forties at a guess. Touches of gray in his short dark hair. Wrinkles around his eyes and smile lines along his mouth. He wore navy trousers and a cool patterned button-down shirt.

"Hi, I'm Andre." He held his hand down to me for shaking, smiling all the while. "Old friend of Joe's. Pleasure to meet you. He's been telling me all about you."

"He has?" I don't think my tone came out right on that one.

"Absolutely. Glad to see you out and about." Andre sat, stretching out his legs and leaning back on his hands. "You feeling better?"

"I am. Thank you."

The second guy wasn't so friendly. Nor did he look approachable. For starters, he was covered in tats. Please note: In no way did I believe a love of ink made someone a serial killer. He was tall and lanky with long black hair, the sides shaved into an undercut. A beard, the length of which left Joe's in the dust, obscured most of his face. And a silver ring pierced his septum. His clothes were uniformly black and kind of ratty-looking. Not unclean, just really well worn. The flat eyes and joyless mouth sealed the deal, however. Scary.

At least they made a perfectly timed distraction from Joe and my too serious discussion. Hoo ya to that.

"Hey." The man tipped his head in my direction and sat also, plonking a six-pack of beer down beside the pizza. Immediately he broke one off, handed it to me.

"Thank you."

"Alex, meet Pat," said Joe, reclaiming his patch of floor. "We went to school together. He owns the tattoo parlor. Andre owns the building and runs the musical instrument shop downstairs."

"I was downstairs with Pat, giving him a hand with the accounts." Andre accepted a beer from Pat as well, drinking deeply. "Heard the footsteps up here and thought we'd come check things out."

"With beer?" Joe finished off his first bottle and held a hand out for a replacement.

"You could have been thirsty robbers, ax murderers, serial killers."

"Ghost hunters," added Pat in a low voice.

Just like that, the guys dug into our pizza. Lucky it was big. Still, I took another slice before it was gone. Andre nodded, taking a bite. "True."

"We did a séance up here once when we were kids." With a sly smile, Joe moved a little closer. "Andre snuck up the inside stairs, making all these freaky noises. Scared the hell out of us."

"That was the intention." Andre grinned. "You little dickheads. Took me ages to get all the wax off the floor from the candles you'd been burning. Dad was pissed."

It sounded like a soft rumbling, Pat's laughter. Thunder coming in from a distance. Here and gone in a moment. I almost thought I'd imagined it. Nice to know the guy could manage some happy, however.

"How about the bird shit?" asked Pat, hiding what might have been a small smile behind his beer.

Muttering obscenities, Andre let his head fall back and gazed at the ceiling with a pained expression.

I gave Joe a questioning look.

"Vaughan had read in a book that you had to have a circle of thirteen candles and then sacrifice something to get a ghost's attention. So he catches a sparrow," said Joe. "Of course, when it comes time to end the bird, none of us could stand to hurt the poor little thing."

"Nell was just about in tears, freaking out." Pat studied his black Converse. "I knew she would. Brought a cricket in my pocket to sacrifice instead. It'd been eating her mom's plants. Wasn't going to live long anyway."

"That's right." A quiet chuckle.

Andre watched Pat carefully, sipping his beer.

"The sparrow got loose and was flying around the room, going nuts. Then Andre starts in with his sound effects," said Joe. "We lost it, bolting out of here like our asses were on fire."

"There was wax and bird shit everywhere." Andre laughed. "Lucky you idiots didn't burn the place down."

"That's what you get for giving Vaughan a part-time job and trusting him with the keys." Joe held out his bottle and Andre clinked his against it in a toast.

"True."

"Has anyone ever seen a ghost here?" I asked, fascinated. Mostly disbelieving, though you never knew.

Andre's tongue played behind his cheek. A droll, dubious look in his eyes. "There's nothing here."

"Tell her the truth," said Joe, playing it serious. "What are you trying to hide?"

"Jesus." Andre sighed. "Legend has it a guy threw himself down the staircase after getting dumped by some woman. Broke his neck."

"Fuckin' love," muttered Joe. "It'll do it to you."

"Hmm. Grandpa said he fell. Apparently it was raining that day and the floor was slippery." Andre drew up his legs, resting his arms on his knees. "Any building old enough is going to have a death or two in it. Though there have been unsubstantiated reports of dear old Dad still hanging around."

Perking up, Pat narrowed his gaze on the man. "I saw something in the bar's basement. Could have sworn someone was down there with me. And if anyone's haunting the place, it'd be your old man."

Hissing out a breath, Andre reached for another piece of pizza. "True enough."

"Andre Senior loved that bar."

"He did the mirrors on the ceiling?" I asked, loving their stories.

Andre barked out a laugh. "Got it in one. You show her the last of the graffiti in the bathroom?"

"Not yet," answered Joe, smiling.

"The old man had a pretty relaxed decorating policy. For thirty years, anyone could leave their mark just about however they liked," said Andre. "Made for a hell of an atmosphere."

"Yeah, I saw the names and dates cut into the bar."

Lots of chuckles. It was interesting, being around people who have known each other for so long. Not to say Joe was a different person around these two men, but he seemed more relaxed. Maybe it was because I wasn't his focus for once. I could just watch him, see how he acted normally. Interestingly enough, he sat cross-legged like someone meditating, only he had a beer in his hand. But his big body was lax, the lines on his forehead, which I seemed to keep causing, gone for once.

He was just hanging, being with friends. It was lovely to see.

"Joe tells me you've got some good ideas for what to do with these rooms," said Andre, blowing my calm to pieces. My gaze jumped to Joe then to Andre and back again.

"They're just doodles, really."

"Well, he emailed them to me and I don't agree. I think they're great and that we should take this project seriously." Andre watched me with interest. "I've been saving for a while, got enough to cover materials if you're willing, like Joe, to take your pay as a percentage of the profits. I think we could at least make a start up here, clearing the space, cleaning things up. Tomorrow suit you, Alex? I'm sure Joe would be happy to bring you by so we could all talk."

"You emailed them my drawings without asking?"

"Yes," said Joe. "Tear into me about it later, if you like. But the fact is, your work is good, Alex."

My mouth opened. And just kind of stayed that way.

"I've got money to invest in something too," added Pat in his low voice. "Especially if you're thinking apartments. Living above the parlor would work for me. No travel time. Keep shit simple. It'd be nice to get the rest of the building fixed up, attract more customers and hopefully fill those empty shops downstairs with new businesses. Having more people around would be good for everyone's businesses."

Lips pressed together, Andre tipped his chin. "I'm sure we could work something out."

"Kind of like that idea of living here myself," said Joe. "Renting a place with Eric is getting old."

More nodding of heads. And then all eyes turned to me.

"Honestly, they're just an amateur's ideas."

"Just a visual designer's ideas," said Joe. "Anyway, ideas are exactly what we need."

Andre took a gulp of beer, still nodding. "What he said."

"Tomorrow works. Around noon, okay?" Climbing to his feet, Pat brushed off the seat of his pants. Obviously about to disappear as if everything had been decided. "Later."

"Thanks for the pizza." Andre followed the other man out. "Good to meet you, Alex. See you tomorrow."

"I, ah . . ."

Joe just smiled.

These people. I threw up my hands. "I'm neither an architect nor a decorator. Mostly I just design logos and stuff."

"You're way more than that," he said. "You're someone with ideas who's excited about the thought of working on the old girl. Bringing her up to date and making her shine again."

"You had no right to send those pictures to anyone."

"I know, but I did it anyway."

"Come on, Joe. Have you even properly thought about this? I live in another state," I exclaimed. "Does it really make sense for you to try and collaborate with someone who won't even be around soon?"

"You said you could work on your laptop wherever." He leaned in closer. "Why are you fighting this so hard?"

"I'm not the right person for the job."

"No. You're just someone who's dreamed of working on a project like this."

Well yeah, he had me there. Those dreams were mine. Here was my chance.

"Andre and Pat, all of us, really, we'd rather work with a passionate amateur than a half-assed professional any day of the week. Besides, we'll get an architect to check over it and do all the boring logistical stuff. Pull some permits and all that." The easy way Joe looked at me was so serene. Confident. "Two of us are lined up to live in these studio apartments already. You get the style of the Dive Bar. All we need to do is bring a bit of that up here."

"There's more to it than that." I brought my knees up to my chest, wrapping my arms tight around them.

"You always this negative?" he asked.

"I prefer *cautious*."

"Sure about that?"

My chin jutted out. "Yes. I know my limits and I prefer not to disappoint people or myself."

For a moment, Joe studied me. His big shoulders rising and falling on a breath. "Okay. If you still feel that way tomorrow morning and you want more time, or you're going to catch that flight home, I'll call Andre and Joe, tell them the meeting's off. That work for you?"

"Yes." Inside me, the panic slowly unwound, slipping out of me. "Thank you."

"No problem." Joe leaned over, clinking his beer against mine. "Cheers."

"Cheers."

He kept on watching me with his lips shut tight. Most people's attention wigged me out, put me on edge. But not Joe's. Or not exactly. He meant me no harm. Somewhere deep down inside of me, I knew it to be true. The man was a straight shooter.

Not that I didn't want to kind of beat him with a wet fish for putting me on the spot like that.

Inside my head, things were winding down, starting to hurt. I pulled some Kleenex out of my pocket and blew my nose. A lovely feminine flower, that was me. Not that Joe ever seemed perturbed. The bearded one was a true gentleman, despite all of the hair, tats, and savage looks. Though realistically we'd only known each other for a few days. Sure, we'd been emailing each other for months, but face-to-face was different.

"You're looking tired," he said. "Want to go back to the hotel now?"

"Soon." The pizza was finished but half of my beer remained. "I do like your friends. Even the ones who play bad love songs."

Quietly, he laughed. "Nell has a lot to answer for."

Reluctantly, I smiled.

"We all thought she and Pat would be together forever. Their divorce was a hell of a shock. They started going out when the rest of us were still worried about catching girl germs. If those two couldn't make it work, I don't know what hope the rest of us have." Joe took a sip of his beer, eyes unhappy. "Apparently Nell and Eric did some drinking after work one night. One thing led to another . . ."

"Pregnant."

"Yep." His eyebrows went high. "No one saw that one coming."

"You think she and Eric might ever get together?"

"My brother should be so lucky." He barked out a laugh. "No. Nell knows him too damn well. They're just friends, I think. She was always more like a sister. Eric and her brother, Vaughan, used to be real tight when they were kids. They had a falling-out after high school."

I stayed silent, letting him talk.

"They're getting along again now. Sorted shit out when Vaughan started working behind the bar and his girl took over Pat's share of the business."

"That's good."

"Yeah." One side of his mouth kicked up. "Now if my little brother would just fix the mess between him and Dad everything'd be great. Or at least Thanksgiving dinner would be a fuckload more pleasant."

"Is that why you liked talking to me?"

No response.

"I didn't know your family or friends," I said. "I was outside all of the drama. Safe. You could unload on me."

Slowly, he nodded. "Yeah. In truth, that was a big part of it. I swear, some days, talking to you, it was about the only thing that kept me sane."

"Glad I could be there for you."

"Please," he said. "After all the fuckery I pulled, disappointing you and everything."

"Ha." A dull ache awoke inside my chest. "Yeah. Good point. You suck."

"I am sorry, Alex," he said quietly.

"I know."

A rumble came from inside his throat and he pushed his long hair back from his face. "I was an asshole to you."

"Pretty much."

"Mind you, I didn't have a clue then how cute you looked in your Little Miss Fucking Sunshine panties."

Huh. I cocked my head. "You flirting with me, Bigfoot?"

A slight smile was all the answer I got. What a goddamn tease.

"Are your parents looking forward to the baby?" I asked, taking my time finishing the last of the beer. Even with the flirting, being around Joe was nice, easy. With just the two of us again, it was relaxing.

"Absolutely. Dad threw a shitfit at first, but they've both known Nell a long time and love her like family." He looked up at me from beneath his thick brows. "Mom would like to meet you before you head off. If that's possible."

"Oh. That's really nice of her." And not the least bit incredibly scary. Holy shit, meeting someone's mother was a big deal. Typical of Joe to be so calm about it. "Wow. Does she know about the whole identity-theft psychic-stripper debacle?"

"That's the official term now, is it? Well, no, she doesn't know about the whole ITPSD."

One shoulder jerked. "See how things go. Your flight isn't until late tomorrow. That'll give you a chance to stop by and say hi."

My throat was so dry. I could barely swallow. "Sure. Why not?"

CHAPTER TEN

Message sent seven weeks ago:

ME: *Have you given anymore thought to the project with the top floor of the Bird Building?*

HIM: *Have you give any more thought to accepting that big job from the prestigious marketing firm?*

ME: *Touche.*

HIM: *Truth is, I'm drowning right now, basically working around the clock. I got talked into covering extra shifts at the bar and I'm helping dad out more with his business. He and my brother had another fight so I can't get him to help. I'm also still trying to spend as much time as possible with my friend Pat, the one that got divorced. And I got caught up helping Nell, his ex-wife, put together a truckload of furniture she felt the need to buy. Need more hours in the day. Maybe Marty should come out east and help me for a while.*

ME: *Sorry, Marty's way too busy gathering nuts for winter. Then forgetting where he put most of them. Sounds like you're taking on too much. You need to slow it down some, hide from*

the world more, and learn how to say no like me. When in
doubt, don't answer the phone or the door. It's always people.
HIM: *Sounds a little extreme, but I could do with hiding for a*
while. Let's swap lives.
ME: *Wait, you want me to leave my couch? I don't see that*
happening. Maybe cloning you in some way would be a better
idea. Get you a friendly cyborg to help around the home or
something. A robotic squirrel to be your new best friend,
maybe? Don't knock it till you've tried it.
HIM: *Speaking of, Blade Runner's on tv. You like?*
ME: *Only about the best movie ever made! Channel please?*

"Nooo," I sobbed quietly into my cell. "Why did you wake me?"

"You didn't call me back yesterday," said Val, unperturbed by
my pain.

"Sorry." I rolled over. Hell. Quarter past ten shone judgmen-
tally from the alarm on the bedside table. The sun-block curtains
were doing their job.

"Are you seriously still in bed?" Val's voice changed quickly
from surprise to excitement. "Oh my God, is he there? He is, isn't
he? About time. I knew all of that anger would turn into kinky
rough sex. Give me all the details. Is he a dirty twisted beast in
the sack? I bet he is. He's got that whole leonine golden hair and
beard thing going on."

"Ah. You can calm down, I'm alone." Slowly I sat up, rubbing
the sleep from my eyes. "I just couldn't get to sleep until, like,
three in the morning or something. So I was sleeping in."

"Well, that's disappointing."

"Sorry."

Truth was, the room had seemed too big and empty. Lone-someness had crept in without Joe's presence. The bed had been too soft, the pillow too lumpy, and nothing seemed to work right. I don't know, it was stupid, really. First, the hotel room hadn't been as comforting as my own place due to the lack of my personal stuff. Now it was even less comforting due to the lack of Joe, which made absolutely no sense. So yeah . . . I'd tossed and turned, deciding to delay my flight yet again. Given I'd already let my clients know I was taking this time off, work would be fine. It gave me no good excuse to run home. My mild agoraphobia, however, had turned into a major commitment phobia. I wasn't certain I was willing to risk a romantic relationship with Joe. Way too scary. But I wasn't actually running home to hide and regroup either. The quandary was lifting my anxiety and confusion levels to an all-time high.

No wonder I couldn't sleep.

Then the fears about the designs had kept creeping back into my mind, and basically my head had been a mess. Desperate to get some z's, I'd popped a sleeping pill in the wee hours of the morning.

"You looked up pictures of him?" I asked.

"Yes. There were some on the bar's Facebook page. Had to see who I was hating on."

"And you really think he's hot?" I asked Val, curious.

"Hmm?"

"Beast man or whatever you called him."

"Abso-fucking-lutely. I'd mount that mountain man in a New York minute given half the chance. And no boyfriend, of course."

"Huh. Your opinion of him seems to have dramatically changed since you got a look at him."

"Are you inferring that I'm shallow?"

"I wouldn't dare."

"Actually," she said. "I was pretty impressed with how he took me ripping into him the other day on the phone. Not everyone can apologize and admit when they are wrong."

"Hmm."

A heavy sigh from Valerie. "Also, now that I've settled down with Liam, I really need you to make more of an effort on the sex front. It's hard to live vicariously through you when you rarely do anything of interest."

I did my usual with the Kleenex, as opposed to answering.

"Don't you blow your nose at me, young lady," she snapped. "It's the truth. Vibrators are no substitute for an actual relationship."

"I never said they were. And I have regular sex with actual people, thank you very much. Or I did up until a couple of months ago." Right up until I got a certain Mr. Collins stuck inside my head. Luckily, that issue was being dealt with. Sort of.

Val groaned. "Please. I'd prefer you just stuck to having sex with yourself. Anonymous-sex-with-strangers stories get boring after a while. Plus I worry about you. Be daring and actually become emotionally involved with someone you're banging for once. Get to know them. Who knows, you might even want to keep one of them around for more than a night."

"The fact that they go away afterward is part of their appeal."

"But there's so much more you're missing out on."

"And maybe someday I'll do the whole commitment thing. But for now, this setup just happens to currently suit where I am in life."

"You've been saying that since you were eighteen."

"Do we have to do this now?"

"Yes. Yes, we do. Apart from me and your folks, your closest relationships are with food deliverymen and the UPS guy. You live your life like you're in a goddamn bubble and it needs to stop," she insisted. "You're going to end up like one of those crazy cat ladies with your apartment smelling of piss and regret."

"You don't think you're being a little dramatic here?"

She harrumphed. "I'm not the one buying birthday cards for my pizza delivery guy."

"One time. Once. And I was trying to be nice."

"Oh yeah? How's he doing?"

"He and his girlfriend got engaged just before I left, actually." I smiled. "Gorgeous ring."

"I rest my case."

I rolled my eyes. "Whatever."

"Normal folk are not this involved in the lives of their takeout deliverymen," she declared. "That's why I pushed you into going. At least Idaho is outside of your apartment."

"Since when did we ever care about normal?"

"Maybe it's time to start."

Deep breaths. That's what was required. Deep steadying breaths so as not to lose my cool.

"Look, I get it," she said. "God, do I get it. It's incredibly hard to take that leap and actually trust someone, knowing that you could get hurt. But we can't hide away for the rest of our lives just because we went through some shit in our younger years. Liam taught me that. Well, him and eight years of therapy. I take it you're still down on the idea of talking to someone about what happened?"

"Val." Memories of blood filled my mind. So much blood. A whole bathroom painted in the stuff. I gagged, my imagination more than happy to provide a lovely flashback of the nauseating metallic scent. "It happened to you, not to me. I don't need fixing."

"Bullshit."

"I can't do this right now."

"We need to talk about it."

Knocking at the door. Perfect timing.

"I've got to go, that'll be him," I said.

"Do not hang up on me."

"I have to go."

"Alexandra Marie Parks, don't you dare—"

"I love you. Say hi to Liam for me. Bye." And *click*. Call ended. Phew.

More knocking at the door.

The day had barely started and I was already over people. I opened it, trying for a polite smile for Joe. It felt closer to a grimace, however. Once I saw him, though, all of the tiredness and yuck in me lightened. Must have been some kind of beard magic. "Hi."

"Hey." Hands in pockets, he just looked at me. Nil expression on his face. "What's going on?"

"Nothing much."

Neither of us moved.

"Really? 'Cause you're looking a little strung out," he said, tipping his head to one side. "Aren't you the 'honesty means everything' girl or have I got the wrong room again?"

I raised my chin. "All right. Do you want to know the terrible truth?"

"Hit me."

"I'm a basket case," I confessed. "A total head job. Might have forgotten to tell you that salient detail in the emails. But I am. A total weirdo nutter with more issues than I can count. Including avoiding having a real live normal sort of relationship with a man. To my mind, romantic relationships and commitment are the black plague. In case you hadn't already guessed."

"Seems like no one has it easy these days. Everyone's got their problems." He didn't even blink. "I haven't dated anyone seriously in years, not since things went to shit with my first girlfriend. We were together a long time and I thought it was for keeps, but . . . things change. Only it took me a long time to change with them. Then, later on, I lied to a woman on the Internet, pretended to be my pussy magnet brother just to get her attention because I thought she was funny and nice and I wanted to keep talking to her. Fuck knows what a shrink would make of that."

I smiled despite myself. "Funny and nice, huh?"

"And pretty. Real damn pretty."

God help me, I was blushing.

"Also, I keep playing family peacekeeper trying to make everyone happy," he said. "It's not working."

"Interesting," I said, leaning a hip against the door. "You try to please people while I just want to avoid them."

Dark eyes assessed me.

"Or at least that's what Valerie said my problem was."

"You think she's right?" he asked.

I shrugged, studied the carpet. "She's spent a lot of time in therapy, so she usually is."

"Hmm. I'm not sure those two qualities necessarily go together."

"He's not handsomer than you." I creased up my face. "Just, you know . . . by the way."

Joe said nothing. There did seem to be a certain light in his eyes, though.

"He's not. So don't think that," I said in a rush. "It's like comparing pizza to Chinese takeout; they're both great in their own way, you know?"

"You're comparing me to takeout?" A little wrinkle appeared between his brows.

"Definitely not. You're the pizza in this metaphor."

A blink. "Okay."

"Gourmet, thin crust. We're talking top quality here."

He nodded. "I can live with that."

"Anyway. You coming in or not?"

"Yes, ma'am," he said, maneuvering past me into the room. "We heading to the airport today or what?"

"Meh." I shut the door, putting my cell on the table, and turned to check out the view across the lake. Blue shimmering water and a pristine clear sky. This crazy insane urge inside of me, wanting to know what would happen next. What if I stayed and . . . just what-if in general. Screw it. I let my mouth do what it would. "But the weather's so nice."

"Yeah," he said carefully. "It is."

The tension in the room, I could have cut it and served it as cake. Shitty cake, but just the same. My hands twisted at my sides. "Seems a pity to waste it sitting in an airport lounge just waiting around."

A small hopeful smile curved his lips. "That would suck."

"And what's another day or so, right?"

He shrugged. "Fine with me."

My phone started ringing. "Just let me grab a quick shower."

"Not going to take that call?" Joe made himself at home in the comfy chair, crossing his legs with his ankle resting on one knee, the way guys did.

"It's Valerie calling to try and deep-and-meaningful me some more. I'm just not up to it right now."

"Ah." He eyed the buzzing phone warily while I gathered a clean set of clothes.

"Feel free to answer it if you like," I joked.

The man did not laugh.

Today's options were jeans or tights and a skirt. I had good legs. A big butt, but good legs. Black tights and a matching skirt, done. A somewhat fancy red bohemian blouse with cool embroidery for the top half. Sometimes a girl just wants to dress up a little. Feel pretty. No biggie.

"Won't be long." I headed for the bathroom.

He pulled out his phone and relaxed back in the chair, just hanging. "No worries. Take your time."

Tools sat in the first large storeroom that was one of the studio apartment options. It sat above an empty shop, on the other end of the building from the Dive Bar. If Joe did wind up living there, he could just about make as much noise as he wanted.

A partition sat in the middle of the room, turning it into two offices, maybe. The little bathroom was a mold- and spider-infested ruin.

"Galley kitchen would work well," mumbled Andre. He, Joe, and Pat were gathered around my laptop, looking over the designs.

"Definitely conserve space." Joe pulled a rubber band out of his jeans pocket and proceeded to pull his hair back and put it into a ponytail. "I think the walk-in shower's a good idea too. Keep things nice and streamlined. Minimum fuss. Nothing I can't handle."

"Okay," said Andre.

Pat seemed less scary today. Just sad. Contained, I guess. He didn't say or smile much. From the brief chat I'd had with Nell, and the mega-fast walk through of her kitchen the night before, I couldn't imagine the two of them together. She came across as so bright and bubbly.

I moseyed on over to the collection of tools, just checking things out. A battered red toolbox sat open, displaying a wide array of goods. Atop a notebook sat a laser meter and measuring tape. A rubber-headed mallet and a saw. Ooh, a sledgehammer.

The men folk were still busy, discussing the designs . . . what the hell?

Quiet as I could, I picked up the sledgehammer. Gave the heavy bastard a swing or two back and forth. Wonder what it would be like to send it slamming into something. To crash it into a sheet of plasterboard.

"Alex," said Joe, startling me.

"Yeah?" All swinging of large manly tools ceased immediately. I felt like a little kid getting caught stealing candy. "Hi."

For a moment he said nothing, just looked at me in the quiet, mindful way he had. Then he nodded toward the partition.

"What?" I asked, eyeing the object of his attention.

"Hit it."

My eyes widened. "Really?"

"It needs to come down," he said. "You wanted to do some of the work, right? Learn some stuff?"

"Yes."

He wandered over to the bit of wall in question, knocked on it twice. "It's not a load bearer or anything like that. No wires in there. Go for it."

Without further ado, he handed me some safety glasses. I donned them, looking beyond cool, no doubt. Then I lifted the heavy sledgehammer, giving him a small, unsure smile. The kind of smile you give a man when you think he's serious but you're not a hundred percent sure. Given life experience, etc., he might just be mocking me.

Andre shook his head and smiled. "Leave her alone, man. She's looking gorgeous today. If she starts in on that she'll get covered in plaster dust and shit."

Interesting. Pat stayed silent.

Joe, on the other hand, gave Andre a hard glance before turning back to me. "Alex."

"Joe?"

He licked his lips. Something low in my belly liked that. The aesthetics of his lovely mouth framed by the golden beard. Maybe I was going a little loopy. Loopier. Or maybe my tastes were undergoing a serious shift.

"Make that wall your bitch," he said, eyes intense. Challenging.

I nodded, hefted the sledgehammer back out to the side, and then let loose. It was a pathetic hit. Sheetrock cracked but that was about it. More swing, more oomph was required. Much, much more. Again, with both hands wrapped tightly around the hilt, I drew back and then swung. Putting my weight behind it this time. Going in hard.

Crash!

The first layer of the wall cracked right open along with the second, a couple of inches in. I even managed to splinter an old length of wood running through the middle. Dust and dirt filled the air. Doubtless it had rained down on my hair, was covering my clothing. Who gave a fuck? The feeling of strength, the shock of destruction. I was hooked. Already my arms were starting to feel the burn from the unexpected workout. But it was all good.

Again, I drew back then rammed the sledgehammer into the wall. *Crash boom bang*. Holy balls. The big-ass hole, all of the wreckage and mess, I'd done that. Me.

I grinned at Joe and he grinned back, watching the proceedings with his thick arms crossed. Poor Andre shook his head while Pat gave me a half smile.

Back to wall breaking I went.

Bam. That's for the people who made me feel small. The ones who overlooked and ignored me. The ones who never let me fit in.

Bash. This was for the ones who put gum in my hair and tripped me in the hallway. Who pushed me and hurt me physically.

Boom. An extra-special hit for those who'd tortured me with words. Because those words, all of those insults, they never left my head. Not even after all these years.

Bang. Here's to the bullies, the bastards and bitches out for attention. The ones who caused me pain just so they could feel superior and powerful in front of their peers. All of them.

The list went on. A strike for those who'd told me to shrug it off, to ignore it and stop whining. Another for the people who'd seen it happen and done nothing. Acted like it was all just a joke, a normal part of growing up, nothing serious. I kept hitting, breaking down the wall, taking the fucker apart. And I didn't stop until I was dripping with sweat and sheeted in dust, three-quarters of the wall laid bare to the studs, smashed to smithereens. My shoulders were screaming and body tired, but my soul was oddly appeased. God knows why, but I loved it. The power, the violence, the ability to well and truly affect my surroundings. Joe standing and watching, keeping out of my way, just letting me do my thing. I could have done it just fine without him there, sure. To have him close, however, made it better.

I doubt Valerie's therapist would have approved. But I felt the best I had in a while.

I don't know how long I spent staring at the remains of my wall, gulping down the bottle of water Joe had passed me, enjoying the afterglow. Sex with strangers didn't even begin to compare to this stress-busting experience. Maybe I'd been a Viking marauder in a former life, or something.

At some stage during my "I am woman, hear me grunt and roar as I pulverize this innocent bit of building" Pat and Andre had disappeared. Only Joe and I remained upstairs, as far as I was aware.

"I see," he said into a phone.

My cell. Shit. I'd told him he could answer it. Sure. Hadn't exactly been serious, though. Nor had he seemed interested.

He noticed me noticing and held my gaze. The look was loaded. Meaningful. Full of what exactly, I couldn't say.

"Okay, Valerie," he said, eyes still on me.

I took a step forward, held out my hand. A swift shake of the head was my sole reply.

"Much appreciated," he said. "Bye."

"That was Val?" I asked stupidly.

"Yeah. Your phone kept ringing. Saw it was her so I answered to get her off your back."

"Oh."

"Earlier you said I could. This a problem?" He passed me the cell and slid it into the pocket of my now white-and-gray-speckled gritty skirt. So much for looking pretty.

"Ah, no." I guess.

"Your first boyfriend lied to you, huh?" He canted his head, eyes narrowed on me.

Shit. My mouth opened, closed.

"He cheated on you?"

"Um. Yes."

"Hurt your feelings?"

"That's right."

Slowly, Joe nodded, taking a deep breath at the same time. "And that was the reason you gave for not being willing to forgive me."

"Lying is a serious offense," I said, inching back just a little. Not that I was scared. Exactly. Definitely not because I thought he'd hurt me physically. Despite all of my sledgehammer girl-power behavior, I could still be harmed in other ways. A woman needed to protect herself. Right. "It's a really bad thing."

"It is. You're right." He took a step forward.

I took one back. "So? What's your point, Joe?"

He stepped forward again. And again I stepped back until my spine hit the jagged remains of the wall. Whatever Valerie had told him, it couldn't be good. And since when had my best friend decided to work against me with this man? Talk about betrayal.

Joe towered over me, arms relaxed at his sides. His eyes, however, they didn't seem so chilled.

"How old were you when you had this lying, cheating boyfriend, Alex?" he asked in a disturbingly calm tone. I didn't trust it one bit.

"Young-ish."

"Do me a favor, Little Miss Fucking Sunshine? Be exact."

I was going to kill Valerie. Sledge her with my mighty hammer. Wrap her in plastic and encase her in a wall. Something like that.

"Hmm?" He waited, looming above me with judgey eyes. "How old, Alex?"

"Twelve," I grumbled.

The man paused, cupped his ear. "Sorry. What was that?"

"Twelve. I was twelve years old when Bradley Moore cheated on me by dating some cow who was friends with his cousin." I did not sound like a sullen little brat. I sounded like something else, vaguely related to the same. Someone who'd just been busted using a piss-weak excuse to avoid getting involved any further with this man. Not that it had even really worked. "It hurt."

"I'm sure it did. How long were you dating him?"

"Not quite a week." I stared straight at his long-sleeve-T-shirt-covered chest. It was dark blue today. The color suited him, brought out the flecks of green in his usually brown eyes.

"Right. This morning you mentioned you have an issue with trying to avoid people," he said, still talking to me in that annoyingly calm voice, despite the skeptical look. "Do you think that you using this no doubt painful event from when you were twelve would be you trying to avoid intimacy?"

"Maybe." I shuffled my feet.

"Or maybe there's a little bit more to it," he said, just sort of gently suggesting. Shit. "Not to diss your twelve-year-old broken heart."

"Fine. Yes, there's more to it. But it's nothing I'm inclined to get into right now."

For a while he said nothing, just stared at me.

"Sorry I lied," I mumbled. "But it was only a little lie."

Nothing from him.

If only I didn't feel such a dumbass need to fill the silence. "I didn't trust you and I needed space."

"Sure. I can understand that," he said in a tone of voice I did not trust at all. "How do you feel about me now, though?"

"Conflicted. How do you feel about me?"

"Confused as fuck."

I huffed out a laugh.

"Alex, I've been giving some thought to our problems while you were doing your bit of construction work there."

"And?"

"And . . . I think we should trade issues."

"What?" I asked, jarred by the sudden change in focus.

"I say yes to too many people," he said. "But you say no to too many people, then wind up alone, missing out on everything."

My gaze jumped to his face. "Safe from everything too. Don't forget that."

"Yeah? Problem is, your safety is bullshit, Alex," he said, voice firm. Harsh even. "What was it you said to me in that email, that you're not some delicate little petal? Well, you're no wallflower either. I've seen you in action and you're more than strong enough to deal with anything that life throws your way. You don't need to be hiding from anything."

Huh. That's what he thought.

"Therefore, I suggest this. You have to start getting out there and saying yes to people."

"Wha—"

"And I have to start saying no," he finished. "No more Mr. Nice Guy letting things slide, fitting in with what everyone wants and fuck what I want."

No words came out. My throat was jammed shut.

"Valerie said you'd planned two weeks off work. You stay here for that time, work with me on this project. Help us out with ideas on design and decoration and such-like." He looked about the room. "In return, I'll teach you about building. So when you go back to Seattle and eventually buy your property you'll know the basics. During that time, we'll put each other to the test, see if we can't push each other out of our comfort zones. What do you say?"

"What, so we take turns daring each other to say yes or no?"

"Yeah, basically."

Holy shit, he was serious. As serious as serious could get. Could I do that? Be that brave? Everything inside me squirmed, saying no, probably not. After all, I'd be effectively putting myself into his hands, but then, he'd also be putting himself into mine. I could easily get it wrong and hurt him. Fuck up his life. God knows I'd failed before. No way was believing in me a safe bet for him.

"What happens if we can't break our learned behavior and step out of our comfort zones?"

He put his hands on his waist, lips pressed tight together. "Unending shame. Shit like that. I don't know, we'll make it up as we go along."

The man made me curious, that much was for sure. About him, the things we could do together, his life here, everything. Deep, deep down in the subcockles of my soul, I'd regret it if I went home too soon and failed to figure out what might be happening between us. If anything was happening between us. Who the fuck knew?

"Alex," he said. "Come on. Try."

Shit.

"If this whole psychic-stripper ordeal has shown me anything, it's that we've both got stuff that needs sorting. So let's do that," he said. "If it doesn't work, in a week and a half you go your way and I'll go mine. We'll be friends at a distance again."

I nodded, taking the leap. "All right. I'll stay on at the hotel for a while longer. See how it goes."

For some stupid reason, the relief on his face nearly brought me to tears. Probably all of the dust in the room.

"Clean slate. We're starting over." Carefully, he brushed the dust from my face, gently tracing his fingertips over my forehead and cheeks, the line of my nose. "Agreed, friend?"

I could run. I could hide. Do the usual. Stick to my bad habits. Or I could stay and try to break down some more walls. Feel more of the rush of excitement and satisfaction.

"Okay, friend," I said. "Agreed."

CHAPTER ELEVEN

Message sent five weeks ago:
ME:
Hi Eric,
It kind of amazes me every time you talk about all of your friends. There's so many of them! I've really just always only had Val. We've been best friends for about as long as I can remember. I guess I'm a keep your circle small kind of person. Relationships wise, I've dated a fair amount, but there haven't been many I'd describe as long term. Maybe I'm just picky. I don't know. What about you?
A xx

Message received:
Alex,
Nothing wrong with being picky. I pretty much still live in the same area I grew up, knowing most people is just the norm. I either went to school with them or met them somewhere else along the way. But I love living in CdA, can't imagine being anywhere else. One major relationship with a girl I was on and

*off with during high school and then for quite a while after. I
was willing to settle down, but she wasn't. Hell, we probably
were too young. She was best friends with Nell so part of our
group for a long time. Last I heard, she was living down in
the south-west somewhere. That's the only relationship I'd
say got really serious.*

xx

People scared me and relationships terrified me. That was the
truth. Also, no was way better than yes. Yes sucked.

Despite these facts, for hours my ass remained stuck to a bar-
stool as promised. Joe had asked me to say yes to a night of hanging out at the Dive Bar while he worked. Confront my whole
dislike of crowds, public places, and socializing in general. The
first step in our agreement. I'd yet to decide what act of no-ness
Joe would be required to do in return. I needed more information
to move carefully but with effect.

"For you." Eric set a small plate down on the bar in front of
me, throwing in a fancy hand flourish, like a magician's assistant.

"What are these?" I asked, eyeing Nell's latest offering.

"Crumbed goat's balls."

I just looked at him.

"Crumbed goat's *cheese* balls." He winced. Drama skills–wise,
the man wouldn't be up for an Oscar anytime soon. "My bad. Forgot to throw in the *cheese* there in the middle."

"Funny," I said flatly, popping one of the warm entrées into
my mouth. Creamy amazing mind-blowing goodness. "Wow. Yum."

A hand neared the plate, fingers making to grab one of my good-
ies. No way. I gave it a solid slap. "Mine."

"Sharing is caring," said Eric, rubbing the back of his hand.

"Well, there's your problem right there."

"Harsh."

I popped another cheese ball into my mouth. Food as art. Ecstasy.

Bartender Eric got busy doing things with bottles and glasses. Down at the other end of the bar, Joe busily filled an order for Rosie, one of the waitresses. Nice woman. She'd apparently been hitched for a few years and showed me pictures of her kids earlier. They were cute. They had the same curly hair and gorgeous dark-colored skin as their mother. I'd never given babies much thought. Considering the lack of serious relationships in my past, it wasn't really an issue. Eventually the hormones would probably start screaming. I'd decide then whether to ignore them or not. Single parenthood, adoption, getting a kitten from the Humane Society. I had options.

By nine o'clock, the dinner rush at the Dive Bar was over. Work had slowed down. I'd chatted with Lydia for a while. Hung out for a bit with Nell. I'd people-watched, head-bopping to the music. Mostly it was alternative and rock-and-roll. The odd bit of pop. No epic love songs, thank God. By midnight, customers were getting thin on the floor.

"You're looking better," Eric said.

"I'm feeling better."

"Heading back to Seattle soon?" He poured sugar and lemon juice into a cocktail shaker. A measure of whisky. "Guess you got work to get back to."

"Actually, I'm on a couple of weeks' break."

Like I'd told Joe, I could still see what had drawn me to Eric's picture on the website. But I could no longer feel the magic. Today he matched a chambray button-down with black trousers and boots. All of it very nice and yet I remained unaffected. Attraction was a funny thing. What did or didn't draw you to a person. I'd thought the neat, hipster-styling Calvin Klein underwear model was my type. How deluded I was. Joe in his black boots, worn blue jeans, and Dive Bar tee now drew my gaze.

Coeur d'Alene was giving me quite the education in my own stupidity.

Next, Eric added ice, put the silver cap on the cocktail shaker, and shook it all up. He strained the mixture into a glass and garnished it with a slice of lemon and a cherry before placing it in front of me.

"What's this?" I asked.

"Whisky sour."

I took a sip. "Nice. Thank you."

"Lydia's got a sweet tooth and Nell's a straight beer girl. But you, you're different."

The way he said it, along with the not so friendly look in his eyes, let me know it wasn't a compliment.

"Is there a problem?" I asked, my chin rising.

"Don't drag it out, Alex. Just go."

I blinked, caught off guard.

"You seem all right," he said. "This isn't personal. But you need to go."

"I do?"

"Whatever you think of Joe lying, pretending to be me, he's a good person. Obviously he likes you and I don't want him getting hurt." With a small, false smile, he rubbed his hands together. "Okay?"

Christ. "You still think I'm playing games with him. Making him pay penance."

One shoulder lifted. The same half shrug his brother did.

"I'm not," I said. "I like your brother. We're friends. Anything beyond that is none of your business."

"Bullshit." Eric leaned across the bar, getting all up in my space. And good God, the way he started looking down his nose at me. Intimidation-wise, his good looks still kind of worked. My shoulders rounded, making me small, making me feel like crap for no goddamn good reason. This was why I hated going out among people. *People.*

"No," I said, my voice thinning out despite my best efforts. "It's not."

"Yeah. It is," he stated, seeming a little bored.

"How do you figure?"

"Because you're into me."

A pause.

"What?"

"It was my picture on the dating site. I'm the reason you came out here." His hands moved to his slim hips. "A few years back, I might have fucked around with you anyway. Not cared that it would hurt Joe. But we've all got to grow up sometime, right?"

Both my eyes and mouth were wide open. Maybe even perfect circles, such was my surprise. "Just to check: This is you grown up now?"

"My brother's a better man than I'll ever be. And I'm not just going to stand around, let you mess with him," the idiot declared. "You know he's worked with our dad, doing the carpentry. Keeping the old man happy all these years with his dreams of Collins and Sons when I turned Dad down. When I needed money to buy into the bar, Joe lent it to me. He hasn't talked interest or pressured me to pay it back even once in three years. And from the moment I told him about accidentally knocking up Nell, he was there for me. He's been nothing but supportive. There've been plenty of times when women wanted me and I played that up. Made sure he knew he came second. But those days are over. That bullshit behavior is over. Do you understand?"

"Yes."

"Good. So, you're cute in a weird, geeky kind of way, but . . . I'm not interested," he declared, winding up his speech. "My brother's a good man and he deserves the best. Go home, Alex."

I had nothing.

Luckily, Eric didn't require a response. He wiped his hands on a cloth and wandered off into the restaurant, leaving me to sip the whisky sour and stew over his words. I couldn't dismiss them completely, as nice as it would have been.

"Everything okay?" The golden boy leaned across the bar. His hair was pulled back in a ponytail, making it much easier to see his face. I liked that. A lot. Sweet baby Jesus, I was liking a whole lot of things about him lately. And sitting here slowly getting tipsy while watching him move about the bar with such efficiency and ease wasn't helping to dull my libido any.

"Ah, yes." I resettled in my seat. "I'm drinking a whisky sour."

"How's that working for you?"

I took another sip. "Not bad."

"I've been watching you," he confided.

"You have?"

"Yep. You've talked to at least five real live breathing people that I've seen. Face-to-face, even. Not on the Internet. Good work."

"Oh. One guy was just apologizing because he nearly spilled his drink on me."

"Nope," said Joe. "Dude was trying to hit on you. Your elbow sort of got in the way and then I guess he lost courage. Ice hitting your crotch will do that to a man."

"Really?" My brows rose. "My human interaction radar must be on the fritz."

"Sitting there in your tight black jeans and sweater, looking hot." He grinned. "Thinking no one would notice."

"You think I look hot?"

Joe studied me in silence. "Friends aren't allowed to think friends look good?"

"Hmm. I guess that doesn't break pal privilege." I smiled. "You've got a customer."

With a rap of his knuckles against the bar he wandered off to serve the latest comer. When he bent over to get a drink out of the fridges under the bar, the denim of his jeans outlined his ass in a very nice way. The backs of his thighs too. And when he reached up for a bottle of liquor off the top shelf the sleeve of his Dive Bar tee stretched around his . . . whatever all those muscles were called at the top of the arms just below the shoulder. Shit, what was the word? I knew it, I did. Great. Now his attractiveness was making me stupid. Stupid*er*. Whatever.

Also, I had a feeling these drinks were encouraging me to take pal privilege too far. Ah, alcohol. The ultimate in social lubrication leading to suspect decisions. Especially when it came to members of the opposite sex.

He looked my way as he turned back around, giving me a quick smile. Next, a beautiful brunette with long flowing locks approached him. She set her hands atop the bar, gave him an award-winning smile, and leaned forward. As various women were wont to do. Words were exchanged and Joe poured her a craft beer from a tap. Then he took her money and put it into the till, gave her a nod. Transaction done. The beautiful brunette returned to her table of friends. Much flipping of hair ensued.

Meanwhile, Joe pulled down another bottle, mixing up a new drink. The ink on his arms danced when he shook up the concoction in the cocktail shaker. Cool. Then he poured it into a glass, garnishing it with a slice of lemon and a cherry.

"Ninth," I said when he returned to my end of the bar, placing a fresh whisky sour in front of me to replace the now empty glass.

"Ninth, what?"

"That's the ninth set of breasts you've been presented with since I've been here. And thank you for the drink."

He laughed.

"I'm serious." I stood, setting my hands on the bar and leaning forward. "You know they intentionally do *this*. How could you possibly miss it? Of course with me, you have to imagine I'm wearing a low-cut blouse, and that I have something to fill it."

His gaze jumped from my chest to my face. "Do that one more time for me, Alex."

"Haha." Demonstration completed, I sat back on the stool and consumed a healthy mouthful of my drink. I'd reached the fun stage of alcohol consumption. You know, when your body feels a little loose and sadly, so does your tongue.

"Thank you for calling me hot," I said. Not meeting his eyes, because there was just no need to get all emotional.

"Thank you for noticing the women hitting on me."

"Nine pairs of breasts versus one guy who wound up with ice on his crotch. Not much of a competition." I popped the cherry into my mouth and started chewing. Sugary goodness. "I'd understand if you wanted to disappear with one of them. Or a set of them."

Not that I'd like it.

He stopped, stared. "I'm a guy so it's kind of hard to tune out breasts when they're right there in front of me," he said. "But if you think any other woman here tonight has my attention besides you, you're an idiot. We're hanging out together. That was the agreement."

I blinked.

"Okay?"

"Relax, Joe. It's not like I was jealous or something." And I blinked again, my suddenly leaden tongue going nowhere. He did not mean that the way I thought (just for a moment) he meant it. But still. Whoa. His smile, holy shit. White teeth, pink lips, and golden beard. It nearly knocked me off my seat. There was definitely wobbling.

"Are you getting tipsy?" he asked.

"No." I laughed. "I'm just slightly happily inebriated. Totally different."

"Right."

"I won't get sloppy. Promise."

"You can do what you like, It's good to see you relax." He leaned in closer. "Between you and me, you can be a little high strung sometimes."

"Which is completely cool and super-desirable, thank you very much."

"Abso-fucking-lutely." The laughter in his eyes was beatific. Delightful. Much more of this and I'd write the guy a sonnet or something, sing him a love song. "I was just about to say that."

"Just as well." I fluffed up my hair. "I wouldn't want to have to get rough with you."

"Oh, I think I could handle you getting rough with me," he said with a sexy-ass smile.

For one long loaded moment, we just looked at each other. Neither of us said anything, but mostly I was just confused. Then without another word he walked away to chat with Eric.

Motherfucker.

What was that? No, seriously. I hadn't even begun to drink enough alcohol to deal with this sort of shit. The two brothers talked about whatever they had to talk about, then he turned back to me, rubbing his big hands together.

"We're good to go," he said. "Unless you wanted to stay a little longer?"

"No, no. Fine with me."

Mind reeling, I climbed down off the stool and gathered my things. We waved goodbye to Lydia and Nell and so on as we wound our way through the maze of tables toward the door. Outside, the crescent moon was high, the stars bright and the air cold.

"Have an okay night?" he asked as we walked toward his truck.

"Yes."

"Good." He unlocked the passenger-side door and held it open for me.

"Thank you." I climbed inside, the seat chilling my ass despite the layer of material supplied care of my pants.

"You're welcome."

In no time at all, we were cruising through the dark quiet streets of Coeur d'Alene, heading toward the hotel. The heat blasted, warming my hands and face. Which reminded me . . .

"Nell said her place still had no heat."

"Yeah," he said. "It's okay. I'll crash on the lounge at home. Think I've pushed your hospitality far enough."

"I don't mind."

"Sure you don't want some privacy?"

"Nuh, I'm good. Keep me company."

"All right." He smiled.

I watched the streetlights cast shadows on the angle of his cheekbone, the furrow of his brow. Strange how his manly beauty had grown on me, redefining or rather stretching my usual boundaries. Perhaps some people's allure came from the inside out. A good thing. Their ways and their words did the wooing instead of their physical appeal. Not to diss Joe's impressive physique. As nice as a pretty face was, though, the personality, the person beneath the skin, should matter more. Anything else was pretty shallow and unlikely to last. Guess that was the difference between my scratching an itch with a stranger and the way this man had me tied up in knots. And not even neat, sea-worthy knots. I'm talking, haven't washed or brushed your hair in forever and there's a big old mess back there.

Shit.

At the bar, he'd flirted with me. Full-on flirted with me, his supposed platonic friend who was not his type. No way did I know what to do. Normally Valerie would be first on my hit list of people to call. But she'd just tell me to jump him, regardless of what else was going on, or any possible consequences. Plus, with him beside me it would be kind of uncool. But a couple of whisky sours or no, I was pretty certain I hadn't imagined his interest.

As Mom had always said, however, best to be sure.

"What are the renovating plans for tomorrow?" I asked.

"Rip out the old fittings and prepare the space for new."

I nodded. "So we'll be doing some pounding and screwing?"

"Ah, yeah." The man cast me a look out of the corner of his eye. "Sound okay?"

"Absolutely. Can't wait to get my hands back on that big hard hammer."

"Great," he said, throwing me another questioning look.

I gave a nice bland smile.

Yeah, pal. Two could play at the what-the-fuck-is-going-on flirting game. I turned in my seat, all the better to face him. "Did you want to bang, Joe?"

"What did you say?" Wide eyes flashed my way.

"Like I did on that wall today. That was fun," I said with all due sincerity. "Will we be doing more of that?"

A pause. "Sure."

"Awesome."

Another quizzical look.

"Something wrong?" I inquired politely.

"No." His Adam's apple dipped as he swallowed hard, shifting in his seat, gaze decidedly unsure. The poor fool couldn't begin to understand the crazy he'd unleashed with his little taunt. Get rough with the man? My starved libido was well beyond the rough-and-tumble stage. No more hiding or denying, sticking to the sidelines of life. It was my time to step forward and be brave. When it came to Joe Collins, I was more than ready to say yes.

"I just . . ." he started. "Never mind."

Neither of us spoke as he pulled into a parking space a short walk down from the hotel. I leaned over, placing my hand on his denim-covered thigh. The muscle tensed beneath my fingers. Shame on me for straying a little close to his loins.

"Thanks so much for tonight, Joe. I'm so glad we decided to be friends. Because you, sir, make a great friend."

"Right. Good." A frown. "How much did you have to drink again?"

"Not nearly enough. Quick, let's get to my hotel room so I can have more!" I threw open my door.

"Okay." Hands stuffed in his pockets, he followed me inside, lingering a step or two behind. Guess he didn't like it when people's moods got all mixed up and mercurial either. Funny, that.

I nodded to the dude at the front desk and pressed the button on the elevator. It opened immediately. Mirrors and old-timey-looking wooden framing decorated the small space. We both leaned against the back wall as it slowly ascended.

"Yeah, sure can't wait to do some banging, and pounding, and screwing around with you, Joe." I smiled. "Sound good?"

He just gave me a dry look from his superior height. All confusion gone from his handsome face. Confined spaces only made him seem bigger, even more imposing than usual. No way, no day, however, was I crawling back into my shell or turning into a shadow. We'd agreed to work on our issues, so fine, I was putting it out there.

Still, my bravado was fading, I could barely meet his eyes. The man affected me in all the ways.

"It's hard, no pun intended this time, because sometimes it feels like you want to be just friends," I said. "But then other times you flirt with me and I honestly don't know what's going on. No huge surprise there, I know. Social awkwardness is my jam. But I thought I mostly understood where you were coming from."

A *ding* from the elevator and the doors opened at our stop. I walked out, his bearded hotness following slowly behind, stalking me almost. For certain his usual cool, easy-going-guy persona was missing in action. The man radiated tension, intensity, even.

And if he didn't, I definitely did.

Inside the hotel room I went for mood lighting, only turning on the table and bedside lamps. I rubbed sweaty hands against the sides of my pants. "What you said back at the bar about me getting rough with you, however. Now, that almost sounded like a dare."

"Did it?"

"It did."

Arms hanging loose at his sides, he just watched me, saying nothing. Jerk.

"So tell me." I stood at the foot of the bed, facing him. Every part of me was wired, wide awake. "What's going on, Joe?"

His shoulders rose and fell on a deep breath. "I realized something tonight."

"What?"

"That I was falling into old habits. Doing what was easy instead of doing what I wanted."

"Huh?"

"It was just before you spilled ice on that guy's pants."

"Sure. I can see how you'd be seduced by my smooth moves," I said, voice filled with much doubt. My insides were ready to spontaneously combust. I swear I could feel sweat breaking out all over me, the man was just that hot. Also, my nerves were on high alert.

One corner of his lips tipped up. "You know how you said you weren't jealous?"

"Yes?"

"Well, I was."

Wow. I had nothing.

"This is the part where you're supposed to admit you were jealous too," he supplied.

"I didn't think it needed to be said. I'm not that good a liar."

"True," he said. "Anyway, I made the pass at you and then I was leaving it up to you to figure out what you want. To be brave and make the next move."

Softly, I laughed and shook my head. Men were such idiots. "Make the first move? This isn't a game. As I said last time the subject of sex came up, previous hurt feelings, etc. It's going to get complicated."

"Yeah, probably," he said, voice deeper than I'd ever heard it. Like subterranean or something.

"What if it all goes wrong?"

"Then you go back to your old life in Seattle and forget all about me."

"I highly doubt that will work." Given my slightly addled mind, the math might be off, but the chances of me forgetting about Joe Collins anytime soon were not good. Two, three percent maximum. You'd have to allow for an episode of amnesia, alien abduction, or something similar. Sexual encounters with men whose names I didn't remember, however, wouldn't replace him. They couldn't.

"Do you want me to leave?" he asked.

"No."

My stomach flip-flopped while everything down low got achy and wanting. We'd made it this far, there could be no turning back. He wanted me to make the next move. Fine. Without further ado, I whipped my sweater off over my head, dropping it on the floor. Thank goodness, I'd packed some nice underwear. My heart beat double time inside my chest.

He'd seen me half naked before, but now the atmosphere was decidedly different. His gaze flickered over me, nostrils flaring at the sight of my black lace bra.

Okay, that was a good reaction.

Problem was, he did nothing else. He just stood there, studying me. He hadn't even taken his damn coat off. Some of his golden hair had escaped its ponytail and hung around his face, lying against his muscular neck. His big solid body seemed locked in place, everything frozen, except for his hands. Strong fingers flexed open and closed, open and closed.

"Joe?"

I moved a solid inch or two toward him. Brave of me, I know. It was impossible to see the look in his eyes. I should have turned on more lights, except something else had me wanting to hide in low lighting. Something involving feelings and other things I'd rather not be thinking about. Ever. Normally, I wasn't shy in the bedroom. My body had its flaws—the same as anyone else's. But no way would I allow dimply thighs or a wobbly butt get in the way of enjoying life. Hell no. I had other neuroses for that.

And he still didn't move.

Maybe this whole risk-taking thing wasn't such a great idea after all. I'd happily been a hermit for many years. Saying no to things that might take me out of my comfort zone had served me well. Shit. What to do? Run and hide or make one last attempt?

"Joe? Hello?"

He licked his lips but didn't speak. Maybe he'd changed his mind.

Meanwhile, I seemed to have suddenly developed asthma. It was getting harder and harder to breathe with all of the emotions building up inside my chest. Lust, fear, and my old friend confusion.

My ribs could barely hold it all in. Any second now my heart and lungs would burst, give up.

And still he stood there doing nothing.

"I made my move," I said, nervous as all hell. "It's your turn."

He didn't speak a word, he just grabbed me.

CHAPTER TWELVE

Message received four weeks ago:
Hey Alex,
How did your date go? I hope it was horrible and he had bad breath, sweaty hands, and only talked about boring ass botanical facts all night. No. Wait. I mean, hope you had a nice time. Right. That's what I meant to say. So?

Message sent:
Thank you for your well wishes. Not sure I should talk about this stuff with you, it feels weird for some reason . . . But okay, the botanist smelled fine and his hands were dry, appreciate your concern. But you'll be pleased to know that he went into far more detail regarding the sex lives of rare orchids than I ever needed to know. Honestly, it was a bit wrong, how into it he was. I wound up feeling he was some sort of orchid pervert or something. It was all stamens and kink. A very odd night. Food was good though.
A xx

Fingers dug into my hair and his mouth covered mine, hot and hungry. There was no going slow. We were a car crash, a catastrophe. His tongue in my mouth and my hands pushing at his coat, tearing at his T-shirt. One large hand slid down over my spine, grabbing my ass and kneading, while the other cradled the back of my head.

Whiskers from his beard tickled the end of my nose and I pulled back, sneezing.

"Sorry," I mumbled.

"You all right?" he asked, eyes darker than I'd ever seen them.

I nodded. "Mmhmm."

And we went right back to it, lips mashed together, my tongue sliding over his teeth. For a moment his hands left me then his coat hit the floor. What a brilliant idea.

"Get it off," I demanded, pushing up his shirt. He ripped it off over his head while I went to work on his belt buckle. What a team effort. The bulge beneath his jeans looked so damn tempting, it made my mouth water. I slid my hand over it, pressing against the hard length of him, stroking him with my palm.

"Fuck," he said, covering my hand with his own, making me work him harder.

His other hand covered the front of my neck as if he were gently collaring me, thumb grazing my skin. Again and again, he pressed his lips to my mouth. Such sweet kisses, I couldn't get enough of them. I chased his mouth, trying to keep contact for longer. The asshole just smiled.

Butterflies didn't cover it. There were pterodactyls inside my stomach, swooping and screeching and flying around. Not even they, however, could compete with the throbbing ache in my pussy.

"We need less clothes," I said, voice shaking. Damn it.

"Yeah."

With one final kiss he let me go and the race was on. He tore open the button on my pants, wrenched down the zip. All the while my blood beat hard, pushing us to go faster, to get him into me quicker. It required more balance than I possessed to toe off my shoes. I clung to his thick shoulders before I hit the floor. Once he had my pants undone and down to my knees, he threw me onto the bed.

I shit you not.

Those big hands gripped my hips and I went flying through the air, landing on my ass with the happily soft mattress bouncing me around. My eyes must have been like twin moons. I'd never been a small, fragile creature; however, people didn't normally just throw me around. Apparently he was in an even greater rush than I.

Off came my pants; he sent them sailing before starting in on his own. Then from his back pocket he produced a condom and threw it onto the bed beside me. We were ready.

"You still with me?" he asked, standing at the end of the bed in forest-green boxer briefs with one hell of a hard-on pointing right at me. "Alex?"

"Y-yes."

A nod.

"Come here," I urged him on, beckoning him closer with my greedy hands.

He climbed onto the bed, situating himself between my spread legs. Much, much better. Our mouths got back together, and it was like they'd never been apart. Wet, feverish kisses. Hot hands slid over my skin, undoing the clasp on the back of my bra. And all the while he rocked against me, rubbing his length along the lips of my sex, making my eyes roll back into my head. God, it felt so good.

Just to be safe, I wrapped my legs around him good and tight. It wouldn't do to let him get away now.

If it weren't for the underwear we were still wearing, everything would be close to perfect. I was so swollen and wet, and we'd barely even gotten started. My bra disappeared, care of his clever hands, and his warm mouth trailed over my chest. The beard was weird. It was sort of soft, not scratchy, yet still made for a bizarre contrast to his smooth lips.

Foil crinkled and he drew back onto his knees, pushing down his boxers and taking his cock in hand. Now, this I needed to see. Thick, long, hard, perfect. He rolled on the condom, not taking his eyes off me for a moment.

"Pretty," he said, trailing his fingers down the middle of my chest, between my breasts, stopping at my panties. "But these need to go."

And so they did.

The heat of his big body covered me, his eyes staring deep into mine. Then the broad head of his cock eased between my labia, pushing slowly but insistently into me, stretching me. All the while, he kept staring at my face like he was trying to memorize it or something.

This was not casual. Nothing about this felt casual.

The thought, no, the knowledge, sent panic rising up inside me. Except Joe's hips were pressing into mine, his body angled just right to put the loveliest pressure on my clit. The thrill of it eclipsed all else. Immediately he started pulling back, drawing the thick length of his cock out of me. Every nerve ending inside of me sung, pleasure racing through my veins. When he pushed back in again, it was a little faster, a bit rougher. And he kept that up until the bed's headboard started shaking.

It felt fucking awesome.

I wrapped my legs around him once more and tilted my hips, taking him deeper. Again and again he thrust into me, and every time it only got better. Sweat covered our skin and the sound of our heavy breathing filled the room. More hair escaped his ponytail, sticking to his face. This man was so beautiful. Also, what he could do with his dick was fucking magical.

Fingers buried in my hair, keeping me right where he wanted me. The man had me mesmerized. I couldn't have looked away from him if I'd tried.

My legs shook, every muscle drawing tighter and tighter as the fire inside me grew. Apparently my heart had been replaced, because my pussy and clit were throbbing like they were the new center of my world. The feel of him burying himself deep, time and again, was the most perfect sensation. From the top of my head to my toes curled tight, nothing else mattered except him and me and this exquisite heat growing between us.

When he reached down between us, sliding his thumb around and over my clit, I exploded. *Boom*. Total whiteout. My breath caught in my throat and my body drew tight. Wave after wave of aftershocks rushed through me. Joe's hand curled tight in my hair and he ground himself against me, hips bucking. His hot breath warmed my neck as he buried his face.

Done. We were both totally done. Dead even.

I was a quivering wet mess barely able to breathe. Yet still those wonderful little ripples spread through me, the muscles in my pussy still weakly trying to seize him, keep him inside. Who could blame them? Joe, the man formerly known as just my friend, was some kind of fucking sex god. It was all too much. Suddenly I needed some space.

"Excuse me." I pushed at his hot, sweaty, oversize body. "Joe?"

Immediately, he got off me, lying at my side. Even his softening cock sliding out of my sex felt right.

"Hey, you all right?" he asked, hand drifting over my hip.

"Yeah, I just, I need a minute." I climbed off the mattress and headed straight for the bathroom, locking the door.

Bright lights blinded me, making dots dance across my field of vision. The cold tile floor and cool air-conditioning made my skin goose-pimple, my nipples harden even more. Hell, the girl in the mirror looked like shit. I mean, well fucked, but still. Swollen lips and messy hair, red marks from his fingers everywhere. It was the look in her eyes, though, that tipped me too far and I burst into tears.

Polite knocking came not too long after.

"Alex, you okay?" he asked, voice subdued.

"Yes," I lied, turning on the cold tap and splashing my blotchy hot face. Ugh, my eyes were a mess, all red and puffy. Charming. I'd totally do me again if I were Joe.

"So that wasn't you who ran from the bed and locked herself in the bathroom to cry?"

Smartass. I didn't bother to answer. Instead, I brushed out my hair and took a few good deep breaths. Put on the hotel robe hanging on the back of the door and tried to pull my shit together. It helped a little. But I still really didn't want to go out there and face him. Maybe I could give myself a facial, it would burn some time. Eventually, the man would have to get bored and leave. Surely.

Then this whole embarrassing episode could be dealt with another day. Or never. Never would be fine.

"Way I see it, you have two choices," he said, obviously standing close to the door. "One. You can come out here and talk to me. Or two. I can go down to the truck, grab my tools, and break the lock or just break this whole damn door. Your call."

"Asshole," I whispered.

"I can hear you."

With a sigh, I gave in and opened the door.

The condom was gone, but otherwise he remained unchanged. Damn, he looked good.

"Hey," he said.

"Hi."

"Did I hurt you?" Concern creased his brow.

"No. No, you didn't. Nothing like that. I like rough, I just . . ." Shit. I had no words. "Sorry."

He shrugged. "Sometimes women cry after sex. It's not a big deal. Just a release of stress or something."

Hmm. Maybe.

Gently, he reached out, taking my hand. Behind him the bed was trashed, blankets and sheets a mess. Also, the room smelled of sex. Typical me to turn something so good into a big heap of bad.

"Tell me what you're thinking," he said, slowly swinging our hands between us like we were children.

"That I have this talent for ruining things."

"You didn't ruin anything." He shook his head. "Nearly gave me a fucking heart attack. But you didn't ruin anything."

"Oh good. That's good." I should probably go easy on the sarcasm. Someday. "I don't normally cry. That doesn't usually happen."

His gaze softened. "What normally happens?"

"I get dressed, say 'it was nice to meet you,' and leave."

Joe just looked at me.

It was the truth. I wouldn't lie to him or try to make excuses. Because the same as any man, women were entitled to a fuss-free sex life should they so choose. And it didn't make us sluts, or whores, or any of the other nasty, misogynistic, double-standard bullshit that got thrown a woman's way when she didn't fit with the traditional ideals of who and what a female should be.

"Do you want me to leave?" he asked.

"No." My fingers immediately tightened around his. Which pissed me off even more. "All of the emotional stuff needs to stop, though."

"It does, huh? So what, you want mindless fucking?"

"Yes, absolutely. And lots of it."

His tongue played behind his cheek while his wonderfully proportioned dick stirred with interest. "O-kay."

"I don't mean to be critical but, last time you did it wrong," I said.

"I did it wrong?" Brows arched high in surprise. "Shit. Here I was worried I'd gotten too rough with you."

"No, no. Hard and fast is great. But what was with all of that eye-gazing stuff?"

Lips drawn wide in disbelief, he tilted his head, staring at me. Again.

"It was totally unnecessary, Joe. How am I supposed to relax when you're doing that?"

The man scratched his head. It killed the remains of his pony-tail, making all that blond hair fall around his face, down to his broad shoulders. "So me watching, to make sure I was doing right by you, ruined everything?"

"Yes."

"I made you cry?"

I shrugged. Surely the evidence was clear enough.

"Tell me, Little Miss. Did I also make you come?"

"Yes. You know you did. It was good, great, even. But . . ."

"But it got too personal." Hands on hips, he stood, unmoving. "Me fucking you and watching you like that."

"I guess so." Though I would have put it in different terms.

"You'd prefer if I fucked you like I hated you, wouldn't you?"

I shrugged. "Well, yeah?"

He said nothing.

"Joe?" Cautiously I stepped toward him, zeroing in on the hard planes of his pecs, the gentler curve of his stomach. Nice to see he wasn't all ripped perfection. The man was intimidating enough.

"Mm?"

Lightly, I slid my fingers through his chest hair, resting my cheek over his heart. It beat away beneath me, strong and steady. His rib cage gently rose and fell on each breath. Bit by bit, my breathing slowed, calmed. His body was warm, even welcoming after a minute or two. Hands smoothed over my back, pulling gently at the fluffy robe until it started slipping off my shoulders.

"Okay," he said, baring me to the waist. Big hands covered my breasts, thumbs stroking my nipples. His eyes were calm, serene, even. "Since I clearly don't know what I'm doing in the sack with you, I guess you better show me. For friendship's sake."

"Sure. I could do that."

Calloused fingers slid down to my waist, pushing the robe off me completely. Next to him, the cool air-conditioning didn't seem so bad. He kept me warm.

"I, um, I prefer to be on top," I said.

He gave me a quick smile. A flash of sharp teeth. "Of course you do."

And without another word, he picked me up and carried me back to the bed.

CHAPTER THIRTEEN

Message sent three weeks ago:
Eric,
Help! Have you ever owned a cat? My neighbors asked me to watch their cat for the weekend while they went away. His name is Misty. Why you'd name a boy cat Misty I have no idea, but whatever. All the poor animal has done since arriving is hide under my bed and yowl. I've tried everything I can think of to lure him out. Biscuits, canned salmon, and calmly explaining that Greta (my neighbor) will be back for him Sunday night. I even tried tough love, telling him firmly that he was being a bad baby and demanding he come out. The little jerk scratched my hand when I reached for him, then went back to ignoring me. I don't know what to do and Google is being no help at all. What if he chokes on a dust bunny and dies under there?? Greta will never forgive me. You know, a plant I could have probably managed, but leaving me in charge of a sentient life force isn't a good idea. I don't think I'm ever going to be ready for motherhood.

Message received:
Alex, calm down. The cat is not going to die. Leave him alone
and he'll come out when he's ready. I promise.

Message sent:
I left him alone and he came out. He's now on the couch
watching an Animal Planet special on humpback whales.
Apologies for freaking out slightly and thanks for the advice.

Message received:
Anytime. I'm sure one day, when you're ready, you'll make a
great mother.

"Can I get you a cushion?"

"No, thank you." I gave Joe a nice calm, bland smile and turned back to his mother. "This meatloaf is wonderful, Audrey. Best I've ever tasted."

"You know, you strike me as the kind of girl who'd really be into meatloaf," said Joe. "I don't know why, you just do."

I ignored him.

"It's Eric's favorite," Audrey told me.

"I can see why."

The birthday boy put down his fork and lifted his bottle of beer in a toast to his mother. Happily, he said nothing. With a mouth full of food, saying nothing was always best. Eric looked part squirrel with his cheeks so full of birthday lunch.

Mr. and Mrs. Collins lived in a nice bungalow a few blocks back from Sanders Beach. A nice part of town. Joe told me how it'd become popular with the moneyed up in the last ten or so years. Some of the houses on the lakefront were amazing. Outside, massive old pine trees kept the house in almost perpetual shade. Inside the Collins abode were comfy couches and pastel walls covered in pictures of the boys. It was nice, homey and relaxed.

Unlike me at that particular point in time.

Unfortunately, Joe wasn't finished with his teasing yet. Sliding his arm over my stiff shoulders, he leaned in and not quite whispered, "Are you sure? The chairs are bare wood. I really don't mind fetching you a cushion to sit on."

"I'm sure."

"But—"

"I'm fine. Thank you."

Concern filled his mother's hazel eyes. "Is something wrong, Alex?"

"No."

Brows pinched, she turned to her eldest son.

"It's fine, Mom," said Joe. "Alex is just a little sore from—"

"Building," I hastily interjected. "Yeah. I'm not used to all that sanding and stuff. My muscles are just a little . . . sore."

"Right. Building." The asshole who would most likely never live to see my pussy ever again grinned. "That's what I was going to say."

Unbelievable. It's like he actually wanted to be attacked with utensils. If he kept this shit up, I'd do a Betty Blue and fork him good, right in the back of the hand. Give him some scars to remember me by.

"Oh," said Audrey. "Would you like some aspirin?"

I shook my head. "I'm fine, really. But thank you."

At one end of the table, Joe's dad, Stan, said nothing, determinedly working away at his plate of food. His father's dark hair was threaded with gray and his face was weathered. Smile lines were definitely lacking. Once upon a time, he would have been a handsome man. His body still looked big, strong, though he moved slowly.

Stan grunted at me when we'd been introduced. Joe frowned and drew me into the kitchen to meet his about a billion times nicer mother. You could see where Joe got his golden hair, despite his mom's being a little faded.

At the other end of the table, Eric's mouth hung open. Empty now, thank God. The mildly horrified look in his eyes, however, was something special. Like it'd never occurred to him that his brother and I might wind up playing naked together.

Not that we'd played, exactly.

As I preferred, I'd been next on top. Reverse cowgirl, yee haa! No way he could ruin things with unnecessary eye gazing in that position. Then he'd turned me around and pounded into me doggy-style. The man made me see stars, I'd come so hard. Three times in one night was a lot. Especially after months of nothing. Once my guard was down, due to complete and utter exhaustion, Joe had cuddled me. It was terrible, disgusting. Fingers caressing me, lips pressing soft kisses to my shoulder and the back of my neck. Normally I'd never allow it, but it felt so good. Plus, I was almost comatose. His surprise attack of intimacy slipped straight though my usual defenses. The way he tempted me, getting me all hot and bothered and twisted up inside in the best way possible. And then, when I didn't think I could take anymore, he calmed everything down and made me feel safe. I wasn't used to being wanted in such different ways. Like I was more than my mouth, tits, and vagina. More than even our friendship.

Holy shit, were we complicating things. We were out of control.

"Building?" asked Eric, voice heavy with disbelief.

"Yes." Teeth gritted, I smiled.

"Banging, screwing," said Joe. "You know."

With a loud huff, Eric sat back in his seat, not taking his eyes off me for a minute. And the look he gave me let me know, I was not making his birthday great.

"Eric?" asked Audrey, gaze racing back and forth between the two of us, Mommy-danger senses obviously on high alert. "Why don't I get you another beer?"

"It's fine, Mom."

"You got a problem?" asked Joe, brow wrinkling.

"She's using you," hissed Eric. "Can't you see that?"

"So?"

I turned to Joe, startled.

"What the fuck do you mean, so?" asked Eric.

"Language," said Stan, not looking up from his plate.

Both of the brothers ignored him.

"What I let Alex use me for is none of your business," said Joe.

"It is if it involves me." Cheeks sucked in, Eric glared at his brother. "This isn't about sex, you idiot. It's about her coming to town for me. Using you, to try and get to me."

My blood, it boiled. "No, I—"

"That's what I'm not okay with." Eric raised his voice, continuing over the top of me. Jerkwad. "And if you'd start thinking with your brain instead of your dick, you'd feel the same."

Stan pounded the table with his fist, making the cutlery rattle. "Language!"

"Boys." Audrey's eyes were wide and her lips thin. "If you need to discuss this further you'll do so later. We're having a family lunch. Enough."

Where they'd ignored their father, both brothers shut their mouths when it came to their mother. It was telling.

"Thank you," said Audrey, picking up her knife and fork once more. "And I'll have no more talk of banging and screwing at the table. I don't live under a rock, you know."

Eric and Joe both cleared their throats, uncomfortable, and I stared down at my plate.

"Sorry, Audrey." I respected the woman. I really did. But so many emotions fired inside of me, warming my cheeks, making my hands tremble. I hated conflict. Funny, given how often I seemed to find myself in such situations. Courage had never been my strong suit. No way, however, would I allow Joe to be insulted. Especially not because of me.

"You're wrong, Eric," I said, studying the remains of my home-cooked meal. "I can assure you that my interest in your brother has nothing to do with you."

Joe's big hand slid over mine, giving it a squeeze. "It's okay."

"No, it's not." I pushed back my seat and slowly rose to my feet, looking down at his brother. "Eric, for your birthday, I'm going to give you the gift of wisdom. Something you should have figured out for yourself years ago."

The man tipped his chin, inviting me to go on.

"You seem to have this misguided idea that a woman couldn't possibly pass you over for your brother. You're wrong." I sucked in a deep breath. "Joe doesn't need to lie and he sure as shit doesn't need to worry about your leftovers. Or whatever it is you're trying to infer. You're so busy over in Eric world, you honestly have no idea. Joe is smart, funny, loyal, sweet, hardworking, kind, caring, and generally amazing in *all* the ways."

"Christ," mumbled Joe, hiding a smile behind his hand.

Audrey's jaw dropped while Stan's brows started to rise.

Eric said nothing.

"And he's a beautiful man, even if he does insist on having a beard," I said. "He's gorgeous. Also, he's a gentleman, earlier comments about banging and such notwithstanding. You did a really good job raising him, Audrey."

Silence surrounded me.

"I think that's about all I wanted to say. Sorry about the language."

Eric's green eyes glared at me.

I glared right back.

Then my hand was lifted, pressed against Joe's firm lips. "Sit down, Little Miss Sunshine."

"Okay." I sat.

More of that pesky silence.

Audrey was staring off at the wall. I hope I hadn't done the woman any permanent damage by discussing her eldest son's awesomeness in *all* the ways. Some things, however, had to be said.

I chewed on my thumbnail, a frown set in place.

Maybe I shouldn't have said that. Crap.

At the end of the table, Eric downed the last of his beer and stood. "Anyone else need another drink?"

"Please," "yes," "hell yes," and last but not least, a grunt of assent from Stan.

It took a while for conversation to get up and going again after my announcement, even with the added social lubrication of more booze. Joe's mom had a strange quirk to her lips. I wouldn't call it a smile exactly. Maybe it was gas. And every now and then Stan would look at me, then frown. Eric and I went back to ignoring each other, which was probably for the best. His I-am-God attitude annoyed the shit out of me. Obviously.

"Stopped by the job you've been going on about this morning," said Stan. "Thought you would have been there. Had to get Andre to let me in, show me around."

Joe finished chewing what was in his mouth before answering. "Sorry. We had a late start."

A grunt from Stan.

"What'd you think?"

Lip curled, his dad shook his head. "No good. Job's too big. Plus I promised the Rosentons we'd get started on their gazebo. Told Andre to call someone else, Peters, maybe. Pick up your tools when you go into the bar next time."

Then, as if the matter had been decided, the man picked up his knife and fork and chased the last of his peas around the plate. Both Audrey and Eric acted distracted, eyes elsewhere. Staring at the family pictures on the wall, the old shots of Joe on his high school football field, a teenage Eric playing the drums. There was even a shot of Audrey with big hair in a white debutante dress.

Obviously, this sort of scene was nothing new for the family. For a long silent moment, Joe just stared at his father. His thigh had turned rock hard against mine, tension radiating. I grabbed his hand as he'd done mine. Solidarity.

"We'll be starting early Monday, Joe." Stan gave me side-eyes. "On time. No excuses."

Joe took a deep breath. "No."

"What the hell do you mean *no*?"

"This job's important to me," said Joe. "I've made commitments to Pat and Andre. No, I'm not walking away from it."

"You shouldn't have given them any definites until I'd been to the site." His father never even looked up from his plate. "You know better."

"I'm not a child, Dad. I can make decisions about jobs."

"Apparently you can't, because the renovation is too damn big." Stan set his cutlery down with great zest. "All of those rooms needing work. What the hell were you thinking? With my arthritis playing up I can barely even get up the damn stairs."

"Then you need to think about taking a backseat. Let me take over and manage things for a change."

Audrey gasped.

Meanwhile, Eric seemed to have frozen in his chair.

"Christ, Dad, I'm doing the bulk of the work as it is," said Joe. "It's time."

Blood suffused Stan's face. "That's my business you're talking about. The business that I built."

"Yeah. The one that I was meant to be a partner in, that's what you said. Collins and Son." Joe sat tall. "You haven't been able to work full-time for nearly three years now. I'm not trying to kick you out, but I'm done building birdhouses and fixing squeaky doors because that's the most you can manage. I'm sorry. But I want more."

"You want." Stan's voice seemed to almost rattle up from his chest.

"Come on, Dad. Be reasonable." Joe pushed his hair back from his face. "It's time to loosen up on the reins a little. Let me take on more. You taught me well, I won't disappoint you or tarnish the family name or something. Trust me."

Nothing from his father.

"I can go out on my own, if you'd prefer." Joe's grip on my fingers tightened to the point of being painful, but I held on. This was what we'd talked about, losing our bad habits, fixing our lives. Finally, he was done doing whatever was easiest, what pleased other people even if it left him with little.

Stan's hands curled into fists. "You'd abandon me, boy, after everything I've done for you?"

"Christ. You can't have it both ways, Dad," said Eric with a sigh. "He's done everything he can to make you happy. To make you proud."

"I don't want to hear a goddamn thing from you." The man glowered at one and all. "Of course you'd be on his side. Too damn lazy and stupid for real work, weren't you?"

"Yes. So you can growl at me all you like," said Eric, jaw set in a harsh line. "But this isn't about me. It's about Joe. Hell, it's about Mom too, though she'd never say it. How do you think she feels, watching you struggle, watching you work yourself into an early grave?"

Their father turned to stare at her, seemingly out of words for once.

"You've been promising her Hawaii since before I was born," added Joe. "Can't count all the times you two have talked about it."

That seemed to stop him.

"Audrey?" asked Stan, voice hesitant.

With a sigh, she watched him with sad eyes. "I'll be sixty-two next year and you're sixty-six. We're getting old, honey. It's not an insult, it's a fact. And yes, I worry about you. Of course I do."

Eyelids blinking repetitively, Stan stepped back from the table. Then, without another word, he turned and left the room.

The house sat in silence. It could have been the calm after the storm, or we might have been in the eye of it. Hard to tell.

"I think that went pretty well." Eric sank back in his seat, hands behind his head. "Could have done without hearing about my brother's supposed super-penis but, other than that, not the worst Collins family gathering ever."

Joe snorted.

His mother huffed out a breath, then took a long sip of beer. A healthy mouthful of the good stuff, actually. Fair enough, seemed justified.

"Mom?" asked Eric. "You okay?"

"Yes," she said calmly. "But none of you deserve cake."

Lunch wound up rather quickly after Stan stormed out. I think Audrey was ready for a little peace and quiet.

Joe had to work at the Dive Bar that night. I set myself up in a corner and caught up on some work on my laptop. Spinach and ricotta cannelloni and a beer were brought to my table first, followed by a five-layer chocolate cake. With my stomach so full, I had to fight off the need to nap, face flat on the table. Luckily, Eric decided they could do without Joe after ten-thirty so we returned to the hotel.

Nothing further had been mentioned about his super-penis or my speech vaguely referring to the same.

Surely, this was why people didn't generally take me home to meet Mom. Not that I generally wanted anyone to. Joe Collins may or may not have been an exception; my feelings regarding him were still a big hot mess. I told Valerie about it, seeing as she was the official keeper of my secrets. The woman laughed until she cried. So much for loyalty.

I unlocked the hotel room door and stopped cold.

"The room is flickering," I said, looking back over my shoulder at Joe.

"Is it?" His smile was secretive, sneaky, even.

"Yeah. Must have been all of those drugs I took in the sixties."

The bearded wonder chuckled, following me into the wonderfully mood-lit room. Tiny little fake candles sat in frosted glasses all around the place, including in the bathroom.

"Pretty," I said, checking out the shadows dancing across the ceiling. "You have anything to do with this?"

"Nah."

I nodded, not believing him an inch.

Bubbles filled the spa bath and a couple of beers sat in a bucket of ice at its side. On the counter sat a vase packed full of roses.

"I really wish my other boyfriend hadn't done this," I said. "Makes it a bit awkward with you being here and everything."

Joe just stared at me.

"What?" I smiled.

"You just called me your boyfriend."

Oh shit. My mouth opened, my mind reeled. Man, was it my day for stepping in it. "Ah, I, um . . . oops. A labeling accident mid-joke. Let's pretend it never happened."

He blinked. "Okay."

"Great. Phew."

He took hold of the bottom of my sweater, carefully peeling it up and over my head. A demure white bra awaited him below. No matching panties. What with the necessary post-conjugal sleep-in this morning, I just hadn't been that organized. Speaking of which, "Who did you get to do all this?"

"Lady at the front desk was happy to help."

"That's nice."

The thing about consorting with giants, they had a habit of just putting you where they liked. Joe grabbed my hips and lifted me onto the bathroom counter, pulling off my booties and socks.

"It's really beautiful," I said, reaching out to touch the petals of a rose. "Thank you."

"Consider yourself wooed."

"Got it."

Then I was back standing on the floor, my jeans disappearing fast. Happily, he didn't appear to be disappointed by my lavender lace boy shorts. Hands down my bare back in a distinctly proprietorial fashion. They certainly weren't shy.

"Hey," he whispered, drawing me in against him. "What you said at lunch, I appreciated it, the way you stood up for me. Next time though, let's not talk ever, even remotely, about sex in front of my parents, okay?"

"Right. Okay. That sounds fair enough."

I checked out the waiting tub again, giving it side-eyes, trying not to be nervous. It was clean and white and lovely. No blood or anything. Nothing to fear here. The past was gone.

"What are you thinking?" he asked.

"That I could do with some good memories in bathrooms."

A grunt. Luckily for him, it sounded different than his father's. Joe's grunt had a vibe of understanding as opposed to Stan's grumpiness and general dissatisfaction. I could deal with Joe's grunt just fine.

"You going to tell me what that's about sometime?" he asked.

"Sometime." Not now. I didn't want to ruin the mood he'd gone to so much effort to create. Instead, I reached up, pressing my lips against his. Once we started kissing there could be nothing wrong. Joe's teeth, lips, and tongue made everything right. Usually I didn't waste a lot of time with the preliminaries. With him, however, all of it was good and worthwhile. When his hands slid into my underwear, cupping my butt cheeks, encouraging me, all was wow. Standing before him almost naked while he remained fully dressed made the power dynamic shift into his capable hands. I'd given it over.

The pterodactyls in my tummy were making their presence known again. Overheating me, turning me into a weak-kneed fool. I don't know if it was due to our closer relationship or his talented dick. Both things probably made this thing with Joe take on so much more meaning than my usual "slam, bam, thank-you man" orgasm exchanges.

The bath might not be so deep, but I'd still be out of my depth. Never mind. My swimming skills weren't so bad. And if they failed me, I was pretty damn sure Joe wouldn't.

"I know you're a little sore," he said, nuzzling my neck, my ear. "Thought we could soak together."

"Aw. Did you have a hard night last night too?"

"Like you wouldn't believe." His soft laughter was downright dirty, making a shiver run up my spine. "Plus, I got this dream of you, bare-ass naked, wearing nothing but bubbles. Had to make that happen."

A thrill ran right through me at his words. Goose bumps covered my arms. "You been having dirty thoughts about me, Mr. Collins?"

"Constantly."

"Since when?"

He looked away, a rosy kind of hue on his cheeks. No. Way. The man was blushing. Mixed with his wild long wavy hair and mountain man beard, it was such a surprise, pure delight.

"I'd rather not say," came the mumble from deep in his large, solid chest.

"Hmm." I rested my chin on his chest, gazing up at him. "Joe, tell me some of your non-PG-rated thoughts, please."

Brows scrunched up, he sighed and tucked my hair behind one of my ears. His breath warmed my neck, teeth tugging gently at my lobe. It tickled.

"Hey." I smiled. "Talk."

"Little Miss Fucking Sunshine, I'm not that original." His nose brushed the side of my face, lips teasing my neck.

Mouth open ever so slightly, I waited.

"Fucking you in all sorts of ways. Different positions." A soft breath. "Pretty much on every surface in this room. And in my truck too."

"Mm?"

"Licking you all over, eating your sweet pussy."

"That sounds nice."

"Yeah?" His lips dragged along my jawline, hands pressing into me. "How about if I wanted to play with this gorgeous tight ass?"

"Um." Not being an idiot, I hesitated for only about half a second. "That could probably be arranged."

The man groaned, burying his face in my neck. Something was definitely filling the front of his jeans in a big way, digging into my stomach.

"Basically," he said, voice little more than a rumble, "with your permission, I just want to hold you down and make love to you for a good long time, watching your face as you come."

I pulled back, wrinkling my nose at him. "Seriously?"

Joe just shrugged. "You asked."

"It's not making love, it's sex. And God, you and the eye contact." My shoulders slumped, body sagging. "Why?"

"Relax, Alex. I still want to kiss, lick, bite, and spank you. Fuck you good and hard every way I know how. A little bit of staring into each other's eyes is not the end of the world." He kissed me on the forehead. "If you gave yourself a chance to get used to it, you might even find you enjoy it."

I huffed out a breath. "Once. But only because I like you."

Slowly, he nodded. "Thank you. I like you too."

"Tomorrow for the rest?"

"Tomorrow, when you're not so sore." His big hands cupped my face, angling me up for a kiss. Such a sweet man. "For now, naked covered in bubbles, sitting on my lap, drinking a beer."

I reached behind my back, undoing the clasp on my bra. "Can I tell you all my sexually twisted dirty thoughts too?"

His grin was pure predator. "I'd like that."

CHAPTER FOURTEEN

Message sent three weeks ago:
ME: *The Man Seat. Your turn.*
HIM: *Cowgirl*
ME: *Doggy style*
HIM: *Lap Dance*
ME: *Spoon*
HIM: *Shoulder holder*
ME: *The handy man*
HIM: *What's that one?*
ME: *Man seat, but do it on the washing machine with a good spin cycle going on.*
HIM: *Holy shit. You've done that?*
ME: *No, but I've always wanted to. Lack of private available washing machine. You know, I've heard of phone sex, but not email sex.*
HIM: *Getting a little heated?*
ME: *Yes. You?*
HIM: *Definitely. Can't talk now, ordering a washing machine.*

Joe had obviously fibbed about only doing a few days of work with his dad and a couple of shifts at the Dive Bar each week. It soon became apparent that the guy bordered on being a workaholic. If I hadn't been in town, he probably would have been renovating the soon-to-be studio apartments whenever he wasn't serving drinks downstairs. With something to prove to his father now too, I doubt I could have kept him away from the place if I tried—and I didn't.

No one else seemed surprised to find us there at it again come Monday.

Joe and Andre got busy spreading sealant around, getting the kitchen and bathroom spaces ready for tiling and cabinetry installation. Andre, as the owner of the building, was every bit as committed to the renovations as Joe was. Meanwhile, I ripped out what remained of the old fittings in the last room down the hall.

Funnily enough, destroying things continued to make me happy. A certain kind of satisfaction could be found in emptying a room of all its detritus. Clearing out the old and ushering in the new. It might have been symbolic of my life, or it might have just been my underlying violent tendencies. I don't know.

Despite our sleazy sex plans, we were talked into attending a nighttime gathering at Lydia and Vaughan's. Pizza and beer were on the schedule. The happy couple lived in a bungalow not far from Joe's folks' place.

On our way over, I thought about how despite my dislike of the outdoors I couldn't get enough of all the trees in Coeur d'Alene. The greenery both blew my mind and soothed it. Seattle was great, but this was different, less crowded and more peaceful. With Joe beside me, a lot of my fears faded. But more than that, some stronger part of me woke up. Coming to this place, meeting Joe, it had all helped to wake me up.

I loved the feeling I got, leaning my forehead against the cool glass of Joe's passenger-side window, gazing up at the greenery and the mountains in the distance. Taking in the colors of the sky as the sun sank low. I'd been focused on being hidden, staying inside for so long. It was like I was looking out at the world for the first time in years, and the view was dazzling.

Maybe my days of being a recluse were done.

Lydia, the blond bombshell, opened the door and welcomed us with, "Boys are out back at the fire pit, girls inside."

"It's tradition," explained Joe, giving the nape of my neck a gentle squeeze before ambling off to be with his bros.

"Oh." Nervousness stirred inside me—I hadn't spent any real time alone with his friends before. Never mind, I'd be fine. Of course I would be. "Okay."

"Down with penises." A smiling Nell heckled Joe from a big old leather couch. "Boo."

"You're the worst," said Rosie. "Get outside."

Oddly enough, Joe seemed unperturbed. "Ladies."

"Let's get you a drink," said Lydia with a light touch on my elbow.

I followed her through the open-style lounge and dining room, into the kitchen area, just as Joe slipped out the door. A glass door led out onto a back patio, flickering flames and the soft sounds of a couple acoustic guitars floating in from beyond. Vaughan, Andre, and Pat were already gathered outside around the fire pit.

"Wine, beer, juice, or water?" asked Lydia.

"Beer, thank you."

"Done." She passed me a bottle from the fridge, while popping off its top.

"Thank you."

We each took one of the remaining single chairs in the lounge. After working on the renovation all day, it felt wonderful to get off my feet. "Into the Mystic" by Van Morrison was playing softly on the record player. Yes, real live vinyl. These people were far cooler than me. My fingers worried the outside seam on my black jeans. All of a sudden my mind was blank. I had no idea what to say so I sipped my cold beer instead.

Nell pouted. "I want a beer."

"There, there." Rosie patted Nell's small round stomach with a smile. "You're having a baby. No fun for you."

"Meh. I don't need that stuff. I'm high on life and pregnancy hormones. A toast," said Nell, holding her bottle of water up high. "To new friends."

"Good one." Lydia drank deep from her beer.

"Welcome, Alex," said Rosie.

"Thanks." I followed her good example. Nothing like cold craft beer to soothe a throat weary from shouting. "Is the bar closed tonight?"

"No," said Nell. "Eric, Boyd, Curt, and Taka are on duty tonight."

"We need nights off now and then," said Lydia, curling her feet up underneath her.

"Sanity breaks." Rosie smiled. She was a beautiful dark-skinned woman with a head full of curls that I would have died for. Mine fell straight and boring. With Nell's coppery-colored hair, freckles, and colorful old-style tattoos, the two women were a gorgeous sight to behold. Lazy me, I'd just chucked on jeans and a long-sleeve T-shirt. I should have made more of an effort. These were Joe's friends, I wanted them to think well of me.

"Speaking of breasts," said Nell.

"We were speaking of breasts?" asked Lydia.

"We are now. Mine are driving me nuts," moaned Nell, eyeing her impressive set. The white chef's coat was of course gone tonight, leaving a body-hugging green woolen dress. "Ever since the tit fairy visited I feel like I'm going to lose my balance and fall on my face. Accidentally gouge someone's eye out with an escaped nipple or something. I don't even have anyone to appreciate them."

With a smile, Rosie wrapped her arm around the woman's shoulders, giving her a quick squeeze. "I think your tits are great."

"Aw, thanks," said Nell with a certain sadness in her eyes. "At any rate, I can't wait to return to normal after I finish feeding the baby."

"You might never go back to normal," said Rosie, stopping to wet her throat with a sip of white wine. "I used to be a B at best, but I've never gotten back below a C. One of my friends is still a double-D eight years later."

"What?" With a soft wail, Nell inspected her breasts and baby bulge. "There's nothing natural about pregnancy. I don't care what they say."

"True."

"Joe keeps sneaking looks at you over his shoulder," Lydia said to me, and gave me a wink.

"It's cute, isn't it?" said Nell. "They get so protective when they meet one they like. I miss that."

With a frown, Rosie rubbed the pregnant woman's arm. "You'll find someone else, Nell."

"I don't know." She sighed. "Honestly, I'm not sure I even want to. I had my one big once-in-a-lifetime sort of love with Pat. But I took it for granted. Well, we both did. Maybe we were too young or something. I don't know. We haven't properly talked since I told him about the baby. I get nods and that's it. Dude'll barely look at me."

"Maybe he's giving you and Eric space to try and be a family." Again, Rosie slipped an arm around the woman, getting close. "Eric has pulled his act together a lot in the last few months."

Making a noise close to strangulation, Nell let her head fall back and stared at the ceiling. "Give it up. We drunkenly bumped hips once by accident. I love him dearly, but only as a friend."

"I hate thinking of you doing everything on your own," said Lydia.

"You planning on abandoning me?" The redhead raised an eyebrow.

"No, of course not!"

Nell shrugged. "I have you, Vaughan, Rosie, Boyd, Joe, Eric, and his parents all dying to help. Relax. We're covered."

"Fine."

With a broad smile, Nell rested her head against Rosie's shoulder. "We're lucky, really. Me and Lydia Junior."

Eyes wide, Lydia laughed. "You would not name the baby after me."

"I might." Another shrug. "Sure, it'll be rough if he's a boy, but he'll get used to it. It'll be character building."

"Very funny." Lydia gave her a sour smile.

"She won't even give us a hint about what she's thinking about for a name," said Rosie, tipping back her glass of wine and taking another mouthful.

"Hell no," said Nell. "You can all know after the fact. Then everyone just has to suck it up and accept it. Tell people beforehand and everyone puts their two cents in. I'm not having people go, 'Oh, I guess that's a nice enough name . . . for a serial killer.'"

"We would never say that." Brows high, Lydia seemed almost insulted.

"Vaughan would."

"Yes, well, your brother's an idiot."

"You're in love with him," Nell pointed out.

"I'm an idiot too. Have you not noticed?"

Rosie and I chuckled as I eased back into my chair. Praise the Lord, I was actually relaxing around strangers. Valerie would be so proud if she could see me socializing like a normal person. Take that, anxiety. The world could be so noisy and full of static. It was easy to get lost and confused. But maybe dealing with it was just a matter of practice.

"So, Alex. Tell us all about yourself," ordered Nell.

"Yeah," Lydia piped in. "What are your friends at home like? What do you do for a living?"

"And what's the deal with you and Joe?" Rosie waggled her eyebrows.

Crap. Three sets of eyes focused on me, waiting. Doubt didn't creep back in, it fucking moon-walked onto the stage. My mind was an empty corridor, lined with locked doors. Behind those doors were all the different things I could say. Torture, thy name is polite conversation with strangers.

No, fuck this. I was queen of my own fate. There'd be no letting Joe down, not tonight. I swallowed hard, wetting my Arizona-dry mouth.

"Um, well . . . I'm a graphic designer," I began.

They all smiled, nodded, encouraging me to go on.

I could do this.

Rain had started falling when we decided to drive back to the hotel. Since the men could no longer sit outside and things were so awkward between Pat and Nell, the night ended rather abruptly.

"You have an okay time?" he asked.

There was something soothing about the sound of the windshield wipers. The hazy way the streetlights looked through the raindrops.

"Yes, I did." It had taken me a while to get comfortable with the ladies' interest in me as Joe's latest paramour. And of course they cared about Joe. Also, they were women so they wanted the nitty-gritty. I gave it to them, up to a point. We had a few more drinks, a couple of slices of pizza, and a pleasant time was had by all. Including me, surprisingly enough. Sharing yourself with people, the right people, felt good. To make new friends also felt good. Maybe there was something to this saying-yes business after all.

"They were nice."

"Good." He smiled.

"Actually they were better than nice," I continued. "They were cool as hell."

A pause.

"I said I'd tell you about my issue with bathrooms." Fingers fidgeted in my lap. Maybe this was my night for sharing, for getting it all out there. Miraculously enough, I'd shared with the women and lived to tell the tale. This was bigger, but it needed to get out of me. Courage would be required, but I'd already indulged in a little Dutch courage back at the party. It would have to be enough. "If you want to know."

Side-eyes.

"It's not pretty," I warned. "I feel like I want to share it with you, though . . ."

"I'd like to know."

I licked my lips, nodded. "Val and I have been tight since we were kids, you know that. I talked about it in my emails. She had a sex change after high school. It's not my story to tell, so I don't normally talk about it with others. But if I'm going to tell you about this . . ."

"Okay."

"We went to a pretty conservative school. Queer kids were given a hard time. Way worse than any of the crap I copped for just being awkward and generally uncool." I shoved my hands beneath my thighs to still them. "When Val was Vince, it was pretty obvious he was into guys. And why should he have to hide it, right?"

Back and forth went the windshield wipers.

"Anyway, some testosterone-fueled bastards decided to hurt him," I said, keeping my voice nice and calm, trying to distance myself from the images inside my head. It didn't work. "People can be so cruel, thoughtless. Clueless about consequences. Especially kids. They ganged up on him, beat him up in the boy's bathroom."

"Fuck," muttered Joe.

"Black eye, busted lip, bruised ribs. He was a mess."

His grip tightened on the wheel. "Assholes."

"Yeah." I gave him a ghost of a smile. Stupid. This was nothing to smile about. "Val's parents were pretty useless, not really present. He got along better with mine. I convinced him to stay at my house that night, so I could look after him, try and cheer him up. We watched movies, ate popcorn, and kept putting ice on his face to keep the swelling down. Once my parents went to bed I raided their liquor cabinet, and we did a couple of shots each. Medicinal, you know?"

Joe just looked at me.

"Val seemed to be doing okay, as okay as someone who'd been through something as horrible as that could be. He said he was going to the bathroom. God, you should have seen the way he moved. It looked so painful. I've never wanted to kill anyone as much as I did those assholes." For a moment, I just breathed. "Val had been gone awhile and I got worried. The bathroom door was closed but not locked."

I turned to Joe, all of the same old thoughts and questions cluttering up my mind. "I figured maybe he was crying, needed some time to himself or something. But that wasn't it. He was lying unconscious in the bath, blood everywhere. One wrist had been cut lengthwise, deep. But I guess he couldn't quite manage the other. That's what saved him. Well, that and the ambulance came quickly, fortunately. I just held his wrists together, screaming for Mom."

"You saved him," he said quietly.

Slowly, I shook my head. "It should never have happened, I should have known he was on the edge. Should have seen something."

"How?" he asked. "You got mind-reading skills I don't know about?"

I snorted. It was better than crying. "Anyway, we stayed at the hospital until they had him stabilized; then Mom made me go home. There was a lot of blood on me and it was all still in the bathroom too so I cleaned it. Didn't seem right to leave that to my parents."

"Christ."

"Yeah, it sucked," I said. "Never thought about it before, who deals with the blood? Apparently there are specialty cleaning companies who can help get it out of carpet and stuff. What a crappy job that must be. I hope they get paid really well."

We pulled up outside the hotel and Joe turned off the engine. The sound of the rain pounded through the silence loud and clear.

"I'm sorry that happened to your friend," he said. "And to you."

"Thankfully, Valerie survived. She's good now, happy. Has a boyfriend who thinks she's Christmas."

"And you?" he asked, reaching for my hand.

I pulled it out from under my leg, meshing his fingers with mine. "I'm learning not to hate people. It's a gradual process."

"Don't think you hate them, I think you're more scared of them." He placed a kiss on the back of my hand, holding my skin against his lips. "After what happened, I can see why."

Outside, the rain kept falling from the night sky. The world kept turning, regardless of people living or dying.

"That's the story," I said.

"Thank you for trusting me with it."

"Did you still want to come inside?" I was not holding my breath. That would be stupid. And yet, after letting all of it out, the story of Val, I could really do with some company. Especially his.

Still holding my hand, he tucked a strand of hair back behind his ear, getting it out of his face. "Yes. But prepare yourself, there's going to be a lot of cuddling tonight."

"Ew." I scrunched up my nose at him.

"I know, I know. But you're going to have to be brave and put up with it."

Quietly, I laughed. "I think I can do that."

CHAPTER FIFTEEN

Message sent two weeks ago:
ME: *I'm having a shit-tastic time right now. Work stress, blah blah blah. Tell me something good.*
HIM: *I've been thinking about you all day, looking forward to hearing from you. Also, whatever it is stressing you out, you can handle it. You're the most badass chick I know.*
ME: *Thank you. I needed that. xx*

"Joe, I thought you said we were going to cuddle."

"We are cuddling." Calloused hands slid around my waist, his lips feeding me soft kisses. And I was hungry for them. So hungry.

"I'm pretty sure foreplay and cuddling are different," I said.

"Christ," he muttered in a rough voice. "Is sex all you ever think about? I'm just trying to comfort you, Alex. Be there for you as a friend. Stop trying to twist this into something dirty."

"That would be easier if we weren't both naked." I laughed and held his long blond hair back from his face, all the better to see him. The cut of his cheekbones and the pronounced line of his nose. Also, his damp pink bottom lip. Perfect for kissing, biting, and sucking on. The man might have had a point about me having sex on the brain. But if I did, it was totally his own fault.

"You're so pretty," I said.

"Pretty?"

"Manly pretty. You know, hairy, and big, and hard and stuff."

The adorable jerk sighed. "Yeah, okay. I'll take that. Thanks."

"You're welcome."

We sat facing each other, me straddling his lap. His back rested against the headboard, his long legs were stretched out. Given the size of the man's thighs, it was kind of hard for me to move much. Not that I wanted to go anywhere. From carrying all his tools and various pieces of building equipment around, he had a rather spectacular body. Thank God for his slight belly. It made me feel better about my own abundance of soft, rounded bits.

In bed, there was an edge to Joe that worked for me like crazy. New life plan, never let Joe leave the bed. Bossy or not, with a little training, I'm sure he'd make a wonderful voluntary sex slave. And oh, the things I'd command him to do.

He collared my neck with his hand, bringing me in closer for a kiss. Deeper this time, longer. His tongue in my mouth and his thumb stroking my jawline. Eyelids closed, my head spun in slow circles. There was only him and me. Everything else dwindled away to nothing.

A hand on the base of my spine scooted me in closer against his body. I might have been on top, but he had all of the control. Against his very nice hard thick cock in particular. If I angled my hips just right, it lined up perfectly with the top of my slit. Tingles shot through me when I rubbed against him.

Caressing his wrist, I watched him through dazed eyes. "I'm starting to notice how much you like to be in charge."

"Hmm." He half smiled. "Did you know, when I have my hand around your throat you get very, very wet? I can feel it on my dick, how hot and slick you are right now."

Hell. Even his words got me wet. When it came to Joe Collins, my pussy was a wanton whore. And seriously, who could blame it? His body was one big beautiful playground. There wasn't an inch of him I didn't want to explore.

He leaned in, nipping my earlobe, making me gasp. "I think you're starting to trust me, Alex."

"Maybe you're just really good at this cuddling and comforting stuff."

"Oh, I'm all for pleasing you." He grabbed hold of my hair, holding me in place for an assault on my neck. Shivers raced down my spine.

"Thought you were done with pleasing people."

"Pleasing you pleases me."

My breath came faster, lungs working harder. I reached down between us, sliding my fingers over the smooth silken head of his cock. Down farther, the ridge, then the more textured thickness of him. Hard and hot, it all felt so good. My insides ached for him.

"Lean back," he ordered, hands beneath my arms, taking my weight. His mouth on my breast was ecstasy. Lips sucking, tongue licking, teeth biting. Pleasure followed by a tease of pain. Just enough to seize my body's full attention, to set my nerves on fire. My head was a mess, my heart beating hard.

I held his head to me, fisting my hands in his hair. Two could play at this game. Also, at this angle, I could rub myself more effectively against his hard-on. Perfect.

"Joe."

"Mm?"

"Enough. In me."

The flat of his tongue dragged across my nipple, making it tighten even further. Then he gave it a quick kiss. "Soon."

Damn him. "No, now."

"Wait. I'm still comforting you," he said, and blew softly over my wet nipple.

My eyes rolled back into my head, probably never to be seen again. Any more comforting and I'd explode. And while I didn't exactly mean to, I'm pretty sure I gave his hair an impatient tug he couldn't ignore.

With an arm around my back, he sat us back up straight. His other hand was busy reaching for a condom. *Finally.* My mouth found his, kissing him deep and wet while his hands shuffled my hips back just a little. So sad to lose contact between my sex and his. That it gave him the room to put on the condom was the only reason I allowed it.

One arm was around me, the other holding his cock. Our lips were close, but not touching. Some of the terrible eye gazing going on. Yet for some reason, I couldn't look away.

The pressure against my labia before his blunt cockhead pushed into me. The feel of him opening me, filling me. However I'd made such things meaningless sex aerobics before, it wasn't happening. Not with Joe. Right then, I didn't have it in me to worry. We were connected, his dick buried deep within, and it felt fucking amazing. He was right. I didn't just want him, I trusted him. And the feelings, the emotions stirring inside of me were building by the minute.

With my hands around his shoulders, my body wrapped up tight in his embrace, I rocked against him. The thick length of his cock sliding in and out of me, making me lose my mind. My nails sunk into the strong planes of his back, as I fought for self-control. But each time he plunged back into me before drawing slowly out again felt too good. Everything low in me tensed, electricity shooting through my veins.

The smell of him, so familiar. The scent of us together filled the space.

Sweat covered our skin, bodies sliding together faster. I gritted my teeth and worked harder, thigh muscles burning, my pussy dripping wet. The sounds of our harsh, heavy breathing was all I could hear. Fingers dug into my sides, his arms crushing me against him. It was a little violent and a lot wild. Loss of control didn't matter, though. Not with the way my blood was racing through me, super-heated and overcharged.

Joe growled and swore. Our motion was frenzied, like he was making a place for himself in me permanently. Every time he kept hitting something sweet inside of my sex. Energy rushed up my spine, all of me tightening, fighting to hit that pinnacle of bliss. I came gasping, grinding myself on him, coming hard enough to scream. All I knew was that my lungs and heart had exploded. My bones were set in place, wrapped permanently around him.

He used my body to finish. Hips bucking, he held me down hard, making me take him as deep as I could. His cock jerked inside of me, pumping out seed. I almost regretted the condom between us.

Wait. No, I didn't. That was insane.

My pulse was so loud, hammering behind my ears. I'm surprised the neighbors weren't complaining. Joe and I were stuck together with various bodily fluids and limbs.

"You okay?" he mumbled.

"Yeah. You?"

A grunt.

Seriously. "What does that even mean?"

"Means I don't really want to talk or move yet." He relaxed against the headboard, gently stroking my back despite his fine words. I lay against his chest. His heart pounded beneath my ear. Nice to know we were both in the same worn condition. Inside of me, his cock softened a little, but stayed put. I liked that, still feeling him.

"I think I'm dead."

The jerk pinched me on the ass.

"Ow."

"Still alive," he said.

I retaliated by pinching one of his nipples.

"Damn it, woman." He grabbed my hand, holding it captive in his. "Enough. I surrender. Let's be friends."

I don't know how long we stayed like that, glued together. Neither of us seemed inclined to move. After a while, I may have even fallen asleep. The man was just comfortable, plus I was exhausted. Ever so gently, my hair was brushed back from my face. A finger traced the sensitive rim of my ear.

"Complicated," said the man.

Had I been more awake, I'd have agreed.

The next day, Joe was back to work at Dive Bar. I was again positioned at a corner table, working on my laptop. Yes, I could have worked in the quiet of my hotel room. Strangely enough, it turned out that people watching actually got my mind going—my creativity rocking and rolling. I kind of liked just being on the edge of things, watching. I never realized that I didn't have to be sucked into the thick of things, surrounded by people and constantly dealing with the frenzy of the big wide world. The fringes were fine too. And so was watching my mountain man hottie (not that he was *my* hottie), and occasionally chatting with Nell or Rosie. It was nice.

Everything had been quiet until Eric arrived just after the lunch rush.

"Come see," he called out from the front door. Smile wide, practically buzzing with excitement.

"What?" Joe paused mid-motion, a couple of beers in his hand for restocking the fridge.

"Everyone!" he yelled.

Eric disappeared back outside while we gave each other confused looks. Out of the kitchen lumbered Boyd, one of the cooks, along with Nell. Rosie and Taka were the waitstaff on duty. With a shrug and a frown, they headed out the door too.

I hunched down in my sweater, shoving my hands into my back jeans pockets to keep warm. A cold wind was throwing autumn leaves around, the sky a clear blue. And parked at the curb was a shiny red muscle car with white racing stripes.

"Two thousand eight Shelby GT500," said Eric proudly. "And I got it for a song, only twenty-five grand. Owner had just died and apparently his wife hated him."

With a nod, Boyd turned and wandered back inside. Guess cars weren't his thing. I kept quiet and stayed back. Cars weren't really my thing either.

"Didn't you already have a reasonably new working vehicle?" asked Rosie, arms crossed.

"It's a guy thing, you wouldn't understand." Taka bent to check out the inside through the open passenger-side door. "Nice. Very nice."

"Take you for a drive sometime," said Eric.

"You better." Taka followed the unimpressed Rosie back inside.

Still beaming, Eric turned to Nell and Joe. "Well? Isn't it beautiful?"

Nell blew out a breath. "Yes, it is. And it only has two doors. That's going to work out great for transporting a baby."

Eric frowned. "I figured you'd just be using your car for the kid."

Nell said nothing. But you could almost see the haze of storm clouds gathering around her head, the frustration and anger wound up in her balled hands—clearly she was experiencing way more stress than was good for a pregnant person. She too went back inside.

"What the hell?" Eric muttered, hands on hips, scowling after her.

Joe just hung his head.

"Seriously? You too?"

"Fuck me." Joe licked his lips, shook his head. "Ever wonder why I don't worry about you repaying the money you owe me? Remember the loan you hit me up for when you wanted to buy into Dive Bar?"

Mouth shut, Eric stared at his brother.

"Because the business was still getting going. Then, when things got out of the red—surprise!" Joe held his arms wide, a vein bulging out of his neck. "You knocked up Nell. You're going to be a father. I figured you need the money, that you'd be help-

ing out Nell with stuff for the baby. You know? Not buying a fucking muscle car."

Eric's lips looked dangerously thin.

"When the hell are you going to grow up and start thinking
about your responsibilities, huh?" asked Joe, voice harsh. "Good
work, brother. Solid effort."

Joe marched back into the bar, leaving me standing there. I
ever so subtly side-stepped closer to the door. Really, I should
have taken the opportunity to run back when Boyd did. The guy
might not say much, but he was smart. Yet, I couldn't help but be
impressed by Joe's hard stance. Sure as shit, his pleasing days
were done.

Jaw set, Eric slammed the car door shut. "What about you,
Alex. You going to give me shit too?"

"No," I said, keeping my face blank. This situation had nothing
to do with me and I was happy to keep it that way.

"He's been different since you arrived."

Lips. Shut. Tight.

The man then mumbled expletives all the way around to the
driver's side, tearing open the door before throwing himself inside. A toddler couldn't have thrown a better tantrum. Engine
growling, he roared off down the street. Sending more leaves into
the air than the wind.

Wow. Conflict sucked. Just being around it made my pulse
manic.

Back inside, Joe was standing behind the bar, staring at the
ground. Not happy.

"Hey," I said, standing on a stool's rung, rising high enough to
lean part of the way across the bar.

"Hey." He took my offered hand, letting me draw him in nice

and close. Then I kissed him. It wasn't a polite peck on the cheek. Hell no. I pressed my lips against his and gave him the kind of kiss best reserved for lovers in private.

Behind us, someone wolf whistled. Another person clapped.

When I finally pulled away, his eyes had calmed, and the beginnings of a smile curved his mouth. Much better.

"Thanks," he said.

"Anytime."

"Your brother is quickly working his way up the ranks toward being an all-time legendary douchebag." Nell slung a handbag over her shoulder, lips tight and eyes as fiery as her hair. "He was supposed to come pick me up at closing. Would you mind giving me a lift back to your place?"

"Not a problem." Joe forced a smile.

"He's probably off somewhere masturbating over his new car." Joe grunted.

I said nothing. It was a disturbing visual, and possibly even true.

It was late, the streets empty. Above us, the stars were spread out across the sky in all their glory. Such a beautiful cold pristine night. Even the wind had calmed down some.

"Sorry, there's probably some crap on the backseat," said Joe, unlocking the truck.

"No worries. I'll deal with it," I volunteered. Fair was fair, the pregnant lady could have the comfy seat up front.

Indeed, there was a variety of paperwork, a set of pliers and some other tools, an empty soda can, a denim jacket, and a baseball cap. I shoved it all over to one side and climbed in while Nell got settled in the passenger seat.

My jaw cracked wide on a yawn at the same time as Joe's. He turned and gave me a wink. I couldn't help but grin back, my partner in tiredness. All of the sexing activities had been eating into our sleep time. Not that I minded one little bit. I'd take shadows under my eyes and a wee bit of morning grumpiness. After all, that's why God invented concealer and caffeine.

The clock had started counting down the time I had left in Coeur d'Alene. Decisions would eventually have to be made about our situation. We could date from afar, take turns visiting. I don't know. While it seemed a likely and even positive option, it filled my heart with dread. Even in this age of technology, long-distance relationships were hard. Unlikely to succeed.

The engine rumbled to life, wonderful hot air rushing out of the vents. As usual at this time of night, most of the houses lay quiet in the dark. We drove under the streetlights as some old Springsteen tune played on the radio. I couldn't wait to get back to the hotel, to have naked time with Joe. To get as close to him as physically possible and forget all about how I'd have to leave him soon.

We'd only gone a couple of blocks when Joe slowed to a roll for a stop sign. After a brief pause, we were off again. From out of nowhere, an SUV smashed into the side of Joe's truck, wrenching us headlong sideways through the intersection. There'd been no headlights to warn us. Nothing. Metal screamed, my head bouncing off the hard glass of the window. Everything went black.

CHAPTER SIXTEEN

Message sent ten days ago:
ME: *Hi Eric, I haven't heard from you for a couple of days. So
I'm assuming you're crazy busy with the bar and your family
and friends. I hope everything is going okay. Talk to you
soon. Best, A xx*

Message sent one week ago:
ME: *Eric, I'm worried about you. Probably silly of me, but
would you mind just dropping me a line so I know you're
okay? It's just been a while. Hey, isn't your birthday next
week? Thanks.*

Hospitals still made me want to puke, that hadn't changed. End-
less white corridors and the scent of bleach and disinfectant.
Nurses and doctors rushing around, so many voices. Somewhere
a child was wailing.

I sat in the hospital waiting room next to Rosie and Boyd. Eric
and his parents sat opposite. Everyone looked worn and pale,
apart from those with red eyes. Despite the cast on his left arm,

Joe insisted on pacing. The fracture was a couple of inches up from the wrist. The doctor said he was lucky that the damage to his arm wasn't much worse. I'd had my right eyebrow glued back together. Otherwise there were some bruises, a few aches and pains, but nothing major. The doctor said I was also lucky. The idiot in the other car who'd been driving with no headlights on had barely had a scratch on him. Of course, he hadn't been rammed in the side by a massive bull bar.

Nell hadn't been so lucky.

"She wants to see you and Alex," Lydia told Joe, her face splotchy from crying. Vaughan stood beside her, their hands wrapped tight together.

Joe stopped pacing. "Right."

I stood slowly, my head still woozy and full of pain. They wanted me to stay overnight, just in case. Mild concussion and so on. Hard to see how me having a panic attack would help anything, though. And if they'd made me stay any longer in a hospital bed, with the whole world feeling wonky and memories of Val's suicide attempt filling my head, it would have happened. So I'd discharged myself against their advice. Now, much like everyone else in the waiting room, I was barely holding my shit together.

"Right," Joe said again before breaking into motion, striding toward Nell's room.

I followed.

She lay propped up by a mountain of pillows. Aside from the bruising on the side of her face and her arm, her skin was paler than the dove-white sheets. Even her red hair, spread out across the pillow, seemed subdued. Machines beeped and little lights flashed, monitoring heart rates and saline drips and fuck knows what else.

It was obvious, the pain she was enduring. My heart ached. Nothing about this was fair or okay.

I knew shit happened to good people, but at the moment, seeing Nell like that cracked my heart into tiny pieces.

"Hey," said Nell, pale face set. She got right to the heart of the matter. "It wasn't your fault, Joe."

Blond hair hanging around his face, he shook his head and said nothing. The slump of his shoulders, his whole body. More than his arm had been broken tonight. It hurt to see him so wrecked.

Oh God. This was way worse than I'd thought.

"Even if Eric had come and picked me up, that car still would have run the stop sign," said Nell. "I could still be in this bed."

"I shouldn't have been driving." Joe gripped the back of his neck hard. "Knew I was tired. Didn't even see the car coming at us. What the fuck was I thinking?"

"It's not your fault." I reached for his elbow, gave his shirt a tug. There was blood on it. From me or Nell, I didn't know. "Don't put that on yourself, Joe. Please."

He didn't even look at me.

"Listen to her," said Nell.

Suddenly, we heard someone shouting down the hall. Then someone was stomping down the corridor, almost running. "Where is she? Where's Nell?"

Pat strode into the room. Black hair, black clothes, face furious. I flinched, taking a step back to stand by the end of the bed. Behind him, Eric hovered, waiting. On the bed, however, Nell's face crumbled, all bravery gone.

"Patrick," she said, tears streaming down her cheeks. "I lost my baby."

"Shit," he muttered, rushing to her side. His arms gently and slowly surrounded her, holding her to him like a precious thing. White-knuckled, her hands clung to his shirt.

"I'm sorry." He lay his cheek against her hair. "So fucking sorry, Nell. My beautiful girl . . . I should have been there. Should never have left."

The sound of Nell's sobbing filled the room. All of her agony set free.

Joe turned, blinking rapidly. I did the same, throat tight and raw. Without a word we left, giving them their privacy. It all still felt like waking from a nightmare, the world hostile and strange, and my body shaking. At least she had Pat now.

"Wasn't sure if I should call him," said Eric in a quiet voice as we returned to the waiting room.

"You did the right thing." Vaughan reached out a hand, squeezed his shoulder. "I'm sorry about the baby, Eric."

Dazed, he nodded and sat back down next to his mom. She immediately took his hand, clasping it between both of hers. Stan sat rigid, face almost confused. Guess it was too much emotion to handle, too many people. His sons were hurting and he did nothing. To be so locked down couldn't be easy. Did he feel like a failure of a father or did he feel nothing at all?

I sat, staring up at the fluorescent lights marching across the ceiling in such neat lines. One half of my face throbbed. Also, there may or may not have been a steel spike shoved through my brain. I'd never had a headache like this.

"Alex?" someone spoke in front of me. Slowly, gradually, Rosie's face swam into view. "You need to rest."

"Hey."

Gently, she took my arm, lifting me to my feet. The world around me straightened. Or at least it stopped spinning for a while.

"Come on," she said in a quiet voice. "I'll drive you back to the hotel."

A few feet away stood Joe, his agonized gaze fixed on his brother. Right. Of course. He should probably be with his family. They probably wanted to be alone right now. Still, I had to check.

I slid my hand over his, tilted my head. "Joe? Are you okay? Is there anything I can do?"

The man had been far, far away. Lost inside his head. He blinked rapid-fire, as if my words were traveling from a distance.

"No." He shook his head. "Thanks."

"Rosie said she can take me back to the hotel. But I'm happy to stay."

Without a word, he lifted his hand, carefully touching the mess on the right side of my face. Lines sunk deep into his forehead. "Fuck, look at you. I'm so sorry."

The look in his eyes killed me. I took his hand, kissed it. "Not your fault. Not even a little. Get that thought out of your head."

"I barely stopped," he said. "If I'd just . . . if I'd waited a little longer I might have seen him."

"You stopped. You did the right thing. He was the one driving in the dark with no goddamn lights on."

Joe just shook his head.

"I'm going to stay," I said to Rosie, giving her a brief smile. Christ, even that hurt.

"No, go," said Joe. Then he shoved his hands under his arms, out of reach. "You should go."

I just looked at him.

"It's okay," said Joe.

Bullshit.

"I should be with my family," he said in a low voice.

"Okay. Call me if you need me." I softly rubbed his arm. We were all so broken and pummeled. No touch was safe. "I'll be at the hotel. Come see me anytime."

A nod.

Eric sat forward in his chair, staring at the ground. His mom had her arm wrapped tight around his shoulders, whispering in his ear. Stan sat there as stiff as ever. Vaughan tipped his chin at me. Lydia was stretched out on the seats with her head in his lap, seemingly asleep.

"Joe!" A blonde strode toward us, a collection of silver bracelets clinking on her wrists, long skirt swishing about her ankles. Guess she was some sort of relative or a friend I hadn't met yet. God, she was a boho queen. Her features were a little sharp, but her hair was long and flowy. And either she hadn't noticed his bruises, or she didn't care, and threw herself at him.

"Star," he said with wide eyes, proceeding to pat her awkwardly on the back. "What are you doing here?"

"I hit the road as soon as I got Eric's message." Stretching up on tippy-toes, she pressed her lips to his. Not family. And certainly not just friends. My stomach dropped straight through the floor. What the ever-loving fuck?

Joe turned his face away, breaking the kiss. Then he looked to his brother.

"She's Nell's best friend and your, ah . . ." Eric just shrugged. "I figured she should know."

"Okay."

"Sweetie." She sighed. "Oh, Joe. What happened?"

"Car crash," he said bluntly, still eyeing her like she'd appeared from another planet. "Pat's in with Nell now, we're giving them some privacy. Where the hell have you even been?"

At that, she inched back just a little. "Arizona, mostly. You know how I love the heat."

"Right."

"But I was only in Montana when I heard, so . . ."

Joe said nothing.

"Star. It's lovely to see you, dear." Joe's mom opened her arms to the woman. Christ, the woman was being greeted like long-lost family. If I hadn't already guessed that Star and Joe had been together in the past, the nervous look Audrey gave me out of the corner of her eye clued me in just fine. Even Stan offered the woman an almost affectionate looking nod. Give me strength.

Next, Star knelt down in front of Eric, holding his hands. They talked softly together. Meanwhile, Joe looked on, brows knitted and gaze glued to the woman.

No way had I been given enough painkillers to deal with this. Someone would need to set me up with a morphine drip at the very least.

"Alex?" asked Rosie gently.

"Who is she?" I whispered. But Joe heard me anyway.

"Hey," he said, face filled with tension and gaze shifting between me and Star. "Alex, we'll talk later. Okay?"

I nodded, on the verge of tears for some dumbass reason. What a night.

"Let's go." Rosie walked me out with a hand on my lower back, guiding me out of the building.

It was something like four in the morning. Almost dawn. Still the stars shone brightly. Fresh cold air flooded my lungs, breathing new life back into me. So much bad had happened in the last few hours. How remarkable that life could just go on.

Back in the hotel room, I did what I always did during times like this—when I felt alone, like I was the last person on earth, lost and hurting. In need.

She picked up on the fifth ring. "Hello? Alex?"

"Valerie. I'm sorry to wake you."

"What happened? You sound weird. What's wrong?"

"We were in a car accident," I said.

"You fucking what?" she screeched in my ear.

Ouch. "It's okay. Everyone's going to be okay, I guess. I just . . . it's been a pretty messed up night. I needed to talk to you."

"Okay." She took a deep breath. "I'm listening. Tell me everything and take it slow."

Joe didn't come over that night. Nor did he call the next day.

Which made sense, really. His family had just been through a terrible loss, his brother would need him, of course. He probably needed time to catch up with Star as well. Besides him just needing to rest and heal. Selfish of me to think otherwise. I wasn't that badly hurt that I needed checking up on. It was hard to move around due to every muscle in my body feeling like it had been run over by a truck. And making any kind of facial expression was out of the question. Resting bitch face was the only safe choice. But I had pain meds and room service, a big hot bath to relax my strained muscles, and plenty of movies to watch if I couldn't sleep. So how bad could life be?

198 | KYLIE SCOTT

I missed him, though.

Yes, I could have called him. Maybe I should have. The thought of interrupting something important held me back, though. Poor Eric. Poor Nell. For sure, I was worrying about Joe not calling for no reason. What a fucked-up situation. It was nothing like the time he'd just dropped off the face of the earth email-wise. We were friends, or something, now. He wouldn't do that to me again. Surely. Hopefully, everyone else was okay. As okay as they could be. Maybe tomorrow I'd go into Dive Bar, see how things were going. On the other hand, that might be construed as me lurking or something.

Gah. There was no set etiquette for this. We'd been sleeping together for a couple of nights and friends for months and months. But this situation . . .

Whatever his silence meant, it didn't feel good or right.

Banging on my hotel door. It was like a recurring dream. I'd been fast asleep—way off in la-la land at only eight o'clock at night. I switched on the light and hobbled over to the door, hurting but excited because finally he was here. Thank God.

Smile on my poor aching, battered face, I opened the door and froze.

"Well, you look like shit," she said.

"Val?" I blinked. She was like a mirage, so badly wanted it couldn't be true.

"I'd hug you, but everywhere looks like it hurts." Instead, she patted me gently on the head. "Holy hell, Alex. I knew this trip was going to be big for you, but this is ridiculous."

"Tell me about it." I groaned, stepping back. "Come in. I'm glad you're here."

"Me too. Go lie down before you fall down."

With a full-size suitcase in tow, she made her entrance. Her makeup was natural looking and not a strand of her dark ponytail was out of place. There wasn't a single wrinkle on her classic black pant suit, nor a spot of dirt on her patent heels. Valerie always had more style in her perfectly manicured pinkie toe than I did in my entire body, and her loyalty knew no bounds. The last few days had been so crazy, it was comforting to know some things never change.

"So, here we are in the wilds of northern Idaho." She collapsed into the armchair, watching me climb slowly back into bed.

"Indeed." I tried to get comfortable, closing my eyes against the light.

"Do you need me to get you anything?"

"No. Thanks."

A pause.

"What are you going to do about the beastman?" she asked quietly.

A stupid urge to burst into tears came over me, eyes itching and nose leaking. No. Absolutely not. Everything hurt and I missed him. Basically, I was being a big baby, but I drew the line at tears. If my voice waivered a little, there wasn't much I could do about that. "I don't know."

"How do you feel about him?"

"Good question." Needy. Pathetic. Confused. Ah, man. "Maybe we should head back to Seattle, give him some space. He's got so much happening right now."

"Is this you running away?"

I gave her question a lot of thought. Or as much as possible, given the dull thumping going on in my head. "I don't think so. I just . . . shit. I want to do the right thing by him but I have no idea what that is."

"Guess you better ask him."

"Yeah."

A long sigh from her. "Go back to sleep. Tomorrow we'll fix your face and your life. In that order."

I snorted. Gently.

It was good to have friends.

CHAPTER SEVENTEEN

Sadly, only so much of your life can be fixed with a makeover.

Val and I went to breakfast at one of the cafés down the street. Care of her mad skills, my bruises were covered and my hair cunningly styled to hide the stitches. Much less Frankenstein than the day before. After much discussion, the decision had been reached. I would call Joe. The only question that remained was when?

"Now," said Val, voice strong, as we stood in the lobby of the hotel after breakfast.

"What if he's sleeping in, recuperating?" I punched my floor number in the elevator. "In a couple of hours would be better."

"You're just delaying. I know all about you, chicken shit lady."

"That's harsh."

"But true."

Unable to deny it, I shrugged.

The elevator pinged, the doors slid open. And I found myself staring at the man of my dreams. Literally. My subconscious had been worrying over the subject of him all night.

"Joe."

He sat on the floor, head hanging low his back up against my apartment door. When I spoke he looked up, tangled blond hair sliding back from his face. Shit, if anything, he seemed worse than he had at the hospital. He looked diminished, like this whole experience had taken and taken from him. Worry bowed his shoulders, sorrow filled his eyes.

"Hey." I stepped forward, Val at my side.

"Hey," he said. Moving in slow motion, he climbed to his feet.

"It's good to see you. How are you feeling? How's your arm?" He waved the cast in my general direction.

Silence.

I just stared at him, soaking up the sight. "It's so good to see you."

Beside me, a throat cleared. "Hi, I'm Val."

"Val." Joe gave her a flicker of a smile. "Hi. Nice to meet you."

"Good to meet you too and I'm going now," she announced, pushing the button for the elevator. It hadn't gone anywhere. The doors slid straight open and Val disappeared without another word.

Joe and I were left alone.

Funny thing about hotels, they're one of those in-between places. People are always coming and going, but no one lives there. Hallways especially seem to be both haunted by the memories of past guests and waiting for new travelers to pass through. So quiet and still, filled with the invisible eyes of security cameras, they've always freaked me out a little.

But the way Joe watched me out of the corner of his eye, like I might attack, like he maybe didn't want to be looking at me but couldn't resist, was far worse.

"Let's talk in your room," he said.

I nodded, dread weighing down my every move. Goodbye had

a feeling, a scent, and Joe was covered in the shit. My moves were mechanical, emotional armor doing its best to keep me covered.

Open door, go inside, wait for him to also enter, close door and face him as best I could. Don't cry, because crying wouldn't help.

I looked at him, and he looked at me, and neither of us said a thing.

Then he moved.

A hand slid over the nape of my neck and his mouth covered mine. Tongues sliding against each other, teeth knocking. The cast on his arm pressed against my lower back, holding me to him. Heaven. Nirvana. All of these things. I clung to him, tears of relief flowing down my face. We were okay. We were fine. Sex could fix anything and I needed him so bad it hurt. Whatever it took, I'd do it for him. I wanted to kiss and stroke every inch of his big body. Show him how much he meant to me, every way I knew how. Not let him leave this room until we'd started to heal him, to put him back together again.

His good hand slid under my dress, feeling up my ass, giving it a squeeze. What a time to be wearing tights. Blue with scattered purple dots, even. I'd been in need of something loud and happy.

"Get them off," he growled.

"Yes."

I kicked off my boots and dragged down both the tights and the Little Miss Fucking Sunshine underwear. Joe's smile was all sharp teeth. My heart galloped.

"On the end of the bed, legs spread," he said.

I backed up the necessary few steps then sat on the mattress. Joe sunk to his knees. Guess we were doing oral. Everything inside of me tumbled and turned. Not particularly gently, he pushed up my denim skirt. Bruises? Sore muscles? Didn't feel a one. Nothing but pure excitement going on here.

"Heels on the edge of the mattress."

"Yes, sir." I grinned.

He groaned and nipped at my inner thigh. "Been needing to eat you."

The things he said . . . everything between my hips tightened. I was most definitely good and wet.

"You should definitely follow your instincts," I said. "They're right on."

Without further ado, he dragged his tongue up the length of my slit, making my back arch. Strong arms circled my thighs, cast and hand resting on my belly. And that beard, Christ, did he know how to use it. Soft wiry bristles tickled and teased while his mouth went to work. As with everything Joe did, he did it damn well. Complete concentration, absolute dedication. He suckled the lips of my labia before slipping his tongue between them to get at the tender flesh below. The man treated my sex like a smorgasbord, he could not get enough. Fingers spread me open and he lapped at and all around my clit, making me squirm.

Fucking good. He was so fucking good and he'd barely gotten started.

Up and down he dragged his tongue, setting me alight. Every nerve ending in me was giving him its complete attention. My toes curled when he flicked his tongue back and forth across me. The sheet fisted in my hands, I held on as if gravity might give way. For sure, my mind had been flung into outer space. Kissing and licking, he left no part of me unloved. A wet thumb pad slid around and around, teasing my back entrance, opening me just a little.

It all felt so incredibly good while his arm in its cast, laid across my stomach, held me down. The man ground his face against me, making me pant, before flicking his tongue over and around my clit. If the man didn't suck on it soon, I might just have to kill him.

"Joe."

"Mm?"

"Please," I begged, pushing my pussy into his face.

His hot mouth covered the top of my sex and I died just a little. To feel his lips drawing on me, suckling that tight bundle of nerves. Absolute pleasure surged through me, racing up my spine, making every nerve in me riot. I came and came as he kept at me, drawing it out. Even when it got to be too much, his hold stayed strong. The man was relentless. I choked out a cry, every hair standing on end. I couldn't stop shaking, muscles jumping and my sex tight. The man owned my body.

I loved him and I hated him, and I honestly hadn't known him long enough for either. But he had me. There could be no fighting this one true fact. Joe had me, whether he wanted me or not.

All I could do was try to continue breathing. It wasn't easy. My body lay limp on the bed, legs dangling off the end of the mattress. Beneath me, the sheet clung to my skin, wet with sweat and cum. And still Joe kept his face pressed against my thigh, fingers digging into me as if he was afraid to let go. Now and then he'd press a soft kiss against my damp skin.

"I'm sorry," he mumbled.

"For what?"

"I want you to go, Alex," he said eventually. "Back to Seattle."

"Wha—"

"This isn't . . . I can't do this with you right now."

"You can't do what with me right now?" Rising up on my elbows, I looked down at him in horror. Wet lips set and eyes sad. Christ, he was serious. This couldn't be happening. "You go down on me and then you dump me? Are you serious?"

Nothing.

"Joe, look at me."

He sighed.

"Is this about Star coming back to town? She's the one you talked about in that email, isn't she?" I asked, already knowing the answer. "The one you wanted to settle down with."

"It's not about Star or you," he said, face turned aside. So much guilt. "It's me."

"You mean it's the car accident," I said, voice rising in volume. "It's Nell losing the baby. It's your ex coming back to town. It's everything. You're overwhelmed, I get it."

He flinched.

"For the first time, you're not everyone's Mr. Fixit and it's messing with you. It's hurting you," I said, trying to go gentle but failing. "I understand, I do. But ending this, us, isn't the answer."

"I'm sorry."

"Joe, please."

Slowly, he got to his feet. I didn't even have the presence of mind to close my legs. After what we'd just done, like decency fucking mattered. Too many emotions warred inside of me. I didn't know who to give the microphone to, anger and frustration or love and understanding. They all had a hell of a lot to say.

"I'm sorry," he said again as if that fixed anything. Then he opened the door, walked through it, and pulled it closed. All without looking back at me once. He was gone.

I'd walked out on a lot of men. I'd also been walked out on by a lot of men. This, however, was the first time it'd ever mattered. If this was what it felt like to have your heart broken, it sucked.

CHAPTER EIGHTEEN

Like hell.

CHAPTER NINETEEN

Awkward didn't cover how it felt walking into Dive Bar the next day, having been dumped by one of their favorite sons. Val may have had to nudge me through the door when I stalled at the entrance. Bravery and I weren't well acquainted. Maybe I'd be in luck and discover he hadn't told anyone yet. Either way, I had to get an idea of where things stood.

Midmorning, the restaurant was quiet. Only a couple of people sat nursing coffee and cake. Despite my skulking, Lydia noticed me immediately.

"Hey." Her smile gentled, her eyes filled with empathy. Never had anyone looked quite so sad on my behalf. Lydia really was a sweetheart. "How are you, Alex?"

So, everyone knew.

"Hi, Lydia. I'm fine," I said through a twitchy grin. "This is my friend Valerie."

Val lifted a hand in greeting.

"How is Nell?" I asked.

At this, Lydia's smile strengthened. "She's at Pat's place, she'll be off for a couple of weeks at least. It looks like she and Pat are

210 | KYLIE SCOTT

back together. Losing the baby is horrible, but it's nice that something good has come out of this."

"Yeah."

"Does that sound awful? It's hard to know what to say at times like this." She worried at her short black apron, turning to glance at Vaughan busily setting up behind the bar. "And you and Joe were banged up pretty badly too."

"No, it doesn't sound awful. And I'm on the mend. Val has concealer and knows how to use it, so . . ."

"Good. That's good." She sighed. "Eric took off. No one knows where to."

"Crap." No wonder Joe was stressed out and taking on everything himself. I looked around the room, as if I were seeing it for the last time. The dark brickwork, the mix of industrial and old style blending so beautifully. The man had made the place perfect and yet avoided any of the credit. I took a deep breath. "Is Joe here?"

Hesitation hit her, her eyes straying upward. "Um . . ."

"Could I get a coffee?" Val smiled, smoothly stepping in to distract her, and earning herself another nomination for best friend of the year. "And Alex tells me you have the best brownies in town. You gotta hit me with one of those."

Lydia laughed, letting herself be swept toward the counter.

Meanwhile, I headed through the kitchen toward the back of the building. The same route Joe and I had taken the infamous night of the red candles, heart-shaped pizza, and horrible music. Boyd and the kitchen kid were busy prepping for lunch. Neither paid me any attention. Out the back door and up the stairs I went. The pounding of a hammer echoed through the upstairs hallway. When it paused, exuberant swearing took its place.

Joe stood in the last room, trying to beat a piece of pine into submission. Unfortunately, while his good hand had the hammer under control, his broken hand obviously made holding the wood in place impossible.

I slipped in beside him, holding the beam steady. Neither of us said anything, but the tension radiating from him almost rattled my teeth. A moment later, the thudding of the hammer started up once again, the wood vibrating beneath my fingers.

"What are you doing here?" he growled, tone low and fierce.

"Helping."

Out of the corner of my eye, his chest rose and fell beneath an old Violent Femmes T-shirt. "I told you to go home."

"I remember."

"And?"

"If you want to end it with me, that's your choice. I can't stop you. But that doesn't change the fact that we're still friends." I dared a look at his face. His eyes were distinctly unamused. Sucked to be him. "And a friend would stay and help, Joe."

He shoved the hammer back into a loop on his tool belt and stared down at me, hands on his hips. "I don't need help."

"Bullshit. What are we doing next?"

"I'm serious."

"Me too." I crossed my arms. "What next?"

With another growl, he shoved his good hand through his hair, pushing it back off his face. My, but the man was agitated. Way cranky, not so cute.

"Would you like me to tie back your hair for you?" I asked. "Put it in a ponytail?"

Teeth gritted, he leaned back against a wall. "Why are you doing this? We've got no future. Never did."

"Okay."

"I don't want you here."

"Duly noted."

He turned and kicked the wall, leaving an almighty hole. The man was going all-out toddler tantrum. "Fuck! Just go, why don't you?"

"No." And yes, his continued rejection stung like a bitch, but this wasn't about me or my pain. "Rant all you like, I'm not doing that, Joe. I'm not leaving you to deal with this alone. Everyone here is hurt and grieving, they're either busy or they're gone. I don't see anyone having your back, and to me that is unacceptable."

Breath coming out hard and fast, he hung his head.

"I'm staying, deal with it." I dusted off my hands. "I'll go grab some more drywall so we can patch that hole."

He didn't say anything, but then, I didn't need him to. He'd stopped arguing and that was enough.

Due to his truck being smashed, Joe had Pat's smaller version of the same on loan. Guess Pat had his bike or Nell's hatchback if he needed to get the two of them around. Only problem was, Pat's truck wasn't an automatic.

"You're not meant to be using your hand," I said, holding my palm out, waiting for the keys, after we'd finished work for the day. "I'll drive you."

His forehead furrowed. "I'm fine with it."

"If you don't rest it, the cast stays on longer," I said. "You heard the doctor. Given you're already ignoring him to a large extent, I think every other thing we can do to cut down on usage needs to count."

The more time I'd spent with him today, the more I realized what an utter bitch it was to have five digits out of action. Especially with him being an especially handy man and all. But also, Joe Collins was a big baby when it came to being sick and/or damaged. He simply did not deal well with limitations.

More growling and grumbling. "Fuck's sake, Alex. You going to spoon-feed me and wash my balls for me too?"

"If you ask nicely." I smiled. He didn't. At least I found me funny.

"Christ." For not the first time, he looked to heaven for help. Shit out of luck there.

Across the horizon the sun was setting, the first star twinkling down over the mountains. Despite the cranky man, it was peaceful here. I don't know that I'd actually had a lot of peace in my life. Plenty of drama and neurosis, but not much peace. Coeur d'Alene had a lot going for it. The nightlife didn't compare to Seattle's, but still . . . the slower pace and the people made up for that. The beauty of the place. I loved this time of day, always had. I also loved the fact that I'd helped lighten Joe's load a little, which made all of my various aches and pains worthwhile. Whether he liked it or not, retreating into himself, dwelling on the accident all on his lonesome, was not for the best.

An icy wind ruffled my hair, teasing strands out of my ponytail. God only knew what I looked like. Dusty, dirty, and all the rest.

"Look, you were right about me working on the apartments," he said in much the tone of one making a great and valiant sacrifice. Such reasonableness in the face of my overwhelming lunacy, bless him. "I did get more done with you there today. And I'm sorry for acting like such an asshole. I just think it's time we stop fooling ourselves, and it's better that we finish this thing off sooner rather than later."

His words cut me to the core, but it's not like he was saying anything I hadn't thought a thousand times before.

"I get that," I said in my best Little Miss Fucking Sunshine voice. "But I'm here, and the least I can do is help you as a friend."

"You got Val here to hang with." His tone softened to something more sweet and coaxing. "There's nothing you need to worry about, okay? All I'm going to do is go home, get cleaned up."

I nodded. "And then come straight back in to work behind the bar. Am I right?"

Ooh, I was so right. Angry little lines radiated out from the corners of his eyes. He was not a happy bearded boy.

"Please," I scoffed. "You're no more likely to leave Vaughan dealing with everything on his own than I would you. That's the thing with friends."

Growly malcontent noises had definitely replaced the grunt as his standby means of manly communication.

"Luckily, I brought a change of clothes with me. I haven't done any hospitality work before, so this should be interesting. Also, Val is quite capable of entertaining herself." Though I had kind of been expecting her to show up to help with the carpentry work at some stage today. On the other hand, who was I to complain about time spent alone with Joe? I clicked my fingers impatiently and held out my hand. "Let's go. Times a' wasting."

"You're being ridiculous, Alex." He threw me the keys, stomping his way around to the driver's side of the car. "Fucking ridiculous."

Turned out he was lying about letting me clean his private parts. Too bad. A tongue bath might have improved his mood immensely.

We pulled up outside a duplex, every light on.

"I thought Eric had gone out of town," I said, grabbing my bag with extra clothes in it, black jeans and a shirt.

"Ah, yeah. Listen—"

"Joe?" Star stood in the now open doorway, wet hair hanging down her back and a seriously short silk robe wrapped around her. Like I needed to see that much of the woman's perfect slender thighs.

Joe swallowed hard. "Ah, Star, this is Alex. Alex, this is Star. You didn't get to meet each other properly at the hospital."

She was staying with him. Living in his house. Fuck me. No wonder the bastard wanted me gone. Not slaying him right then and there took some real effort.

"Hi." I put on my best smile, moving forward to shake her hand. "Lovely to meet you."

"Hi." Star gave me a limp hand and a disgruntled once-over.

"She's using Eric's room while he's away," inserted Joe.

"How nice. Give you two a real chance to catch up." My cheeks hurt from smiling. "That's great. Just . . . great."

"How was your day, baby?" The winsome smile she gave Joe as she felt up his cast almost makes me puke. Let's not even go near her calling him *baby*.

"Ah, fine. Thanks." Joe cleared his throat. "Better get in the shower. They'll be needing me in at the bar."

"You have to go out again?" Pouting, Star followed him into the living room. "But, I made dinner for us."

"I told you I'd be busy. Alex, make yourself at home. I won't be long." With all due haste, he grabbed some clean clothes and then locked himself in the bathroom. Goddamn coward.

I plonked myself down on the couch, quietly steaming. Men. Had any species ever sucked quite so badly? Meanwhile, Star fussed around, giving me looks out of the corner of her eyes.

"You're a friend of Joe's, Alex?" she asked.

"That's right."

"How nice."

"Isn't it?" I worked the kinks out of my sore neck.

"I forgot, you were in the crash too." She leaned her hip against the edge of a table. "You poor thing, no wonder you're such a mess."

I huffed out a laugh. "I spent the day helping Joe. Building tends to make you messy."

"You're a carpenter?"

"No, I'm a graphic designer," I said. "I helped them with the layout for the apartments at the Bird Building."

Slowly, she nodded. "Yeah, he told me a little about those. So you're a business friend and you're helping him with the construction work now?"

"He's injured. He shouldn't be working at all. Someone has to."

"And that someone is you? Surely his father—"

"Stan's arthritis makes it difficult to do much these days."

Her head tilted to the side. "How close are you and Joe?"

"That's none of your business."

Brows knitted, she stared me down.

"Your turn, Alex." Joe reappeared, beard wet, hurriedly pulling on his shirt. Then he stopped, sensing the crappy mood in the room. "Everything all right?"

"Absolutely," I said, rising to my feet. "I won't be long."

One cold shower later, I was ready. By gently patting my face clean with a damp cloth, I'd managed to save some of the makeup Val had skillfully applied. Enough for me to not look too Frankenstein's bride.

Star was holed up in Eric's room when we left.

We didn't speak much on the ride back to the Bird Building. But then, Joe hadn't spoken much all day outside of giving me orders. I caught him lost in thought often, however, frowning into space. Wincing, grimacing, he displayed all sorts of unhappy. I'd have suggested he talk to someone about it, but the man could barely handle me helping out. Plus there was the fact I'd never been a big believer in therapy. Also, there was Star. His long-lost one true love, apparently. No, hiding from all of these problems and letting myself die a little on the inside made much more sense.

I'd said I'd stick by him, and that's what I was going to do.

I guess Pat had already been by to pick up Nell's things, because Joe's bedroom was all man. No sign of any incursion by Star whatsoever, thankfully. There'd been a big king bed with a dark green bedspread. An assortment of jeans, boots, and shirts filling a small built-in wardrobe. A couple of photos on the wall of the local area that I guess he'd taken. They were beautiful.

I pulled into the first open space within walking distance of the bar. The continued absence of noise seemed too loud. Guess my nerves were just really on edge.

"There's nothing going on between me and Star," Joe said, startling me slightly.

"No?"

"No." He exhaled loudly. "I just, I wanted you to know that."

I nodded. "Okay."

"She didn't have money for a room anywhere, so . . ."

"Right."

He scratched his head. "Alex, I meant it when I said I can't deal with this, you and me, right now."

"I know you did." And God, did that hurt. "I'm not going to put any pressure on you. I just want to help."

Another heavy sigh. "I hate that you were in the accident too. I don't want you getting hurt anymore."

"I know. But I care about you, Joe, and for now, I'm staying." I pushed open the truck door. "Let's go do this."

The strangest sight met us when we walked into the restaurant: Valerie pouring drinks behind the bar. Someone had even thought to slap a Dive Bar T-shirt on her. As usual, the woman wore it well.

"Isn't that your friend?" asked Joe, scratching at his chin.

"Yeah." I tilted my head; the scene made no more sense. It did, however, explain what she'd been up to all day. "I recall she briefly did a stint bartending when she was putting herself through the cosmetics course."

"How brief?"

And that'd be best not said. "Let's go say hi."

We wound our way through the tables, heading toward the bar.

"Oh my God," I said, with all necessary exaggeration. "They'll let anyone work here. This is fantastic, I'm asking for a job."

"Yes-s-s." Val grinned. "Do it. Then we can be bartending besties."

"Christ," mumbled the grumpy bear behind me.

"Has he been that happy all day?" asked Val.

I shrugged. "Pretty much. Thought you were going to come upstairs and help?"

She got busy filling glasses with ice and lime again, pouring in nips of vodka before finishing them off with soda water. "I got talking to Lydia and found out that her fiancé, Vaughan, has gigs in Seattle and Portland for the next week that he can't cancel. He was just waiting on Joe to come take over the bar so he could hit the road."

"So you volunteered."

"Yep. But I have to head back tomorrow." She raised a brow at Joe, though she kept talking to me. "I take it you're going to insist on helping him with the bartending duties as well?"

"Yes, I am."

A heavy sigh. "You're seriously going to run yourself ragged looking after this jerk that just dumped you?"

"Okay. When the jerk is standing right next to me, probably not the time to have this conversation, Val." I got my ass behind the bar. Not checking out whatever look was on Joe's face, because I didn't want to know. "But Joe and I are friends. Friends help friends."

"Mmhmm." Both brows high this time, Valerie remained skeptical. "Vaughan's away for a week, this Eric dude is MIA, and your friend not only needs to be here every night, but he's apparently determined to carpenter all day, every day too. Let's not even go near the topic of this ex-girlfriend coming back to town."

Joe said nothing. A whole lot of it.

"I can handle it." And the less I said about Star the better.

"You also have your own business to see to," said Val.

"I can delay taking on new jobs for a while."

"Three jobs. Three." She even held up three fingers just to emphasize her point. Either that, or to help me out with the counting. Sweet of her. "While still paying for that hotel room."

"His hand is broken." I pointed at Joe, then gestured to the room at large. "Half of their staff are missing."

Joe opened his mouth to speak, but Val got there first.

"And these are your problems how?" Hands on hips, Val stared me down.

"Because if I let him go on his merry way he'll spend twice as long with a cast on. That's if he doesn't screw up his hand somehow permanently. It's my problem because I decided it was and I need to respect that decision."

"You're stupid about him." Val took to pointing at Joe too. Her bloodred fingernail looked downright dangerous. "Aren't you?"

Head hanging low, Joe muttered obscenities.

"Val, stop," I said, hands shaking with anger and other emotions I didn't care to define. "You're embarrassing me."

"No, I'm staging an intervention. Your experience when it comes to relationships of this nature is somewhere between none and sort of fucked up. It makes me worry." Taking a step closer, she lowered her voice. "Does he even appreciate you?"

"He does. Very much." A muscle jumped in Joe's jaw as he spoke. Oh dear, the tension coming from the man was not good. "But you can both get out from behind there. I'm here now, I've got it."

"Please, you haven't got shit. You look an even bigger mess than she does." Val reached down for a bottle, popped off the top, and placed it on the bar in front of him. She did not smile. "Sit down, shut up, and drink your beer."

Mouth open, Joe froze.

"Ouch. Told." With her black tray at the ready, Rosie waited in the service area. The look of surprise contorting her face would have been hilarious if only the drama unfolding hadn't included me. Three tables full of customers waited on the other side of the room. Well, mostly on the other side. Let's just pretend they hadn't heard. Given the way Lydia and Boyd were sneaking looks from the direction of the kitchen, I was probably well out of luck.

A moment later, the volume of the music in the room rose substantially. Thank you, baby Jesus.

"Your two vodka, lime, and sodas." Val squeezed past me, placing the drinks on the tray.

"Thank you, ma'am." Rosie smiled. "Looks like it'll be a quiet night anyway. Vaughan got all of the fridges fully stocked and everything sorted downstairs before he left. You might as well sit and relax, Joe."

A grunt. He eyed the beer as if it might be poison.

Beside me, Val's shoulders rose and fell on a deep breath. "I think you're doing the wrong thing."

"Okay," I said.

"And you." She turned to Joe with a glint in her eye. "Let her do what she wants to do for you. If you screw up that hand so she has to stay here a minute longer than necessary, I will come back and hurt you."

Saying nothing, Joe sat and started drinking his beer. Wise of him.

Val stomped off toward the ladies' bathroom.

"She doesn't share well." I grabbed a beer for myself. Necessary after the last few minutes. "You should have seen what she did to this kid in middle school when he tried to use one of her scented gel pens. Total carnage."

"She cares about you," said Joe after a moment.

"Yeah." I took a sip of beautiful cold beer. All the while, staring off at nothing.

222 | KYLIE SCOTT

"So do I."

My gaze darted back to him, something squirming inside my chest.

"You're determined to stay and help?" It wasn't really a question, more of a statement.

"Yes."

"All right," he said. "You take my room, I'll sleep on the couch. At least you won't have to cover a hotel room."

"Thanks. But no. I prefer having my own space."

"Then I want to pay for your room. And for your time working with me."

"Oh. No." I drew closer, giving him an awkward smile. "Look, I'm not doing it for the money."

"I know you're not. But you're still getting paid." His tone left no room for *maybe*.

We both drank in silence for a moment, just listening to Solomon Burke singing "Cry to Me." That man knew things about loneliness and pain, relationships and feelings. Maybe I should get all morose and listen to a bunch of sad songs. Probably an effective way of working through the clutter of emotions Joe inspired. Val was right, my knowledge in this area was crap. I could only go by feel, do what seemed right. And while Joe probably deserved a good ass kicking followed by abandonment, that wouldn't help anyone in the end.

Love or like really did suck.

Joe cleared his throat. "I'm not used to needing someone . . . to needing help, I mean . . ."

I kept quiet.

"Sorry for being an asshole to you earlier and not warning you about Star staying with me."

Huh. "Apology accepted."

We both took another mouthful of beer, swallowed it down.

"Your friend scares the living shit out of me," he said.

I choked out a laugh, snorting beer from my nose. Very cool, very lady-like.

The edge of Joe's mouth curled upward and he passed me a napkin from farther down the bar. I'm pretty sure it was the first time I'd seen him smile, really smile, since the accident. It was almost worth publicly dribbling alcohol out of my nasal passages for. Almost.

"Hey," said a bright, bubbly voice from behind us. Star in a slinky orange dress, her hair all bundled up on her head with two chopsticks artistically sticking out. "I got to thinking after you left, and . . . I'm here for you. With the bar, the building work, whatever you need, baby. I want to help too!"

CHAPTER TWENTY

When it came right down to it, getting dirty and being loud with tools didn't really mix with Star's vibes. Plus, she had experience bartending and waitressing. As much as I think she'd have liked to keep a closer eye on Joe and me, her being upstairs didn't make much sense. Especially once Val headed home. Bummer. About Val going, that is; not having Star in my space was a complete win.

So instead, Star took to interrupting us every chance she got. First came coffees. Or coffee. Star accidentally forgot to make one for me. Oops! Next came cake and whipped cream, which she spoon-fed to Joe, apparently so he could work and eat at the same time.

Whatever.

He blushed pretty beneath his beard, but let Star do her thing complete with cooing and Marilyn Monroe smiles. The temptation to barf was huge, let me tell you.

"All finished," she finally (thank God) said.

"Thanks," grunted Joe, rubbing at the back of his neck.

"Are you in pain?" Much eyelash batting on her part. "Do you want me to give you another massage like last night?"

I froze. Then went back to painting the wall because it was neither my business nor my problem. Joe and I were just friends. The fucker.

"We don't have to do it lying down on your bed, you could just sit there for me," she said. "You'd have to take your shirt off, of course. But I don't think Alex would mind."

"Nooo. I don't mind." My smile was all sharp teeth.

"Star's a masseuse," said Joe.

Of course she fucking is. "Great."

"Uh, yeah."

"Why don't you just pop off your shirt for me?" Star stretched her fingers, warming up her hands. "You know it'll make you feel good."

"That's okay," said Joe, going back to sealing the kitchen countertop. "We're pretty busy. Thanks."

"Later at home, then. I look forward to it." And with a wink, she was gone. For now.

The main problem with painting aggressively to unleash pent-up emotions is that the bulk of the paint wound up flicking off the brush and onto the painter. I wiped a particularly large dollop off the side of my nose, trying to calm my shit down.

"Nothing's going on," said Joe.

"None of my business."

"Alex—"

"I'm just here to help out until your cast is off." Because I was an idiot. Also, because I'd said I would and I simply had been born that stubborn. No hippie-handy-hipster would be running me out of town anytime soon. I'd leave when I was good and ready. Like it or not, my hiding days were behind me. At least when it came to Joe Collins.

Still, no wonder Joe suggested I paint, as opposed to letting me near a hammer, screwdriver, or anything else that could easily be used as a weapon. To think, I was normally such a calm and mild-mannered creature. Well, mostly. But turning serial killer on anybody's ass wasn't something you'd immediately associate me with. Until Star.

Sighing and pained looks from the man with the beard.

"Really, Joe. It's fine."

"Are you fucking kidding me?" he asked with a touch of anger.

"What?"

He walked over to where I stood, looking down at me with a cranky face. "Do you honestly believe I'm that clueless when it comes to you?"

I just shrugged.

"Just because I'm in no shape or position to sort shit out with us right now does not mean I'm completely ignorant of your feelings, Alex," he said in a stern voice. "Okay?"

"All right."

"I know this isn't easy for you."

Yeah, no. It might be the only thing on my mind. But it was not the conversation I was interested in. In the aching body/aching heart stakes, things weren't well with me. And bursting into tears or yelling abusive things at him wouldn't help. "You're right, Joe. But I think that's also a conversation for another time."

"I need you to trust me."

"About what? You said we were over." Just repeating it hurt. "And you told Star nothing about us whatsoever. What exactly is it I'm meant to be trusting you about?"

He did some more of the looming and staring.

"You can't have it both ways, Joe," I said. "You can't distance yourself from me emotionally and then demand that I be open with you. That I trust you."

"Alex—"

"I know you're hurting and that there's nothing I can do about it. I accept that." I took a deep breath. "But you need to accept that I'm hurting too, and there's nothing you can do about that right now."

He swore under his breath.

"So I say we make the best of this situation and get this done, okay? Let's just work. I'd really like to get this part finished today." With the brush dripping on the drop sheet, I indicated the outer bathroom wall. Things were coming together fast. At least I could feel a little satisfaction from achieving something.

"Hey," he said, his gaze softening. "You mean a lot to me. Hell, it'd probably be easier if you didn't. But I appreciate you having my back through this. I do."

What the ever-loving fuck was that supposed to mean? That it'd be easier if I was shit on his shoe, something he could scrape off when times got hard? Give me strength. I could have screamed.

After a final unhappy huff, he headed back over to the kitchen counter.

"You're welcome," I said. Then with gritted teeth added, "Baby."

The man stopped cold, looking back over his shoulder.

Splat went my paintbrush against the wall. "Do you like being called that, baby?"

Jaunty happy whistling approached, Andre wandering into the room.

"Things are slow downstairs," he said. "Thought I'd come up

and see if I could help?" He drew to a halt, looking between Joe and me. The smile fell off his face. "Right. You know, I'm going to come back later. I just remembered something I need to do. Somewhere else. Urgently."

Andre fled. Fair enough.

"Got some attitude there, Little Miss Fucking Sunshine," said the bearded one.

"Oh, I think I'm entitled to just a little bit of attitude. Don't you?"

Head cocked, he looked me over, taking in the paint-splattered jeans and oversize T-shirt. No expression crossed his face, however.

"Maybe even a big bit of an attitude."

"That so?" he asked, voice a low rumble and a predatory gleam in his eyes.

"It is. Baby."

"Christ, you drive me crazy," he growled.

"Ditto."

He took a step or two toward me, moving straight back into looming over me. Not that I'd ever admit it for feminist reasons, but I kind of liked it when he did that. Made me feel small and helpless in a way. Though it also put me in just the right position to grab his nuts and twist them. Probably not something that ever occurred to him, the poor man.

Poor man, my ass.

"Must be awesome having Star staying with you. All that catching up you two can do," I said sweetly. "Not to forget the massaging. Full body?"

"Does it matter?"

Wow. His balls were so about to go through the wringer. "Just a little."

"You're awful cute when you're jealous," he said with a sharp smile.

"Am I now?" My hand grabbed his essentials, giving them a squeeze.

"Shit. Um. Alex?" His face paled a wee bit. "Let's just take it easy. Calm things down a bit."

"I'm calm. I'm perfectly calm."

"I only had my shirt off. Nothing happened."

"Did you?" Gently, I rolled his balls, massaging them through his jeans. "Tell me the truth, baby. Can I trust you?"

"You can. I swear."

"You know, I want to believe you, but . . ." I tightened my grip. "Your history when it comes to being honest with me isn't the best."

"Swore I wouldn't lie to you again and I haven't."

"Is that so?" I asked.

"Yes."

"I could make a hell of a case here for guilt by omission, baby."

"Nothing is happening with Star," he said. "But if you were me, would you have told you about the massage? Come on, honestly?"

My fingers dug in, making him suck in a breath and swear.

"It was only therapeutic, I promise. The minute she tried to turn it erotic, I shut her down." His words came out in an almighty rush. "That's the whole truth of it."

Easing up, I turned to rubbing his cock with the base of my palm. A reward, if you like. Almost immediately, he started to harden against my hand. The sick puppy. I think he actually enjoyed having me threaten his manhood in this manner. Then again, I was absolutely loving this, so who was I to talk?

"Do you believe me?" he asked, ever so subtly leaning into my hand and widening his stance.

"Maybe."

"It's the truth."

I shrugged. Like whatever might be happening between his legs left me unaffected. My increasingly damp panties, however, declared that a lie.

"Christ, I thought my dick was dead," he mumbled, eyelids half closed.

"Hmm?"

"Pretty much all I've had since the accident is guilt and pain. Which, let's be honest, I deserve."

"Joe." I stroked his face with my free hand, the beautiful curve of his cheekbone, the smooth skin of his temple. "It wasn't your fault. You have to let that go."

Nothing.

"I didn't see the car either. I should have, but I wasn't even looking."

Eyes wide open, he all but growled at me, "You weren't driving."

"But I knew you were tired," I persisted. "I should have been paying attention, helping you. It's on me too."

"No."

"If I'd been sitting in the front instead of Nell, she might still have her baby."

"Alex, no. That's not your fault."

"Because sometimes things just happen." I placed my hand over his heart, forgetting for the moment where my other one remained. "Joe, you didn't cause that accident. The idiot thinking it was okay to drive in the middle of the night without any headlights caused that accident. The blown streetlight, which the council hadn't fixed, caused that accident. Not you."

His Adam's apple bobbed as he swallowed. "Thought you'd said you'd accepted you couldn't help me with this hurt."

"I changed my mind." Also, I was a bit of an idiot when it came to him. Let's be honest. The still hand on his crotch got back to work, grasping his balls in a firm grip. "Are you listening to me, Joe? Are you taking this in?"

"I'm too afraid not to."

"Good. Because you blaming yourself is only going to wind up hurting Nell and your family and friends in the long term. How do you think they're going to feel watching you self-destruct over this?" I asked, keeping his family jewels held tight. "Do you think Eric would be able to deal with that? Watching his brother tear himself to pieces."

"Okay, okay." He gripped my wrist. "I'm listening, Little Miss. Ease up just in case I want to have kids someday."

I did as asked.

"This is the strangest conversation I've ever had with a woman's hands on me."

"You're welcome." I smiled. "I like to think of it as a type of aggressive sex therapy."

"Do you now?"

Interestingly enough, now that I'd started fondling him through his clothes, I didn't want to stop.

"It's scaring me how much I like it." He leaned down, brushing the tip of his nose against mine.

"Want me to threaten you some more?" I asked, undoing his belt buckle, followed fast by his jeans. Hell yeah, sliding my hand down into his boxer briefs felt like finding heaven. Everything hot and hard and good in this world. Even if he did piss me off sometimes. I wrapped my hand around his cock, giving him a firm stroke.

He groaned. "I'm at your mercy."

"Damn right you are." I smiled, reaching up to plant a kiss on his lips. Very nice. "Don't forget it."

"Never."

If only it were true.

His whole body leaned toward me. His focus on what my hand was up to, buried in his pants, complete. Something so good about the feel of a man in this state. The smooth skin leading down to the ridge around the head of his cock, how swollen he felt with my fingers wrapped around him. It got me high, touching him and turning him on more and more. Just being this close to him. His breathing hastened, hands gripping my shoulders like he needed the support. Poor baby.

Slowly, I eased his jeans and underwear down, freeing him. "Alex, someone could come."

"That's the idea."

He chuckled, down and dirty. "I mean, someone could walk in."

"Yeah, they could." I sank to my knees, keeping a firm grip on him. A bead of pre-cum sat on the head of his cock, just waiting. Tongue darting out, I dealt with that. Salt, warmth, and masculinity. There was nothing else quite like it. "You want me to stop?"

"Fuck no." Eyes beautifully dark, he stared down at me, mesmerized.

I took him into my mouth, suckling the tip. His skin against my lips was divine, his big body towering over me, yet completely under my control. Even the smell of him made me wet, all heat and him. Very much up close and personal. I traced the rim of his cockhead with my tongue, exploring, while he mumbled cuss words along with my name. Things got down right blasphemous when I massaged the sweet spot, digging into the dip in the ridge with the tip of my tongue. The boy would be burning in hell at this rate.

Still, he'd told me not to stop. Not that I had any intention of doing so.

Let Star give all the therapeutic massages that she wanted to. Only I had him like this. Or only I better have him like this if he wanted to keep his balls intact. Such soft, sensitive things. I rolled them in one hand, tugging gently to remind him who was the boss right here and now. A dazed grin appeared on his face in response. Kind of hard to smile back with a penis in your mouth, but I tried.

One hand stroked him while the other played with his ball sac; I worked him hard and fast. Despite my brave words, I could do without being caught giving Joe a blowjob by one of his friends. The only sounds were my wet sucking and Joe's heavy breathing. Again and again, I dragged my firm lips up his cock, tongue swirling over the tip. Hips rocking forward, he eagerly edged closer, making me take him deeper.

"Shit. Sorry," he panted. "Fuck, that feels good."

I hummed my approval and apparently, that felt even better. His fingers fisted in my hair, pulling apart my short ponytail. Sucking on him hard, I pushed him closer to the edge. And finally, over it. He came in my mouth with a strangled sort of sound. His pelvis pushing his cock deeper despite his best intentions. Quickly, I swallowed, taking his cum into me. The time for delicate excuses or spitting had passed. Plus, I loved him.

Oh God. No. No, I didn't.

Sitting back on my heels, I slapped a hand over my mouth. Breathing through a panic attack was hard enough. Breathing through a panic attack while giving a blowjob was even harder.

"Hell. Alex, are you all right?" Joe quickly pulled up his pants, tucking his softening dick out of sight. Then he handed me a bottle of water. I swallowed a good half of it down, stopping only to slump over and give the whole breathing thing another go.

"I should have pulled out," he said. "I didn't even ask. Sorry."

I held up a hand. "It's fine."

Poor man probably thought he'd nearly choked me with his cum or something. Which kind of had happened but not in the way he was thinking. My heart hammered, sweat sliding down the side of my face. All good. No problem. I was not in love with Joe Collins. That had just been some strange mental aberration brought on by proximity to his magical, truly talented cock or something. Let's not get all emotional and start feeling things we shouldn't be. I'd given the man head, not my heart. Because falling for him would be dumb, stupid, careless, and more.

He already had too much going on in his life right now. Exactly as he'd said.

"Went down the wrong pipe," I whispered, patting my chest.

More heavy-browed concerned looks from him.

God, how embarrassing. I finished off the rest of the water, slowly getting myself back under control. "Let's get back to work."

"Are you sure?"

I nodded, as weak and jittery as a bobble-headed doll. Offering me a hand, he helped me to my feet. Sad to say, I think I needed the assistance. Gently, he brushed my hair out of my face, watching me oh so carefully. I had the stupidest impulse to cry, to hide my face in his chest and bawl like a baby. Not good.

"Painting," I said, retrieving my brush from out of the tray. The shaking went away after a while, but Joe's eyes kept returning to me for the rest of the day. Never mind. He didn't need to know about my dumbass revelation. Hell, once we'd finished up here, I had every intention of drinking until I no longer knew about it either.

This was no time for love. Not for him, and therefore, not for me.

The knock on my hotel door came around ten o'clock that night, disturbing my intense study of the ceiling. My mind hadn't been able to settle on anything else. Apparently, no movie or book currently available could distract me from the overwhelming misery of being in love with Joe Collins. It was just like being fourteen again, minus the pimples. Everything sucked and I was doomed.

Surprisingly, I opened the door to find him standing there. His hands were stuffed in his jeans pockets. "Can I come in?"

"Sure." I stepped back, closing the door after him. As the usual, he took up all of the space, all of the air in the room. There was only him and me. "How did you get here?"

"Cab."

"Is everything okay?"

He didn't respond immediately.

Since I was doing all of the driving, I'd dropped him off at his place over an hour ago. We'd gotten out early, it'd been a pretty quiet night at the bar. A good thing, since his one good hand and my lack of experience behind the bar did not make for speedy service.

He sat on the end of the bed, a hand braced on his knee, eyes troubled. "Star and Mom went to visit Nell tonight."

"How is she doing?"

He winced. "About as well as you'd expect, I guess. They've given her good pain meds, apparently. She's comfortable enough. But that doesn't help with knowing she lost the baby."

"She's grieving."

"Yeah."

"It's horrible." I sat opposite him on the chair, not quite know-ing what to do with myself. God only knew what my lovelorn heart might attempt if I plonked myself down beside him. Sonnets, bad poetry, or just a random declaration. Whatever happened, I couldn't tell him about my feelings. The poor man's back was al-ready bowed under the weight of all of the current emotional pressure; adding my earlier revelation to the mess would not help. I wanted to be his wonderwall. His place to rest and heal. The per-son who had his back, no matter what. That's how I'd show him my love without doing any damage.

"Has anyone heard from Eric?" I asked.

"Ah, yeah." He offered a brief smile. "That's the good news. He texted earlier, said he'll be back in a day or two."

"Good. That's great."

"I've been really worried about him." He cleared his throat. "Alex . . . when Mom dropped Star back, she was upset. Crying."

My insides tensed. The old enemy, anxiety, shooting through me. "She and Nell are close, right? You said they were good friends."

A nod.

"It must have been upsetting for her to see Nell hurting."

He just stared at me.

"What happened, Joe?"

"I just, I was just trying to comfort her. Holding her, you know?" His mouth tensed. "Then she started kissing me and . . . I stopped it. I, ah, I did."

"Okay."

"She wants for us to try again. We used to be really good together before shit fell apart," he said. A simple statement, though it hurt like hell. "She says she made a mistake, leaving."

Not a surprise. Joe might have chosen to be oblivious, though Star had made her intentions pretty damn clear.

His fingers speared roughly through his hair. "I told her I'd forgotten something at work. Got out of there."

Questions poured through my head, but I said nothing. I had no rights in this situation, not really. Despite today's accidental oral, he'd made it clear we were over, or unofficial, or whatever the hell exactly we were. And I'd said I accepted it, but would stay to help him anyway.

Yet here he was, confessing. The situation was beyond confusing.

"Do you believe me?" His gaze pinned me to the chair.

"Yes."

"Good." Slowly, his shoulders relaxed, lowering. "I can't handle this coming from her, any more than I can continue things with you. Sooner or later, you're going to have to go home. Who the hell knows when we'll see each other again. Eric's going to need me to have his back; the baby's funeral is the day after tomorrow. It was a little girl, did you know that? I had a niece."

"I'm so sorry."

"I haven't even heard from Dad, but I know Mom is just devastated. God knows when Nell will be back on her feet," he said. "My family need me here."

My heart at my feet, I nodded. "I know."

"But I haven't even told you the best of it."

"What?"

"The idiot that hit us found out his insurance won't cover the cost of repairs," he said. "So he's suing me."

"Wha—" I shook my head, my forehead scrunched up. "How the fuck is that even possible? What planet is he calling this in from?"

He rubbed the back of his neck. Suddenly, pain filled his eyes and he winced, carefully bracing his cast with his free arm. "I don't know. Got an old school friend who is a lawyer. I'll call her tomorrow, see when we can talk."

"That's insane that he would come after you." Fury filled me from top to toe. "God damn it."

"Yeah."

"He was the one driving with no fucking lights on!"

Joe said nothing, a wide yawn cracking his jaw. "Christ, I'm tired. I don't remember ever being this tired before."

"Lie down," I ordered, getting to my feet, then kneeling at his and undoing his shoes.

"Alex." Worry lined his face.

"We're not having sex or doing anything fun. We're sleeping." I pulled off his boots and smelly socks. Such is the joy of love. "Go on."

"I'm not sure. I know things got intense between us today, but—"

"You don't want to lead me on," I said. "Relax, Joe. I'm not going to try and start something, launch a surprise attack or something. Can you say the same of Star?"

The dubious look on his face said everything.

I yanked off his second boot and sock with a smile. "Your virtue is safe with me. Lie down."

"Thank you," he said, rising to his feet.

I turned down the bed then stepped back so he could lie down. There were shadows under his eyes I hadn't noticed earlier. More lines on his face than there had been previously. I fetched him an extra pillow for his broken arm, making sure he was comfortably settled for the night. Eyelids closed, he looked slightly more relaxed. Not much, but a little.

When I crawled in beside him, I made sure to leave a definite couple of inches between our bodies. Switzerland, the no-go zone. After all, the man needed his space. Despite this, he reached out, grabbing my hand and holding on tight. The warmth of his skin and the rough patches of his callouses, even the contained strength in his long fingers; I did my best to memorize it all.

Somewhere in the darkness, the sand was slipping through the hourglass, my time left in Coeur d'Alene disappearing to naught.

CHAPTER TWENTY-ONE

I don't believe I'd ever seen anything sadder than the tiny white coffin sitting up in the front of the church.

Roses in every color of the rainbow overflowed from vases and a pianist played softly. The minister spoke, her voice soothing, flowing straight through me. No idea what she said, though. What could you possibly say to help during a time like this? At the myriad of possibilities such a small life would never get to explore. A beloved daughter, a granddaughter, and niece. She was all of these things and yet none.

I sat near the back, leaving plenty of room for family and longtime friends of Nell and Eric. Tears flowed from almost everyone. Nell sat up front between Patrick and Eric. Vaughan, Lydia, Rosie, and Andre sitting on the left, and Joe, Star, and his parents on the right. Afterward, over a hundred colorful helium balloons were released by the mourners. Set to drift off up to the sky, disappearing into the heavens.

Life didn't last anywhere near as long as we thought. For all its occasional drudgery, it could be so fleeting. Nothing was certain.

Like Patrick, Star remained at Nell's side during the wake. Nell clutched her hand fiercely, obviously grateful to have her there. I hoped for Nell's sake, Star did decide to stick around for a while. The Collins' house was packed with mourners, Taka, Rosie, and Boyd from Dive Bar seeing to all of the food and drink. Joe's mom seemed so pale, a ghost of herself wandering in and out of rooms as if she didn't know where she belonged. Stan sat in a lounge chair, staring off at nothing.

It hurt to see Joe's family and friends like this.

Wrapped up in a woolen jacket, I headed out onto the back patio to get some air. Crying had helped let out some of the emotion and tension filling up inside of me. But it didn't do anything to ease me feeling like an outsider. Nor the growing anxiety over me needing to get back to my work. The mother of all jobs had fallen into my lap via email the night before. Fortunately, the customer was willing to give me a week to finish up here in Coeur d'Alene before getting down to business. It felt good, to have fresh ideas flooding my head, to get the creative juices flowing. But having the job hanging over my head, the customer's expectations, everything just waiting, got my nerves all amped up.

Maybe part of me had accepted it was time to go home, even if the thought of leaving Joe cut deep. Gah. Too many thoughts were going around and around in my head. Maybe I should just chop it off.

"Hey," said Joe. "Wondered where you were hiding."

I shrugged. "There's a lot of people in there."

"Yeah. Thanks for coming today."

"Of course."

He sat down on the cool old porch swing beside me, making it gently sway. Last night, he'd slept with me in my hotel room again. And again, nothing had happened. Joe's libido had gone on hiatus while he dealt with everything. I didn't really blame it.

"Shit." He winced, feeling out the best position for his cast. "Man, I can't wait to get this thing off."

"When do you go back to the doctor?" I asked.

"Checkup in a couple of days."

I nodded. "How's Eric doing?"

Another wince. "I don't know. Having Star staying with us seems to help distract him a little. They always got on well."

"That's good."

He raised a brow.

"Just because she and I aren't besties doesn't mean I don't think it's great she's here for Nell and Eric."

With his free hand, he gave my knee a squeeze. "Thanks, Little Miss."

"I just don't want her hurting you again."

"I know." He gave me a halfhearted smile. "Don't worry, that's not going to happen. Right now, I'm just taking it one day at a time. Relationships aren't even on the horizon."

Didn't I know it.

"Mom's going to go see Nell's grief counselor," he said. "Have a talk with him."

"That's good." I gave his hand a squeeze. "She seems so lost."

"Mm." He sighed. "Eric's throwing himself into the bar, keeping busy. Wants to help out with the construction as well."

"I guess I'd want to keep busy too."

A nod. Followed by another flash of a not-so-believable smile. "Maybe I'll come visit you in Seattle once the job's finished. We could celebrate, go to a nice restaurant or something."

"That'd be great."

He didn't say anymore and neither did I. There didn't seem to be any need. We sat in silence, enjoying the afternoon light. Brilliant autumn colors were slowly coming in, turning the green trees shades of blazing orange, red, and pink. I bet winter here was beautiful. A pain in the ass sometimes to deal with, but beautiful nonetheless. Maybe Joe could send me some pictures since I wouldn't be here to appreciate the view.

Surely we'd still be friends from afar. I couldn't imagine losing him from my life completely.

"Alex, can I have a moment?"

Well fuck. I put a calm smile on my face and turned to face her. "Hi, Star. Sure."

It was my own fault for coming downstairs in search of caffeine. Except Joe and I had gotten desperate and apparently Star's deliveries to upstairs had dried up ever since he'd refused her romantic advances. Fancy that.

I leaned my hip against the service counter, waiting on Lydia to make the two take-away coffees. Over behind the bar, Eric was keeping busy. Seemed like he never stopped moving, finishing one job then rushing on to the next.

"What's up?" I asked.

"I'm worried about Joe." Silver bangles tinkled on her arm as she tightened her regulation ponytail. "I know you're trying to help him. But I don't think you understand him as well as you think you do."

I just blinked.

"Men like him, they need the time and space to sort things out for themselves," she said, her gaze searching me intensely. "You know?"

"All right."

"I don't know if you realize, but, he's taken a lot of blame for the accident on himself."

"Mm."

She wrung her hands, taking a deep breath. "And what with Stan . . . that's his father, by the way—"

"Oh, okay."

"Well, Stan is a bit of a moody silent type himself," she said. "So Joe's always used his work time to think things through, you know?"

I said nothing.

"But now, with you being here, and I know you're trying to help and that's so great of you," her smile turned anguished, "it's just, I'm worried you might be hindering more than you're helping."

"I see." I frowned.

"Also, Joe's told me a little about your business and how you're from Seattle and everything. Eventually, sometime soon, you're going to have to go home, right?" A certain light shone in her beady little eyes. The day after a funeral with all of this heartbreak happening around her and she wanted to throw down with me over this flimsy bullshit? What a woman.

"Yes."

More wincing. "Is it really fair to Joe if he gets used to having you around and then you have to leave?"

More nothing from me.

"I'm guessing you and Joe are close?"

"What is it exactly that you want to know, Star?"

Her mouth opened and closed. "Oh. Well. It's not really any of my business."

"No, it's not."

"I just worry about him."

"That's nice." I wiped my dusty hands off on my equally dusty jeans. "And I can see you've really given this a lot of thought."

"I care about Joe a lot. I love him, I always will." She gave me a pitying look. "We were together a long time, Alex. A bond like that doesn't just disappear."

"No, it wouldn't." I wanted to smack the prying, manipulating cow down so bad. But I didn't. "But I don't think leaving him alone to mess his arm up worse trying to keep up with the project is the answer. Thank you for your concerns, Star. I'll give them some thought."

"You don't know when you might be leaving?" she asked with just a touch too much eagerness. If ever I'd been tempted to scratch someone's eyes out, this boho bitch was pushing me right up to the edge. "The fact is, I'm here now, Alex. He doesn't need you. He has all of his family and friends. You putting your life on hold isn't necessary. Surely you can see that."

Well. "Wow. I'm glad you feel you can be so open and honest with me. But the thing is, Star, having an opinion doesn't automatically make you right."

"Here you go." Lydia slid the two take-aways onto the counter, giving us both wary looks.

"Thanks," I told her with a genuine smile. At least not everyone here would be chasing me out of town with pitchforks. "I better deliver these while they're hot. Star, I'll be sure to give what you said lots and lots of thought."

Her smile was a fleeting thing.

Whatevs.

I stomped back up the stairs, just a wee bit pissed off.

Joe looked up from coating the freshly sanded wooden window frames. "You okay?"

"Living the dream, baby."

"Mmhmm." He cringed ever so slightly at my use of the endearment.

I winked at him, throwing in a slightly tired smile. "Here. Caffeinate."

"Thanks." He took a sip. "I think you're real pretty with all that sawdust in your hair."

"Do you, now."

"Oh yeah. Brings out those cute little freckles on your nose."

I smiled for real this time. "Took me hours to get it looking just right."

Pain filled his eyes and he gritted his teeth, bracing his bad arm. "Damn it."

"I think we need to move up your doctor's appointment."

"It's tomorrow. Why bother?"

From his back pocket he pulled out a strip of painkillers and popped a couple. "Stop frowning, Little Miss. It's first thing tomorrow morning and I'm definitely going."

"Good. What time are we meant to be there?"

His gaze softened. "Mom wanted to drive me."

"Okay."

"You sure?"

It stung a little, of course. "Yeah. Whatever works."

"Thank you." He placed a soft kiss on my forehead. "I think you're the best female friend with occasional benefits I've ever had."

"Shucks." I quickly ducked my head, hiding the hurt. I was

not going to cry. It was just all of the emotion going on these days getting to me, that's all. My heart had taken one knock too many. But no biggie, I'd survive. So that's where we were right now. Of course I'd known, it just sucked to hear him say it out loud. Especially after Star's bullshit inquisition downstairs. "You're a sweet talker, Mr. Collins."

"Hello?" called a voice, followed by Stan stepping into the room. For some reason he seemed hesitant. "Morning."

"Hi," I said.

"Dad." Joe stepped forward, dusting off his hands.

"Looks like it's going well." Stan wandered about the room, inspecting everything.

"Yeah, with Alex's help we're pretty much keeping to schedule."

"That's good."

I took a sip of my coffee, uncertain if I should be here or elsewhere. In the end, I picked up my paintbrush, turned my back on them, and got back to work. Rembrandt had nothing on me these days. My painting expertise was moving ahead in leaps and bounds.

"I wanted to talk to you about that," said Stan. "I've, ah, been giving some thought to what you said about the business."

"Right?"

"And you're right. It's time for you to take over." The shuffling of feet. "You've been doing the bulk of the work for a long time, heading up projects. I just didn't want to admit it."

Holy shit.

"Huh," said Joe, surprise clear in his tone.

"I'd like to keep helping out where I can, but with my arthritis, I'm not up to doing anywhere near as much as I used to. It's the truth." Stan sighed. "Think it's about time Collins and Son became Collins and Father."

"Dad . . . I don't know what to say."

"Don't say anything, put me to work," said Stan in his gruff voice. "Let's get these apartments done. After that, I'm taking your mother to Hawaii for a couple of weeks. About time we had a proper vacation."

"I'm glad to hear it," said Joe. "Mom'll love that."

There came the sound of backslapping, low happy chuckles.

"Hey," said a deep male voice. Patrick stood in the doorway, checking out the almost finished apartment.

"Pat, man. How is Nell doing today?" asked Joe, going over to do some more of the dude backslapping and handshaking.

"Better. Your mom's visiting with her," said Pat. "Nell told me to get out of her face for a while. To go do something. I've closed the shop for a few weeks and it seems like they've got downstairs running pretty well. Figured I'd come see if you could use a hand."

"Always."

The three men huddled together, discussing the ins and outs of the project. Joe looked so happy. The happiest I'd seen him since the accident. Star had been right, his friends and family really did have his back. Now. And she might be happy to hang around and keep trying to get something started with him despite his being in no condition to deal with any more emotional upheavals. I certainly wasn't going to be that person.

No. It was time for me to do what he'd asked for in the first place and leave. To go back to my own life.

"I'm just going to get some air," I said.

Joe nodded, the other men still talking the how's and why's of construction. Damned if it didn't even make me feel like more of an outsider. Me and my delicate little feelings were ready for some breathing room. I picked up my bag, slinging it over my shoulder. Given we'd barely hit midmorning, I'd have plenty of time to make the afternoon flight to Seattle.

And I sucked at goodbyes. Seriously sucked at them. Probably another reason why I'd tended to avoid entanglements in the past. One by one, all of my rules had gotten broken for Joe Collins. Now even my heart was starting to show some cracks.

Without saying a word, I left.

I sent him a text a couple of hours later from the airport saying goodbye. He didn't respond.

CHAPTER TWENTY-TWO

Dear Joe,

I know you're probably angry at me for leaving the way I did. What can I say? I guess we both wound up needing some space. Honestly, the thought of saying goodbye to you face-to-face was too much. Maybe it was me reverting to my old ways and running and hiding. But please try and understand that at the time it's what I felt was best for both of us.

Any news from your lawyer friend about the idiot trying to sue you? I hope she can send him packing. And how is your arm, what did the doctor say at your checkup?

I hope everything is on the improve and that the work on the apartments is going well. If you could send me some photos sometime, that would be great.

Love, Alex

Hi Joe,

I don't know if you're reading these, but I'm going to keep writing anyway. My work is going great, the job that came through while I was in CdA is a lot bigger than my usual.

The initial company logo package I designed was approved and now they want me to look at several more of their businesses. They're great to work for and pay on time, what more could I ask for?

How is your work going? I bet you're making much better time with your dad on board than you were with my dodgy renovation skills. Please say hi to everyone in the Dive Bar and to your family for me. Is Star still staying with you and Eric? I hope Nell is back on her feet and doing okay.

Val says hi. She's doing well, busy doing makeup on a couple of TV shows being made locally. The hours are crazy but she's loving the challenge. Her and her partner Liam are as happy as ever.

You'd be impressed, even with the crappy cold weather I've been going out a bit more to movies. Actually eating dinner out instead of living on delivery. I haven't been going on any dates, I'm not open to anything like that right now. Maybe what happened between us is never really going to be resolved. Maybe you're going to stay mad at me for a long time. I don't know. But if you finish the apartments and you think you'd maybe still like to come visit Seattle, you'd be very very welcome.

Love, Alex

P.S. Marty says hi too.

Dear Joe,
I miss you. Please write back to me. Even just something short to let me know you're okay.

Love, Alex

CHAPTER TWENTY-THREE

Nervous didn't cover what I was feeling. Terrified came closer.

A week before Christmas I stood outside a monster-size log cabin situated on Lake Coeur d'Alene. This had to be the place. Security at the gates had checked my name off an invite list and the cab had dropped me at the wide front steps. If Liberace had a log cabin, it'd look like this. Completely over the top.

Time to be brave and go inside, it was too damn cold to stand outside in the icy wind any longer.

The main room was roughly the size of my apartment back in Seattle, but three stories high and with a rustic chandelier. Flames blazed in a massive fireplace framed by floor-to-ceiling windows overlooking the water. Flashily dressed people mingled with champagne flutes and martini glasses in hand. In one corner, Vaughan sat on a raised platform playing guitar. Okay, so I was definitely in the right place.

"Miss, may I take your coat?" asked a man in a spiffy three-piece suit.

"Thank you."

At least I hadn't over- or under-dressed. The dark blue velvet fit-and-flare fifties-style dress might be simple, but the new YSL black stilettos and Mom's black-pearl necklace amped things up nicely. I fit in. A woman also in a three-piece suit came past with a silver tray loaded with a variety of beverages. I grabbed a cut-crystal glass with two fingers' worth of scotch in it and downed it in one. Ooh yeah. Feel the fire.

Right now, Dutch courage was my one and only friend. Well, along with the cute little black-and-white dog sniffing at my shoes.

"I didn't step in anything, I promise," I told the dog, reaching down to pat him. He immediately rolled onto his back, giving it up for a good belly scratch. "Yeah, baby. You know you want it."

"He really does," a man with shoulder-length wavy blond hair told me. Not Joe, this one was actually smiling at me. "Hi, welcome to my home. Well, actually it's my wife's place, she made me sign it over to her because apparently I'm not *responsible* enough to look after things. Accidentally burn down one kitchen trying to make popcorn old style and you never hear the end of it. Like I had a clue a pan full of hot oil left unattended would catch on fire. Crazy, right?

"Um."

"But no, I get the blame same as always. She's all, like, you're why we can't have nice things. Actually, between you and me, I looked pretty fucking funny with no eyebrows for a month. That's Killer, by the way," he nodded at the dog, before continuing on with barely a pause for breath, "such a lady's dog. He's always chasing tail."

Eyes wide, I just stared. "Don't take this the wrong way, but are you Mal Ericson from Stage Dive?"

"Hmm? Yeah. That's me." His brow furrowed. "Hang on, why would I take that the wrong way?"

"Oh. No, well—"

"Hey," said a guy with dark, slicked-back hair and a cool gray suit, who looked like he'd just stepped off the cover of *GQ*. Apart from the two toddlers. I don't think they usually accessorized with those. "Man, can you take Zeny for a sec? Lena's just chilling with Anne and Lydia and I don't want to disturb them. But Steph needs her diaper changed."

Holy hell, it was Jimmy Ferris. Also from Stage Dive. Mind. Blown.

"Sure." Mal took one of the twins off his hands. Lord knows how he knew which was which, the gorgeous girls were absolutely identical with their dark curls and cherub mouths. "Who loves Uncle Mal best? Yes, you do. You're helpless to resist my charm, aren't you?"

The toddler giggled, then smacked him in the face. Honestly, I kind of liked her style. Funny thing, though, even when Jimmy strode off blowing bubbles on the other baby's neck and making her screech with glee, the bad smell didn't dissipate any.

Mal just sighed. "You've done something bad in your pants too, haven't you?"

"Da-da-da-da," said Zeny.

"Z, your da is a big naughty word that starts with *d* and ends with *k*." Mal turned back to me with a pained expression. "You'd think being a millionaire rock star would save me from having to deal with poopy diapers, wouldn't you? But no. My life is a complete misery ever since everyone started popping out babies. Total chaos. It's not okay."

He searched the crowd, eyes narrowing in on someone. "And she knows about it. She's laughing at me, Z. Why, I bet your Auntie Anne sent you over here for me to deal with, didn't she? They're all against me."

Zeny smacked him in the face again, following it up with a big wet open-mouthed kiss to his cheek. Talk about slobber.

"You're lucky I love you," he told the baby. Meanwhile, the little dog, Killer, yipped joyfully, jumping at Mal's feet, making the baby laugh even more.

Zeny reached for the dog with one chubby fist. "Kiy."

Beyond us in the main room, the party kept on keeping on. I hadn't seen Joe yet, but he had to be here somewhere. Ever so calmly, I clutched my hands together. Hopefully that'd hide the worst of the shakes. Ah, anxiety, my old friend.

"Go, frolic, have fun," Mal told me somberly. "I have to deal with Miss Smelly Pants here."

"Okay. Thanks." I smiled, trying not to laugh at the broken look on his face.

Which left me confronted with the large room full of people again. Ugh, parties. Worst. No, none of that nonsense, I could do this. One step at a time, I made my way toward the gathering. Why, a knight in shining armor facing down a dragon horde couldn't have been as brave. There were a whole lot of people here I didn't know. Fortunately, there were quite a few people here I did know too.

"Alex." Lydia threw her arms around me, her cheeks a rosy hue. A color suggesting the lady had a few drinks before I arrived and was thoroughly enjoying herself. "I'm so glad you came. We weren't sure if you would."

"'Course I came." I'd only finally made the decision the night before. But Lydia didn't need to know that. "Couldn't miss seeing Nell and Pat re-tie the knot."

"Isn't it great? Love, thy will be done."

"Why are you quoting eighties song lyrics?" asked Rosie, giving me a quick side hug.

"Because Mal got the expensive champagne and I'm making the most of it." Lydia grinned. "That redheaded guitar man is so getting drunk sex tonight. *Rawr.*"

"Okay, Tiger." Rosie laughed. "Settle down."

"Soooo," I said, dragging out my last moments of happiness, etc. "How's Joe?"

Dating Star. No, married to Star. God help me, he was probably pregnant with Star's baby somehow. I wouldn't put anything past modern science. They were all out to ruin my life.

"Good," said Rosie, ever so succinctly.

"Oh. Great." I grabbed another scotch off a passing tray. "Good to know he's still breathing."

"Yep. He's definitely doing that."

"Is he still working on the apartments?"

"Mmhmm." Rosie nodded.

Taking another sip of champagne, Lydia tried to hide a smile. Not so successfully, as it turned out. Mostly she just wound up nearly dribbling the good French stuff.

I frowned.

"Why don't you just ask me what you're really dying to know?" said Rosie.

"Fine." I sniffed. "Is he with Star?"

"Nope." She grinned, showing lots of white teeth. "That turkey-brained girl is gone."

"Once she realized Joe wasn't going to fall at her feet, she suddenly had to be somewhere else," said Lydia. "Maine, was it? Or New England?"

"Somewhere over that way." Rosie shrugged. "As long as it isn't here, we're happy."

"You should have seen her flirting with everything that had a penis within a fifty-mile radius."

"Gag worthy," said Rosie. "She even tried that shit with my husband when he came in to pick me up one time. He just ignored her, but still . . . not cool."

"No," I agreed. "Wow."

"Feel better now?" asked Rosie, giving me a wink. "Your man is still a swinging single. Pissed at you. Still single, though."

"Oh."

Brows high, Lydia nodded. "He really hasn't gotten over you leaving without saying goodbye."

"Okay." Bummer. Not a surprise, but still. I took a sip of the scotch. "It's been over two months. I was sort of hoping—"

"No," said Rosie.

"Nuh," added Lydia. "Alex, with all due love and affection: that was not your best move."

Rather dramatically, I sagged to one side. "I know, I just . . ."

Both women watched me, waiting for some amazing, all-revealing explanation. Sadly, I didn't actually have anything resembling same. I'd needed to run at the time. Everything had been too much, too painful, too *gah*. Not a great word, but sadly, it fit.

Rosie gave up waiting first. "Okay, well. I hope you brought your ass-kissing lips with you."

I nodded. "It's a stay-on lip gloss. Chanel. Val bought it for me."

"Great shade."

"Thanks." I offered a glum smile. "Exactly how angry is he? Say, on a scale of one to ten, where one is rock-and-roll wrestling where it's mostly just posturing and finger pointing, to ten, where Godzilla is trashing Tokyo?"

The girls pondered for all of about a minute.

"Eleven?" asked Lydia.

"Sounds about right," said Rosie. "You hurt his delicate man feelings. Given Star took off only leaving a note a few years earlier, it wasn't pretty."

"Shit." My shoulders sagged. Maybe I should just hide and drink for a while. Delay the unhappy reunion. "I didn't mean to hurt him."

"Best of luck, my friend." Lydia clinked her champagne flute against my glass. "And remember, when in doubt, get the girls out."

I cocked my head. "What?"

"Tits," whispered Rosie.

"Ah." I checked out the small amount I had on offer. "I'm not sure that'll work in my case."

"Apparently size doesn't matter," said Lydia, who had enough going on for two women with some to spare. "If they're into breasts, then all are great."

Maybe. "I think Joe's more of an ass man, actually."

Lydia sighed dreamily. Dreamily or drunkenly. Tricky to tell which. "Nothing says I love you like anal."

I downed some more scotch. It was worth a thought.

"Okay." With one hand on top of the other, Rosie made the T for time-out symbol. "There are small innocent babies here somewhere. Let's keep butt sex out of this, please."

"Sorry," said Lydia, chastised.

All of a sudden, from the stage situated in the corner of the room, Vaughan started playing the "Wedding March." Amid much whistling, clapping, and cheering, people moved to either side of the room, leaving an aisle. Andre, in a sharp blue suit, stood beside Nell, resplendent in a slinky simple ivory gown. The woman was beaming, her whole face lit up with love. Up front stood an Elvis impersonator, strangely enough. And Patrick, in black jeans and a black button-down shirt.

"Mal insisted they get married by the same Elvis who married Anne and him in Vegas," whispered Lydia. "He said the dude knows how to make vows stick."

"Elvis hoodoo?"

She shrugged. "Guess so."

I frowned. "Oh, have I gone mad or is half of Stage Dive here?"

"No, all of Stage Dive is here," said Lydia.

"They're buddies with Vaughn. His old band toured with them."

Nell and Patrick deserved to be happy. I had another mouthful of scotch, smiling at all the love in the air. Peace, happiness, stuff like that. Contrary to those emotions was the big strong hand gripping my arm, drawing me back through the crowd.

Crap. I'd been found.

Sooner rather than later might have been quite acceptable under some circumstances. Just not this one. Thunderclouds were friendlier than the look on Joe's face. Tornados, tsunamis, all sorts of natural disasters. The bearded one was indeed pissed. Though it should be noted he looked downright delectable in his black suit and tie.

Without a word, he marched me away from the wedding taking place. Down a corridor into another wing, far, far away from anyone else. And all the while, his grip around my upper arm remained not painfully tight, but definitely iron strong. As awesome as my new YSL heels were, they'd not been meant for jogging.

"Slow down," I hissed. "Joe."

He ignored me, looking this way and that into the rooms as we passed. An office, a media room, a bathroom, and a room with nothing but a drum kit set up in it.

"Goddamn it," I said, nearly tripping over my two feet. "Let go of me. Stop!"

Finally, we reached a room he was apparently happy with. A bedroom. Having dragged me inside, he slammed the door shut before turning to face me. This happened at about the same time when I'd had more than enough. As fury blazed in his eyes, the palm of my hand smacked into his cheekbone. I honestly don't know who was more startled by the crack of sound, him or me. Either way, talk about a reaction.

That Zeny kid knew her stuff.

Hand stinging and breathing hard, I just stared. "If I say stop, you stop. You do not keep dragging me around like some sack of shit answerable to your highness. Is that clear?"

"My highness?"

I just shrugged. "You get what I mean."

He dragged the back of a hand across his mouth, eyes all ragey. The red blossoming on his cheek was quite the beauty. "What are you doing here?"

"Apologize for not listening to me."

"You're right, I should have stopped. I was angry, but that's no excuse. I'm sorry." His nostrils flared. "Now, what are you doing here?"

"Well, I was watching Nell and Pat get remarried. But apparently you decided we needed to have a chat and it couldn't wait."

"They invited you?"

"No, Joe. I just showed up because I thought it'd be funny to fuck with you," I said, thoroughly riled up by now. "Of course they invited me."

The man about-faced and started pacing. "They shouldn't have done that."

"Oh my God, are you kidding me?"

"What?"

"You don't own these people," I said. "Yes, they're your friends, but you don't make their decisions for them."

"Like a little loyalty wouldn't be too much to ask for. Though I guess you're the wrong person to be understanding that concept."

My mouth formed a perfect O.

"You left without saying a fucking word." He pointed at me in particularly aggressive fashion. Douchebag. "After everything we'd been through."

"You'd told me to go. Time and again, you told me in no uncertain terms," I said, not backing down. Not this time. "So when the time was right, I left."

"You said you'd have my back."

"And then your dad took over working with you. You didn't need me there anymore."

He huffed out a breath, hands on hips. "You couldn't even say goodbye?"

"You couldn't even tell Star we'd been involved with each other?"

"Goddamnit. You left because you were jealous?"

I sighed. No point going for anything less than total honesty. "That was one of the reasons, yes. Plus, you'd made it pretty clear that there wasn't room for me in your life right then. With your arm, and Eric and Nell dealing with the loss of their baby, and that idiot trying to sue you, it was all too much for you and I got that. I understood. Your life was crazy complicated just then. But I couldn't afford to put my world on hold any longer. Not once Eric came back to handle the bar and I knew your dad would start helping you with the renovations."

More pacing. "You thought I wouldn't understand that?"

"No. I knew I couldn't handle that," I said, my heart breaking all over again just from thinking the words. Let alone saying them. "I mean, I couldn't handle saying goodbye to you. Leaving here was one of the hardest things I've ever done. Okay?"

"So you took the coward's way out."

"Surprise," I yelled. "Hi, I'm Alex Parks. Nice to meet you. In case you haven't noticed, I happen to be one of the biggest scaredy-cat, angst-ridden idiots of our age. Not the most noble title, but hella true just the same."

Teeth gritted, he shook his head. "Fuck's sake."

I said nothing.

"If you're so damn frightened of everything, then what are you doing here?" he asked.

Good question. Very good question. Not one I really wanted to answer.

He leaned down, getting in my face. "Well?"

"I couldn't stay away, okay?" I cried. "You wouldn't answer my emails, and I needed to see you."

"Why?"

I looked to heaven. "Come on, Joe. Work with me here just a little. Why do you think?"

He held his hands out wide. "Little Miss Fucking Sunshine, I don't have a clue. You leave me without a goddamn word and now suddenly months later you're back and I'm supposed to just be cool with that?"

"So don't be cool with it," I said. "Be mad at me. Tell me to go back to Seattle, that you never want to see me again."

"Alex—"

I pushed at his flat belly with both hands. Guess he hadn't

been expecting that, because he stumbled back a step. And if it worked so well once, then what the hell, let's go for it again. I pushed him until his back hit the door and both of us were wearing our fiercest faces.

"Tell me I mean nothing to you, that I never did," I said. "Go on. You were acting cold enough toward me before I left. It shouldn't be a reach for you. Give me some fucking closure."

He blinked, surprised or something, I don't know. When I went to push him again, however, he grabbed my wrists, holding on tight. "Stop it."

"Tell me I'm a shit friend and you don't want me as a lover anyway. Do it."

"That's enough."

"Break my heart one more time, Joe Collins. Come on," I jeered. "I'm good for it."

His mouth firmed. "What the hell are you talking about? How did I break your heart?"

"By not being ready. By shutting down completely just as I was opening up to you," I said, throat tight with emotion. "Making me think I meant nothing to you by acting like an absolute asshole after the accident. Necessary or not, you fucking broke me, Joe."

He just stared at me.

"And the worst of it, it's not even all your fault," I said, tears welling in the corners of my eyes. "It's mine. First for coming out here and getting involved with you. For wanting to fix everything and not being able to. For taking on so much after the accident that I felt like I was coming apart and the only thing I could do was run."

Brows drawn tight, he cupped my cheeks in his big hands. "You're right, I should have had your back with Star. I'm sorry,

Alex. Christ, I'm sorry for everything. I acted like a heartless bastard because I couldn't cope with us right then. I should have just . . . shit. I should have waited, kept you close. Not make you think what we had was nothing. I'm sorry, Little Miss, I was a fucking idiot. Can you forgive me?"

"You're sorry?" I'd been so ready to kiss his ass I couldn't quite believe it. "Really?"

He nodded. "Worst thing I ever did, pushing you away."

And the whole gazing into each other's eyes was getting to be too much again. I couldn't take it. *Gah,* talk about an overload of emotion. I closed my eyelids tight, breathing in deep. Just when I thought maybe I'd gotten a handle on myself, Joe's lips brushed against mine and I lost it all over again.

God, he could kiss.

Mouths searching, tongues gliding against one another, and his hands . . . holy hell, his hands. They went from gently holding my face to fingers stroking down the sides of my dress. Next thing I knew they were under my skirt, sliding into the back of my black lace underwear.

With an ass cheek in each hand, he groaned long and loud. "Fuck, I missed you."

"You did?" I panted.

"Yeah. Don't disappear on me again."

" 'kay."

"Promise me," he demanded, a hand moving up to collar my throat, fingers and thumb pressing in just a little.

"I promise."

In one not even remotely smooth move, he spun us around, reversing our places. My spine hit the door and his teeth sunk into my neck. Punishing me in the best way possible. Hands tore my panties down my legs, hesitating only when he got to the stiletto heels.

He looked up at me, a smirk on his face. "More stripper heels?"

"Joe, they're designer," I said, wiping away a tear, stepping out of my fancy underwear. "Have some respect."

"Sure thing. Just give me a minute."

"Huh?"

Thick fingers slid between my legs and the man disappeared beneath my skirt. Oh shit. I was a goner. Hot mouth, wet tongue, and a determined man of many talents. Don't even get me started on the feeling of his beard, brushing against such sensitive skin. I was a blissful mess there in no time. More than ready for him, needing him immediately.

"Joe." Holding up my skirt, I stroked his hair. "Come on."

"What?" he asked, flicking his tongue up and down along my slit. So damn good. If it weren't for his hands and the help of the door, I'd be on the ground. Honestly, my knees were barely up to the task of keeping me upright in the face of such overwhelming pleasure.

"Sex. Now." I pulled on his hair some more.

He wiped his mouth with the back of his hand and stood, before getting busy undoing his zipper. Out of his wallet came a condom and onto his impressively hard cock. "Right now?"

I nodded, twining my arms around his neck.

"You sure?"

"Don't make me hurt you," I said in a warning tone.

"Yes, ma'am."

Strong hands lifted me and I wrapped my legs around him good and tight. Heaven help me, given half a chance, I'd never let him go. Once my skirt was out of the way, we were good to go. He directed the head of his cock to my opening, both of us moaning at the exquisite sensation. He was hard and I was soft. We both wanted it bad. Slowly he lowered me onto him, the heavy length of him filling my insides just so.

Mouth open, I gasped, everything low in me tightening. This was what I'd needed since the moment I'd left. Him. There'd been no dates or distractions, I hadn't even tried. Joe Collins had my heart whether he wanted it or not. With his big cock moving deep into my delicate insides, lighting up every inch of me, we might as well just cancel Christmas. Nothing else could be this perfect, bright, and special.

"Okay?" he asked.

"Oh yeah." I smiled, my mouth trembling just a little.

Ever so sweetly he lowered me onto him, then lazily withdrew. Thrusting into me with the kind of knowledge I'd imagine only long-term partners knew. I was safe in his arms. There could be no doubt. And I knew his hazy eyes wouldn't leave my face for a moment, registering every minute detail and reaction. Absolute ecstasy. The kind of sensation I could find with only one person.

"I love you," I said, gazing into his eyes. It never even occurred to me to hide.

"Thank fuck for that."

I clenched the muscles in my pussy tight around him, making things even better, hotter. Christ, what a rush. It nearly sent me cross-eyed.

"Shit," he mumbled. "Do that again."

I did as told. His hips ground against me, fingers digging into my ass cheeks. There'd be the best bruises later for him to kiss better. Gradually, his thrusts came harder and more often, pounding me into the door. I could barely breathe, let alone think. Inside of me, every muscle, every atom, coiled tight, reaching for that high.

Heels digging into his butt, I wrapped myself so tight around him the man couldn't possibly escape. The heat and the smell and the everything . . . it was perfect. I yelled out his name, squeezing his cock tight. My mind was up among the stars, circling the galaxy. Yet still, I could feel him coming inside of me, his pelvis pinning me against the door.

Heaven. Absolutely positively heaven. I'd found it at last.

"Okay, that's not suspicious at all."

"What?" I asked, giving Rosie my very best attempt at innocence. Big eyes, fluttering eyelashes, that sort of thing.

Joe just quietly chuckled, the traitor.

I sat on his lap with a fresh drink in hand, his arm draped across me. All was good. Nell and Patrick had been successfully re-hitched in our absence. Both of the twins' diapers had apparently been changed. On the impromptu dance floor, Stan and Audrey were swaying arm in arm to some cool old blues music. Alongside them, Vaughan and Lydia were doing likewise. Mal and his wife, however, were attempting to tango. Though I think mostly it was just Mal while his wife laughed her ass off, arms wrapped tight around him.

Love was ace.

"I think Rosie's referring to the fact that your hair is a mess and half of your makeup is gone," said Nell, sipping from a glass of water. "You look distinctly rumpled. And here I thought only the newlyweds were meant to sneak off and bang in a cupboard or something."

268 | KYLIE SCOTT

Patrick just raised his eyebrows. "They have beds, baby. Why do it in a cupboard?"

"True," she said. "How long do you think it would take us to do it in every room of this mansion, anyway?"

"Dunno." Pat sat with his arm slung over Nell's shoulders, his face serene, at peace with the world. Also, speculative. "We should investigate that later."

Nell grinned.

Sitting on the arm of the couch, Eric just shook his head. "Married people don't have sex. You two should know that. Minute you sign that contract, boom! Life as you knew it is over. No fun. No nothing."

"Ah, my brother," hummed Joe. "That patron saint of love."

Eric gave him the stink eye, including me in on it too. Then he raised his bottle of beer in the air. "Fine, I'll be nice. To love."

Everyone else raised their glasses, clinking them against each other's.

"To Nell and Patrick," said Eric, his bottle again held high. "You two deserve every happiness this world can give you. And I mean that."

"Thank you." Nell's eyes misted over.

Being manly, Pat gave him a nod.

"Here, here," said Andre.

And the moment felt right. Old tensions laid to rest, no one in pain. Or at least, I didn't think anyone was. A shadow lingered in Eric's eyes, however. His usual surliness or something more, I couldn't say. Today could have just as easily been the day his and Nell's child was born. Not the kind of thing you can easily set aside and forget about. Heartbreak like that had to linger.

"And to you two," continued Eric, pointing his near-empty

bottle in my and Joe's direction. Oh God, here we go. If he even started down the "she's using you to get to me" road, I'd brain the idiot. But instead, he gave me a half smile. "Best of luck."

The two brothers did the chin-tip thing to each other.

"Won't be easy, living in different states," said Rosie.

I smiled. "We're used to being pen pals."

"It'll work," said Joe, tone brooking no doubts. "I'll spend some time there, you spend some time here. Eventually, we'll work out which town suits us better."

"You'd really leave?" asked Eric, frowning.

Joe just shrugged.

"Nuh." I laid my head on his shoulder. "I don't see that happening."

He brushed his lips against my forehead. "I'm serious, Little Miss. If you need to be in Seattle then we'll work it out."

"You've got your work here, mine's portable."

"You've got Val and your folks there."

"Yeah. But Val loves jumping on a plane and going somewhere. Whereas I hate flying with a fiery passion," I said, because blatant truth, it'd taken a Valium and a huge serving of self-determination to get me here. "I think my parents would like visiting Coeur d'Alene. If, maybe, someday, I decided to move here. We'll see."

"I want you with me." Another kiss was placed on my face. "But don't rush into making a decision. I don't want you regretting anything."

"We'll figure it out." I smiled, soaking in the scent of him, the feel of his slick suit and thick shoulder beneath my cheek. The brush of his beard against the top of my head. Heaven.

"Yeah," he whispered. "Love you."

"You do?"

"Without a doubt."

"Good. I love you more though," I said. Because it's important in relationships, especially those that felt like forever, to show that you were the better person. Ha.

"He's a no-show."

"Hmm?" I moved over to the window, standing beside Joe. Mostly patiently, he stood waiting by my office window wearing only boxer briefs. The man was lucky there were so many trees in the neighborhood shielding us. Otherwise, he could have caused a goddamn stampede.

"Guess he's shy," he said, slinging an arm around my shoulder.

"He's probably intimidated by the size of your nuts. Maybe if you put pants on?"

"Haha." He kissed the tip of my nose.

"Marty will come out to say hi sooner or later. Have patience. He's a busy squirrel."

Joe sat on the edge of my desk, one of the few remaining pieces of furniture left in the apartment. Strong arms slid around my middle, drawing me back between his legs. "How you doing with all this?"

"Okay. No freak-outs." My gaze tripped over the myriad of boxes containing all of my worldly goods. I was moving to Coeur d'Alene to live in one of the Bird Building apartments with my boyfriend. Whoa. My heart double-timed. "Mostly no freak-outs."

"Haven't changed your mind?"

I hummed, leaning back into him. So much warm skin to skate my fingers over. Heavenly. "No. I mean, my business can move, no worries, and you and I are solid. Everything is good. I'm still a little anxious, but—"

"I love you." Warm lips pressed kisses into my shoulder. So good, shivers raced up my spine. The man knew things, deliciously good things. "I could help you out with that anxiety."

"Relax me?" I asked in a husky tone. Shame on me, the room still reeked of sex from the last time. Having finished up the bulk of the packing, we seemed to have descended into some crazed competition to see how many times we could do it in my apartment while it was still my apartment. So far, we were both winning.

His fingers dug into my hips demandingly. "Mm-hmm."

"Distract me?"

"Absolutely."

"Val and her man will be here soon to help carry it all down to your truck." I arched my neck, giving him better access. "Though we do still have the mattress."

"Be a shame not to use it," he mumbled, his hard cock poking into the small of my back. The man was insatiable. But hey, when it came to him, so was I. We were a perfect lusty match.

Out of the corner of my eye, I saw a flash of fur race by on a tree limb. I pushed out of Joe's hold, rushing to the window. "Marty! Hey, fam."

From behind me came a heavy sigh. "Cock blocked by a squirrel."

"Oh, but he's so cute," I cooed. "Aren't you, Marty? Yes, you are."

Once more, arms came around from behind me, holding me tight. "I appreciate you leaving him for me, Little Miss."

"It was a hard choice, it's true. I'm just . . . Honestly, I'm still not sure if maybe I should st—"

Teeth nipped at my shoulder and I giggled like some lovelorn schoolgirl. I couldn't help it. Joe had me, heart and soul. All of my phobias had fallen to him, one by one. He helped me be a braver, better person. Someone more open to the world and all of its experiences.

"I love you," I said, giving in before my hickey count went sky high. Constantly wearing scarfs around my parents was starting to raise some awkward questions.

"You better," he said, voice gruff.

"All the way, Mr. Collins." I grinned, my heart overflowing. "I'm going all the way with you."

Stay tuned for

CHASER

Book #3 in the Dive Bar series

Visit Kylie Scott at

www.kyliescott.com

for updates!

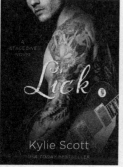